Striking It Rich

THE STORY OF THE CALIFORNIA GOLD RUSH

For all my aunts and uncles—S. K.

For John, Matthew, Andrew, and Megan Templon—A. D.

Text copyright ©1996 by Stephen Krensky
Illustrations copyright © 1996 by Anna DiVito

Simon & Schuster Books for Young Readers
An imprint of Simon & Schuster Children's Publishing Division
1230 Avenue of the Americas
New York, NY 10020

READY-TO-READ is a registered trademark of Simon & Schuster, Inc.
Also available in an Aladdin Paperbacks Edition.

Designed by Chani Yammer
The text for this book was set in 17 point Utopia.
Printed and bound in the United States of America
10 9 8 7 6 5 4 3 2 1

The Library of Congress has catalogued the Simon & Schuster Books for Young Readers
Edition as follows:
Krensky, Stephen.
Striking It Rich : the story of the California gold rush / by Stephen Krensky ;
illustrated by Anna DiVito.
p.   cm.—(Ready-to-Read)
Summary: Describes the discovery of gold in California and its impact on the development
of California and the West.
ISBN 0-689-80804-6 (hc)   0-689-80803-8 (pbk)
1. California—Gold discoveries—Juvenile literature. [1. California—Gold discoveries.
2. California—History—1846-1850.] I. DiVito, Anna, ill. II. Title. III. Series.
F865.K894   1996
979.4'04—dc20   95-52432
CIP   AC

Striking It Rich

THE STORY OF THE CALIFORNIA GOLD RUSH

By Stephen Krensky

Illustrated by Anna DiVito

Ready-to-Read

Simon & Schuster Books for Young Readers

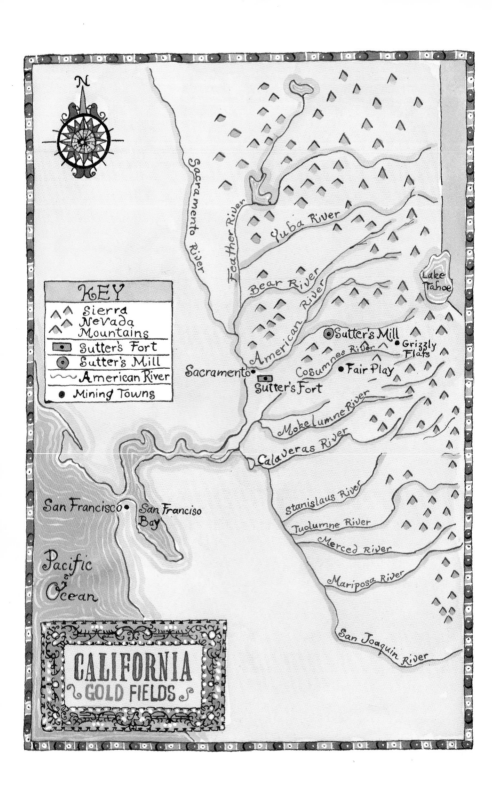

· 1 ·
News Travels Fast

GOLD!

The news was big if it was true—but was it? San Francisco might be a sleepy little town, but it had heard these stories before. There were always plenty of rumors, boasts, and outright lies when it came to finding gold in the hills.

The facts behind this latest story were plain enough. They began with James Marshall, a carpenter. He was helping to build a sawmill on the American River, a hundred miles to the east.

Marshall had little education, but he had sharp eyes and was nobody's fool. On January 24, 1848, he was digging in the

riverbed. There he spotted a glittering yellow rock, no bigger than his thumbnail.

Gold, thought Marshall, or maybe iron pyrite, which looks like gold but is more brittle. He struck the metal with a hammer. It flattened but did not break—a good sign. But Marshall was a busy man. He stuck the rock in his hat and went back to work.

Later, he rode to Sutter's Fort to see his boss, John A. Sutter. Born in Switzerland, Sutter had been a farmer, a trader, and a fur trapper. He had never been too successful.

Sutter and Marshall carefully examined the rock. They bit it to see if it was soft like gold. It was. They dabbed it with acid to see if its shine would dim. It didn't. Then they weighed it against silver and other things they knew were lighter than gold.

The rock passed every test. It was gold, all right.

Sutter told Marshall to keep the gold a secret. It might not amount to much, but it could still distract the men from their jobs.

But secrets like that don't last. Sutter's men soon learned what Marshall had found. On Sundays, their day off, they began to look for nuggets and gold dust. Some workers collected enough gold in an hour to equal a month's pay.

By the spring of 1848, more and more

tales were reaching San Francisco, which was home to 800 people. Miners were bragging about scraping gold off rocks with their knives. Why, one fellow had hit a $50 nugget while digging a hole for his tent pole.

Didn't there have to be a little truth to these reports? Many people thought so, and the gold fever spread. Lawyers dropped their clients and soldiers deserted their posts. The schoolhouse closed after its only teacher ran off. Then the mayor disappeared. And nobody could complain to the sheriff because he was gone, too.

By the end of June, San Francisco was almost a ghost town. Stores were empty. Doors blew open in the wind. Dogs roamed the streets and wooden sidewalks with only their shadows for company.

Everyone, it seemed, had left for the hills.

• 2 •
Heading West

During the summer of 1848, the news spread slowly eastward. It rode across the prairie on horseback. It paddled up the Mississippi River on steamboats. It blew around South America on sailing ships.

At first, people back East were not much impressed. Nobody was sure if the stories were true. After all, talk was cheap, and California was far away.

Most Americans didn't know much about California. The territory had only been part of the United States for a few months, since the end of the Mexican War. Its population was small and scattered—a mixture of native tribes, Mexican settlers, and a few American pioneers.

Before long, though, California was on everyone's mind. By November, the New York City newspapers were filled with stories about gold. There was talk of streets paved with gold and nuggets as big as apples lying on the ground.

Then in December, President James K. Polk spoke to Congress about the gold strike. Based on reports from the army and government officials, his speech mentioned "extensive" mines. "The abundance of gold . . ." he said, "would scarcely command belief. . . ."

That settled it. Even those people who didn't believe the newspapers had faith in the president. He was bound to know the truth.

Now California was the place to go. In 1848, a decent job as a store clerk or farmhand might be worth $7 a week. A miner could collect four times that much between breakfast and lunch.

It all sounded so simple. Spend a few months in California and then return home, pockets filled with gold. The thousands of dreamers who believed this were almost all men and were mostly young, though one was a ninety-year-old Revolutionary War veteran. Few traveled with their wives or children—if they had them—because they didn't plan to stay very long.

First, though, the miners had to get to California. One hopeful inventor offered a trip by flying machine. But his balloon-floating ship never got off the ground.

Instead, travelers went by land or sea.

The sea route, the favorite of Easterners, went down around South America and back up to San Francisco. Hundreds of ships, from elegant clippers to leaky barges, made the trip. The 15,000-mile voyage took from six months to a year.

Most ships were cramped and crowded. One put so many people into a single room that they had to sleep standing up. Sometimes the passengers were from the same town and knew each other. Often everyone was a stranger, wary of other travelers.

On such a long voyage, many passengers got seasick and could not eat. The rest weren't much luckier. The meals had odd names, like *lobscouse* and *hushamagrundy*. The ingredients—including salted meat and moldy bread—were even odder.

One passenger wrote that his favorite food was anything with dark molasses, because it hid the mold and killed the bugs.

By the end, most sea travelers were tired, sick, hungry, bored silly, and in need of a bath. Some had gambled away their savings. Many were in poor health. But almost all the hurts or hardships were forgotten at the first sight of San Francisco Bay.

People from the Midwest favored the

land route to California. From Missouri the trip was 1,800 miles by wagon train—although one man walked the distance with his belongings in a wheelbarrow. A typical wagon was ten feet long, four feet wide, and pulled by oxen or mules. The wagon train might have just a few wagons or several dozen.

The wagon master led the train and settled any problems along the way. He

also gave out chores—gathering firewood or water, keeping lookout, or cooking food. One wagon train even made its members change their underwear each week and carry three pounds of soap for baths.

Days on the trail were long, dusty, and hot. The ride was bumpy. Travelers carried

weapons to defend themselves from rattlesnakes, grizzly bears, and Indians. But more men were killed by accidents with guns than by any run-ins they had along the trail.

One big killer on the trail was cholera, a disease caused by a bacteria found in

water. It passed through rivers, wells, even canteens—and it acted fast. A man could feel feverish in the morning and be dead by sunset. Cholera claimed thousands of lives among the gold-seekers during the spring and summer of 1849.

The third route to California took the least time if things went well, but they rarely did go well. Travelers took a boat ride to Central America, walked sixty miles across Panama, and took another boat ride up to California.

The sea trips held few dangers because they were brief. The overland walk was the tricky part. The Panama jungle was hot and filled with mosquitoes that carried malaria, a usually fatal disease.

The jungle also was home to flamingoes, parrots, and monkeys. But most travelers were in too much of a hurry to notice.

Whether they came by boat or wagon train, about 80,000 people reached California in 1849. These were the Forty-Niners, hopeful miners who had survived the worst trip of their lives. They could afford to smile and shake one another's hands. Now, they thought, their worries were over.

· 3 ·
The Mining Life

Most of the gold-seekers had rushed to California without much thought. Some brought all the comforts of home: wooden chairs and tables, fancy dishes, even crystal lamps. Others were more practical. They brought raincoats, heavy boots, canvas tents, and cooking pans.

But almost no one knew how to mine for gold.

And nobody cared. Everyone was still dazzled by the wild success stories they had heard. One miner had fallen down a hill, dug into the dirt at the bottom, and struck it rich. Another had seen his mule pulling up tufts of grass—and flecks of gold, too. The biggest nugget found in 1849 weighed 161 pounds and was worth $38,000, so anything seemed possible.

Wise travelers spent little time in San Francisco, where a small hotel room rented for $1800 a month, the price of a new house back East. Even a house cat cost $8 to $12.

Instead, hopeful miners took a three-day ferry ride to the hills, where they began hunting for gold in and around the mountain rivers. One newcomer was amazed to see a seasoned miner "pull" a nugget from the bark of a tree. He had climbed halfway up a nearby pine to try his luck before he saw the miner laughing at him down below.

When a gold-seeker started mining for real, the first thing he did was stake a claim. To do this, he would drive four pegs into the ground at the corners of a piece of land beside a river. To hold his claim, he had to keep working it. A claim left untended for a week was up for grabs—unless the miner was sick.

A miner's day started early. Up at dawn, he wasted no time getting dressed because he never changed his clothes. After a quick meal of bacon, biscuits, and strong coffee, he headed for the river.

If the miner was working alone, he stood in the river wearing high boots to keep out the cold. As the water rushed by, he scooped sand and water into a metal pan with raised sides, which often doubled as his frying pan. Then he carefully swished the grit around.

The sand or dirt was swept to the edges of the pan, leaving the heavier gold or gold dust in the middle. The miner would empty the pan and then scoop up another load of sand and water.

Some miners worked in teams. Three men could sift through sand and silt more quickly than one if they used a *rocker* or a *Long Tom*.

The rocker was a wooden box about three feet long that sat in a rocking cradle. It had cleats and screens to separate the dirt from the gold. One man shoveled in the dirt, a second poured in the water, and the third rocked the cradle.

The Long Tom was a bigger box, eight to fourteen feet long. It had sieves and screens and cleats, too. But it didn't rock. Instead, a Long Tom required a steady stream of running water.

Digging, rocking, or swishing a pan was tiring, and the river water was painfully cold. In many places the mosquitoes were so thick, it was said they could lift a hat off a man's head if he wasn't paying attention.

After sunset, the miners staggered back to their tents or slept under the stars. In the few boarding houses, miners were stacked like wood in low bunks without pillows or sheets.

On Sundays, the miners rested. They washed and put on their best clothes. They even combed out their beards, braiding or coiling them in tails. One miner was known for dividing his beard in

half and tying it in a bow under his chin.

If enough miners settled in one place for a few months, they called it a town and gave it a name—like Fair Play, Bedbug, or Grizzly Flats. Soon someone would open a general store, and someone else a saloon.

Although storekeeping was not as exciting as mining, it was much more dependable. Most goods in the hills were traded for gold dust. One pinch was worth a dollar, but not everyone's pinch was the same. Many storekeepers got rich by selling shirts for $40 and boots for $20 in gold dust, ten times their price back East. Sugar, potatoes, and apples were $2 a pound, fifty times the usual price. For a hungry miner who couldn't wait, a slice of bread cost $1. Buttered bread cost $2.

Over time it became clear that not everyone was suited to mining. Some miners gave up after a day of hard work. Others endured months of empty stomachs, blistered hands, and crushed fingers before quitting.

These men could still earn a living, though. Some became messengers, charging busy miners fifty cents to mail a letter and $2 to pick one up in San Francisco. The few women in the camps could cook for $30 a day. And one former miner made $14 a day by playing the violin in a gambling house.

But most miners didn't quit, even for a well-paying job. There were 6,000 of them at the beginning of 1849, and tens of thousands more by the end. Each was searching for the one lucky strike that would make his fortune and send him home a hero.

· 4 ·
The Dust Settles

The miners of 1848 found the California hills pretty friendly. Their needs were simple, and there was enough gold to go around. No robberies and few fights were reported. When winter came, the miners gathered their savings and brought them to banks in San Francisco.

By 1850, these same miners could only shake their heads or scratch their beards at the change. San Francisco built 600 new buildings in 1849, and its population jumped to 34,000 by 1852, larger than Washington, D.C. Land lots that once sold for $16 were now worth $15,000. A miner in town had to stay alert and be prepared for trouble. It was a slow news day when no one was killed and no robberies were reported.

In 1849, the average miner earned $16 a day. In 1850, it was roughly half that. The mines and cities were built on success, but they also were jammed with poor and desperate men.

News of the gold strike had drawn miners from around the world—from Europe, Australia, China, and South America. Most of the Chinese came from southern China, where crops had failed and jobs were few. The Chinese described California as *Gum Shan*, the "Mountain of Gold." It was a land of hope to a starving peasant.

The land offered little hope to some. The hundreds of Yalesumni and members of other native tribes, who lived in the hills before anyone else, had already been pushed aside. But anyone whose skin was not white or who spoke English with a strange accent was badly mistreated. They had to pay special taxes and did not have the freedom to mine where they wanted. Some new towns even posted signs to keep these miners away.

The government should have stepped in, but there wasn't much government to go around. No police had been hired, and few laws had been passed. The army had its hands full keeping soldiers from deserting to the gold fields. A few *alcaldes*—a mixture of judge and mayor— who had retained their positions from the days of Mexican rule were scattered through the countryside. Their power was limited, however.

The most serious crime in the mining camps was claim-jumping. Murder came next. Once a suspect was caught, a judge and jury were picked, usually from the miners themselves. A quick trial was held. Since there were no jails, those who were judged guilty were punished at once. One stubborn thief, who refused to reveal where he had hidden a stolen sack of gold, was tied to a tree barebacked. Three hours and many mosquito bites later, he finally talked.

But even this rough justice varied. If an American stole a mule, he was whipped. If a Mexican stole one, he was hanged, even if nobody had proof.

Back in San Francisco, street gangs, like the Sydney Ducks from Australia, terrorized many people. In July, 1849, they attacked and looted a Chilean neighborhood. Several people died, and dozens more were hurt.

Slowly, things began to change. At the end of 1849, a governor was elected and a constitution was passed. Less than a year later, on September 9, 1850, the territory of California officially became a state.

The new state had a population of 92,000. Its future capital, Sacramento City, which hadn't even existed two years before, was booming. A visitor could take a long nap in Sacramento and awake to find a new building had gone up while he had slept. It was a wild and woolly time. Laws seemed to change every day, and

when people shook hands on a deal, they counted their fingers afterward to make sure none were missing.

In the meantime, the work of mining

became more organized. By 1851, teams of men were damming rivers to mine their bottoms. Other groups drilled tunnels in the hillsides.

Mining was becoming big business. Thousands of solitary miners still clogged the riverbeds, sifting sand in their tin pans. They didn't know it, but their greatest days had already passed.

• 5 •
The Country Moves On

Even after 1850, tens of thousands of people arrived in California each year looking for gold. They tended to stay whether they found it or not. Life in California was exciting, and even failed miners were reluctant to give it up.

San Francisco survived several major fires, rebuilding itself with alarming speed. During the 1850s, granite and brick gradually replaced rickety wood buildings. Solid wharves stretched out into the bay.

Some people saw there was as much money to be made from the miners as from the mines. Charles Crocker started with a general store in Sacramento and became one of the richest men in California. Collis Huntington sold shovels to miners in Sacramento, Mark Hopkins supplied them with hardware, and both men made vast fortunes through trade, real estate, and transportation.

Meanwhile, a former pots-and-pans peddler from New York came West with a

shipment of thick tent cloth. His name was Levi Strauss. The market for tents was bad, so Strauss turned his canvas into sturdy denim pants and sold them for $1 apiece. By the 1860s, hundreds of people worked for Levi Strauss & Company, making thousands of pants and work shirts a year.

In 1850, there were fewer than 1,500 California farmers. Californians imported much of their food—flour from Chile, for example, or vegetables from Hawaii. It took time for Eastern farmers to adjust to California's growing season. But they learned fast. By 1860, there were 20,000 farmers, and more land was used for farming every day.

The West was opening up faster than anyone had expected. In 1869, a new railroad connected the East and West Coasts. The trip took only a week—a speed undreamed of twenty years earlier.

As the former Forty-Niners settled down, most realized they had never made the fortunes they hoped for. Neither James Marshall nor John Sutter ever became rich from their discovery. Marshall never again struck any gold worth mentioning, and he ended up a poor blacksmith.

Sutter, meanwhile, made and lost several fortunes before moving back East to live out his last years in Pennsylvania.

But successful or not, all the miners had one thing in common. From city slicker to grizzled mountain man, each had played a colorful role in a truly American adventure.

tend to overemphasize fiction as elementary teachers have already done to the neglect of most kids' natural inclinations.

Nevertheless, the need for story is as strong as the need to know, and it, too, can be satisfied by print so long as the stories are easy to read. So the reading teacher keeps a good supply of stories on hand that are easy to read, ranging from PAL Paperbacks,[4] for example, to TV tie-ins to adult mysteries and Westerns. The reading teacher never uses these to "teach" skills for reading literature or to teach literary criticism—that's the English teacher's prerogative. Questions that the reading teacher asks about a particular novel should stem from genuine interest in the novel and in the student's reactions.

In order to serve students' needs better, the reading teacher has to know who is reading what. And students like to know what books their peers would recommend. So, while there are 101 ways of having kids report on their reading, the one we like best requires simply filling out two index cards, each with the title and name of author, number of pages, and the answers to two questions: On what page did you stop reading? When and where does the story take place? The reason for the first question may not be as obvious as for the second. The teacher's best clue to a student's reading interests is the kind of book he or she cannot finish. Further, this question tells students that you don't expect them to finish every book and they shouldn't pretend to have done so. Some kids may want to add a brief bouquet or brickbat, expressing their reactions.

The reason for the two cards is so that one may be filed by the title or author's name; the other by the student's. Thus anyone using these two files can ascertain which authors and titles are popular in this class; and Joe can get an idea for a book he'd like by checking behind Fred's name and avoiding the books that Lou reads.[5]

Reading teachers as well as English teachers have to know what books are popular with adolescents and what is being published for the young adult market. We wish we could devote more space to this topic in this text, but the most we can do is to advise that if you haven't taken a course in reading for adolescents recently, you are underprepared as a reading teacher. (You can become an expert without taking a course, but it's easier under the guidance of an instructor.) To catch up on your own, we recommend several good sources in Box 15-5 (pages 450–52).

If you want help with selecting a range of paperbacks and hardbacks, consider the sources in Box 15-6. The teaching materials which accompany these selected kits of trade books are more rightfully the domain of the English teacher, but they will help you (the reading teacher) to ask intelligent questions, and will, in fact, illuminate *your* reading of the books. Some reading teachers require individual students to react formally in writing or in discussion groups to

---

[4]Xerox Education Publications, 245 Long Hill Road, Middletown, CT 06457. Send for list of these high interest/low vocabulary *thin* paperbacks that include short novels and collections of short stories as well as nonfiction.

[5]The idea of the double file system was suggested by Paul Diederich in "What Does Research in Reading Reveal about Evaluation in Reading?" *English Journal* (September 1969).

reading which satisfies the need for story. We prefer not to do so, but for those of you who want suggestions for follow-up activities, we refer you to the sources in Box 15-6 (pages 454–55).

Comic books   A kind of subtopic here is that chunk of the "competing curriculum" known ironically as "comics." Obviously, comics satisfy the need for story among good readers and poor. Do they belong in school, even in classes that focus on out-of-school reading? We would give them high priority in a few classes, no priority in others. A teacher who is an expert on the comics might create a fascinating, intellectually demanding course on the comics as a social phenomenon. The readability—and respectability—of the comics run the gamut from almost illiterate to highly literate, satirical, witty, politically acute. As part of the pop culture, comics in the classroom run the same risks we discussed in relation to rock lyrics, but risks that you may be prepared to take. I can make a better case for comics than for pop lyrics, but I would not bring them into my classes until I had given myself a crash course on the kinds of comics my nonreaders might read, and until I had ordered my priorities for a particular class.

Reading to Forget

Most of this book is concerned with reading to remember, with using reading as a means of learning. I once worked in a K-8 school that had a Learning Center at one end of the building and an Unlearning Center at the other. They were both necessary to the mental health of the inhabitants. The Unlearning Center was really a place for unwinding, where kids could work out aggressions, learning blocks, and other problems by strenuous physical exercise under supervision. That school maintained a balance that we sometimes overlook in our zeal for learning how to learn.

So let's remember that a very valid use of reading for personal satisfaction is the book or magazine as escape hatch. Many literate adults seek emotional release in one kind of escape reading or another: whodunits, sci-fi, fantasies, travel books, popular biographies. And masses of young and old adults turn to print equivalents of the TV soap opera. Critics are quick to point out that addiction to print is no more laudable than addiction to TV when the same levels of violence, sensationalism, smut, sexual explicitness, and detachment from reality are found in both. To be sure, any addiction is to be avoided; both books and drugs can be used addictively or therapeutically. Yet, addiction to print, however damaging it may be to the addict, is almost never destructive to others, as is the case with other kinds of addiction.

Teachers should recognize the therapeutic values of escape reading. When college professors realize that the midnight oil is burning in the dorms for Harlequin paperbacks and Barbara Cartland and Heyerly romances, not for *The Culture of Narcissism* or *A Distant Mirror* or *The Ascent of Man*, they should move swiftly through the first reactions of despair and on to the reasons why ordinary students, overtaxed by college texts and collateral assignments, escape into fantasy worlds. Our hope is that future college students will be less taxed because they have learned better reading/study strategies in high school, but from sixth grade to sixteenth, teachers should respect the need for escape reading.

In middle school, where so many students need to consolidate beginning reading skills by easy reading of any kind, good teachers take advantage of reading to forget. In balanced counterpoint to reading to learn, they encourage escape reading, find time for it, and ask no questions.

RECAPPING MAIN POINTS

Although production of print in the United States has reached staggering proportions, critics charge widespread illiteracy among American adults. Meaningful estimates are hard to come by because definitions of literacy have changed since the time when functional literacy was set as equivalent to completing fourth grade. Today's definitions stress the ability to function in a "high tech" society and to learn through reading.

Most students develop on their own the literacy skills needed in life outside of school since these are an extension of skills learned in school. However, poor readers need instruction in "survival skills." Many of these can be taught in courses that permit real-life applications. In reading classes, where survival skills must be taught out of context, lessons should be subordinate to learning how and why to read for broader purposes, including personal satisfaction.

Reading and English teachers have responsibility for promoting reading for personal satisfaction. For students who take both reading and English, personal reading may be more strongly emphasized in the former and study of literature in the latter. To stimulate personal reading, teachers make classroom collections of books, magazines, and clippings related to their students' out-of-school interests. They teach units on newspapers and magazines and, like content teachers, make these media basic instructional resources. School publications, especially those with links to the community, provide reasons for reading, and even poor readers can contribute to their production. Word processors are proving their worth in this endeavor.

Students' need for information of all kinds, including trivia, can be satisfied by almanacs, popular reference books, and trade books.

The need to know and the need for story are strong in all human beings. Because the need for story is easily satisfied by films and television, the accessibility of stories in print is a major consideration, especially for poor and reluctant readers. To promote this reason for reading, teachers need to know what is popular with adolescents. Students' reports on their reading should not only inform the teacher but motivate their classmates.

To start a reading habit from the need for story, teachers have to tolerate subliterature, including comics. Even mature readers turn occasionally to reading for escape. Especially in the secondary years, teachers must take advantage of every reason for reading, even reading to forget, if they are to win ground for eventually developing the will to learn through print.

FOR DISCUSSION

1. Discuss the many issues involved in the controversy over whether secondary school curricula should include instruction in how to read materials that are not integral to subjects like history, math, literature, and science.

2. In recent years courses like Driver Education have come under attack for diverting students' time and energy from basic education. What other electives might provoke similar criticism? Defend these courses as necessary settings for the teaching of basic literacy skills.

3. What questions are raised in this chapter about teachers co-opting materials from the "competing curriculum" to teach literacy skills? What additional materials of this kind might be used to teach reading? What arguments can you present for and against their use in school?

4. Chart your own reading habits over the past twelve months. Use such headings as Title, Type, Assigned, Self-selected, Source, Time Spent, and so on. Which reasons for reading referred to in this chapter are revealed in your chart? When you share your chart with colleagues, consider why you read more or less than you used to and how your habits and interests might compare with those of other occupational groups.

5. Why must teachers do all they can to motivate every student to spend more time reading? Are there limits to what teachers should expect of themselves and their students in this regard?

6. How can content teachers in academic as well as nonacademic areas encourage students to read beyond their school assignments?

7. Read and report on one of the first three books listed under Further Reading at the end of this chapter.

8. What is "the new literacy"? Read the essay of that title by Benjamin Compaine in the Winter, 1983, issue of *Daedalus*. (We hope you will be attracted to other essays in this collection and that these, too, will enliven your discussion of how reading fares in a high-tech society.)

FURTHER READING

Chambers, Aidan. *Introducing Books to Children*. 2d ed. Boston: Horn Book, 1983.
    Don't be put off by "children," which as used by this English author refers also to teenagers. Part Two, "The Reading Environment," contains many practical suggestions on browsing, recommending books, and setting up a school bookstore.

Donelson, Kenneth and Alleen Pace Nilsen. *Literature for Today's Young Adults*. Glenview, IL: Scott, Foresman, 1980.
    See especially Chapter 12, "Using and Promoting Books with Young Readers."

Fader, Daniel. *The New Hooked on Books*. Berkeley: Berkeley Publishing Co., 1976.

Hunter, Carman St. John with David Harman. *Adult Literacy in the United States: A Report to the Ford Foundation*. New York: McGraw Hill, 1979.

Thomas, Ellen Lamar and H. Alan Robinson. *Improving Reading in Every Class*. 3d ed. Boston: Allyn and Bacon, 1972.
  Chapter 18 describes Coach Sandy Patlak's ideas for developing lifetime readers among sports-minded young people.

12 The Word Factor in Reading and Writing

By March of my first year of teaching, I was convinced that I'd made a terrible mistake: I should have chosen first grade instead of tenth. It would be better, I thought, to catch them before they know anything instead of struggling with 14-and-15-year-olds who half-know too much. Little did I know then that six-year-olds have already passed through their richest learning years and come into first grade with staggering amounts of knowledge about language and vocabularies that have beer estimated to run as high as 17,000 words.[1]

But you understand why I was frustrated by March of that first year, especially with respect to language development. Vocabulary is such a frustrating matter. Oh, great fun to teach, especially if you love words—but are they learning anything?

Now, many years later, I feel almost equal frustration as I consider how much we know about the word factor in reading and writing, and try to sort out what parts of that knowledge can make a difference to teachers and their students in secondary schools. When I began to teach, there was a mounting accumulation of research studies and instructional materials supporting the importance of vocabulary building. Now these resources threaten to overwhelm us. In this chapter we'll try to sift through the essential understandings about vocabulary growth so that you can decide how much effort and what kinds of materials will pay the greatest dividends in "word power" for your students. We'll refer you to books for students and sources for teachers. We shall also give you lists of do's and don't's. In an effort to be brief, we shall sound positive—even dogmatic—about matters that are not yet that clear-cut.

The section which follows gives a minimum of theoretical background; the next two sections comment on practices for developing word meanings, first as

---

[1]Estimates of the size of children's vocabulary at given ages vary widely because of differences in sampling methods and in kinds of responses accepted as evidence of "possessing" vocabulary. Probably the estimate that average children learn at least 20,000 words in their first ten years of life is not only realistic but useful for teachers to keep in mind. Excellent information is contained in "Vocabulary Knowledge," an article by Richard Anderson and Peter Freebody in *Comprehension and Teaching: Research Reviews,* John T. Guthrie, ed. (International Reading Association, Newark, DE 1981): 77–117.

like the concepts to come first and the appropriate vocabulary to follow, but it
the reading teacher operates, then as content teachers handle the word factor;
and we close with a section on words as entities which can be pronounced and
spelled.

Understanding the Word Factor

While research has not yet cleared up all the mysteries about how people
"process information" and which factors contribute most heavily to the process
of comprehending print, every study identifies "word knowledge" as a necessary component. Teachers must be concerned with three aspects of word knowledge: words as physical entities, words as meanings, and concepts which may or
may not be expressed in words.[2] Postponing until the last section our concerns
with words as symbols to be pronounced and spelled, we shall remind you in
this section of what you have observed about the ways in which people acquire
vocabularies for reading and listening, writing and speaking.

Words as Meanings

When we use terms like "vocabulary development" and "word power" in
this chapter, we refer to understanding what words mean in particular contexts.
"Meanings," Carroll reminds us, "stand in complex relationships to . . . words.
These relationships may be described by the rules of usage that have developed
by the processes of socialization and communication."[3] Meanings are agreed
upon by those who share a common use of the words. See Box 12-1 for Oliver
Wendell Holmes's metaphorical definition of "word," which illuminates this
point about the relationship of meanings to words.

The reason for laboriously defining "meanings" in connection with words is
that we need to distinguish *words* from *concepts*. We are not talking about
concept development in this chapter—that comes in the next—but since
teachers often identify concepts by words, and all too frequently by one-word
labels, it is essential that we try to make a clear distinction between our use of
word and *concept*. Concepts are classes of experience *formed in individuals*, says
Carroll, sometimes independently of language processes but more often (we
would say) in close dependence upon language processes. As an example, think
of three-year-old children who understand how plurals are formed in English;
because they have had the necessary "classes of experience" we say they have
the concept of pluralization. What they don't have is the vocabulary to say that
some words are *plural* and others *singular*.

Nevertheless, it is very difficult to disentangle "words as meanings" from
"words as concepts," and it may not be practical for us teachers to belabor the
distinction. It may be sufficient simply to recognize that students can learn the
vocabulary of a subject without understanding the concepts. Generally, we'd

---

[2]John B. Carroll, "Words, Meanings and Concepts," *Harvard Educational Review* 34:2 (Spring 1964):
178–202.
[3]Carroll, p. 185.

BOX 12-1

> A word is not a crystal, transparent and unchanging; it is the skin of a living thought, and may vary greatly in color and content according to the circumstances and time in which it is used.
>
> —Oliver Wendell Holmes (in the case of Towne v. Eisner)

often happens the other way around. When our tests of learning are wholly verbal, we may not know whether students have mastered the concepts *and* the vocabulary or just the vocabulary.

How Young Children Acquire Meaning Vocabularies

Why must we "teach" vocabulary anyway if children acquire thousands of words before they enter school and presumably go on adding to their vocabularies with or without us? Children's early acquisition of vocabulary is aided by two conditions: first, they learn words by direct experiences for immediate use in satisfying real needs (such as hunger, thirst, protection, love, curiosity); second, young children have phenomenal memories that diminish, alas, as their lives grow more complex. Their vocabularies are made up partly of words they can use in speaking but mostly of words they can understand when they hear them in the meaningful contexts of their own lives, and in stories read them or seen on television. As children learn to read, the number of words that they can recognize in print grows until it overlaps with their listening vocabulary. Gradually, their reading vocabulary outstrips their listening vocabulary because reading takes them beyond their experiences. The proportion of their meaning vocabulary that they use in speech remains comparatively small, and their writing vocabularies grow only to the extent that they have reasons for writing.

When they are very young, children learn words purposefully. They internalize word meanings and organize them into semantic systems of similarity, contrast, and hierarchy.[4] They acquire concepts, not merely vocabulary. This kind of growth continues in most people until about age twenty, though at a decelerating rate, and then it stops. We go on learning new words after we are out of our teens but we learn many of them not as the language of ideas but as labels, like the names we attach to acquaintances. In short, as adults we chiefly learn synonyms and jargon. We learn to say "visual display" when referring to print on the page. We vaguely connect *holograms* with transmitting whole images from one point in space to another. Joos suggests that some people, whom he calls "academics," continue to add new words to their personal vocabularies and to refine their understanding of them for the rest of their lives, but that "normal" persons don't increase their personal vocabularies after age twenty. "Both normal and academic persons have been president of the United States;

---

[4]Martin Joos, "Language and the School Child," *Harvard Educational Review* 34:2 (Spring 1964): 203–10.

for example, Eisenhower is a normal person and Truman is an academic with a vocabulary considerably more than twice as large. Similarly, both types are common in fairly low-ranking employments. . . ." We would guess that Spiro Agnew, Nixon's first vice president, whose speech was studded with sesquipedalian words, is another example of a "normal," learning words as labels, not as shaping one's language to a growing wisdom. (By the way, if you just looked up *sesquipedalian* or figured it out from context, you've learned a new label.)

Vocabulary and I.Q.

Teachers should love words and foster vocabulary-building but not mistake this for growth in real language, which comes through concept development. We remind those of you too young to remember Spiro Agnew that a large vocabulary is not a sure sign of wisdom or even intelligence. But they are related. If intelligence is the capacity to see interrelationships in minimal data and to apply what is learned to new situations, we can see why intelligent people have large vocabularies. Bright youngsters draw inferences about word meanings from minimal clues; that is, they "pick up" words from fewer encounters than not-so-bright kids need. Anderson and Freebody, in the article recommended on the first page of this chapter, say that the strong relationship between vocabulary and general intelligence is "one of the most robust findings in the history of intelligence testing." They summarize the evidence to show that correlations between vocabulary subtest scores and total scores on a number of different IQ tests range between .71 and .98 at different age levels.

Fifty years ago a psychologist named Johnson O'Connor, reacting to the unpopularity of IQ tests, decided to look elsewhere for a common factor that would account for some people having larger vocabularies than others. By means of standardized testing, he sampled the vocabularies of persons in all walks of life and found that in any field the persons who got ahead were the ones who recognized the meanings of most words, that is, all the common words in the sample and more of the infrequently used words like *hirsute* and *syzygy*. The common factor among the high scorers was not years of education or chronological age, but high position in their fields. The self-taught shop foreman had a higher score than the college-educated sales representative.

Does this imply that teachers cannot affect vocabulary development since it comes naturally to those with verbal aptitudes? No, because aptitudes are affected by interest and opportunities. Take two 14-year-olds with roughly equivalent "mental ability." One has a much larger vocabulary than the other because (1) he is alert to words; (2) he meets more words in a greater variety of contexts; (3) he helps himself to remember words. These habits can be inculcated by the schools. Research shows that schools do this job best when teachers systematically plan for vocabulary development and do not leave the matter entirely to incidental learning.[5]

---

[5]Walter Petty, Curtis P. Herold, and Earline Stoll, *The State of Knowledge about the Teaching of Vocabulary* (National Council of Teachers of English, 1968).

Vocabulary and Environment

How large a vocabulary you can acquire depends on *when* you live as well as *where*. The difference between Shakespeare's vocabulary of 15,000 words and the 45,000 words of a contemporary graduate student is explained by the four hundred years of exploration and invention that lie between the Elizabethan age and the age of telecommunications. These four hundred years have seen an astronomical multiplication of ideas and artifacts that required naming so that by the 1960s the editors of Webster's *Third New International Dictionary* (1961) could select 450,000 words for inclusion. For the next edition (1976) they kept the same number (replacing some old words with new entries), though they had amassed definitions for more than 600,000. The example of Shakespeare reminds us, of course, that it's not the size of one's vocabulary that matters but how well it fits one's needs.

Just as the Elizabethan Age limited the size of Shakespeare's vocabulary, so does society in the narrower sense of family, community, and associates determine a student's vocabulary. In the 1960s a London teacher named Basil Bernstein observed the "restricted code" of some families and the "elaborated codes" of others. He noted that some poor families living all their lives in close quarters used very few words to communicate with each other, while other families, usually better off economically, needed larger vocabularies to communicate what they were doing and thinking and feeling in a much broader world. One's expressive vocabulary is very much bounded by one's audience, so that a mother isolated with young children on a camping trip uses a very different vocabulary from the one she employs after returning to a job outside the home. But even on a camping trip, an adult's receptive vocabulary is constrained only by the books he or she carries and the ability to read. It is difficult to conceive of persons in the United States being so isolated that they receive no messages from the world outside when we recall that 99 percent of American homes have at least one television set.

How Interest Affects Vocabulary

Yet even with similar access to words through books and the mass media, people vary greatly in the number of words they notice and remember. Granted that intelligence and life experience are factors, an equally important influence is interest in words. Readers of similar levels of ability can have different degrees of interest in words. One reader is interested in what happens in a novel; if a new word appears which is not absolutely crucial to meaning, he scarcely notices it. Another reader is more interested in style than plot; she is alert to new words and turns of phrase.

The teacher's main effort in developing vocabularies is to arouse students' interest in words. This is more important than teaching specific word meanings or even vocabulary-building techniques. Any vocabulary exercise which is boring and injurious to interest must be discarded. What is tedious to some will be interesting to others, of course, but, by and large, most students—even those who don't intend to go to college—see value in improving their vocabularies. And even those headed for college find looking up words in a dictionary and using them in sentences a boring procedure. What is worse, this practice may cause them to misuse vaguely understood new vocabulary.

In addition to stimulating a general interest in words and language, teachers want to prevent the skipping of words which are crucial to understanding an assignment. That is why they alert their students to those words *before* they begin reading.

Chances are you never "saw" *sesquipedalian* before reading this chapter. We're willing to wager you will see it at least once in the next six months, if only on one of those graffiti cards found in gift shops: Eschew Sesquipedalian Obfuscations. You know that the frequency of *sesquipedalian* has not suddenly increased. Why didn't you notice it before? Why will you notice it now?

Levels of Word Knowledge

Planned instruction should be based on expectations for growth that are neither too demanding nor too slack. Knowing the different levels of word learning helps you to set appropriate goals. Let's review these levels by thinking of yourself as the learner.

Minimal understanding is represented by the ability to categorize. You may not know the meaning of *ohm, lintel, gusset, slalom,* or *colander,* but you recognize that they are associated respectively with electricity, architecture, dressmaking, skiing, and cooking. These words are on your threshold of meaning. They probably got onto the threshold through fairly passive reading and listening. Really to understand the meaning of *slalom* you would have to do more than half-attend to the Winter Olympics broadcast on television; you might have to be a skier yourself.

Just below this threshold are words you can categorize as to their part of speech. If you came across the sentence "Have you ever seen a kinkajou?" you might not have the foggiest notion of what a kinkajou is, but you know at least that it is something that can be seen, a concrete noun, not an abstract one. As you try to find out what students "know" of a word, be sure to credit them with threshold meaning, when it exists, and understand its limitations. A person who can categorize words like *ohm* and *lintel* probably reads widely and is relatively alert to words. He or she may also have wide interests and really know something about electricity and architecture, but you cannot be sure.

Another indication of minimal awareness is mistaking the meaning of a word or term by assigning an opposite meaning. Very often the distractors on a vocabulary test consist of an antonym and two or three other words not connected at all with the key word. The student who misses the right meaning and chooses its opposite is closer to understanding than the student who selects one of the neutral distractors.

Beyond recognizing the category to which a word belongs, students may recognize its meaning among several choices. At a still higher level of understanding they may recall a word's meaning without cues. It is easier to use a word in a phrase or sentence than it is to define it. A student who may not be able to define *environment* can say: "You ought to live in a clean environment." Abstract nouns are harder to define than concrete ones, and consequently you

BOX 12-2

VOCABULARY TOOLS FOR TEACHERS

Word Frequency Counts

Dale, Edgar and Joseph O'Rourke. *The Living Word Vocabulary: A National Vocabulary Inventory*. (Field Enterprises Educational Corp., 1976). Distributed by Dome, Inc., 1169 Logan Ave., Elgin, IL 60120.

Kucera, H. and W. Nelson Francis. *Computational Analysis of Present-Day American English*. (Brown University Press, 1967).

Thorndike, Edward L. and Irving Lorge. *The Teacher's Word Book of 30,000 Words*. (Bureau of Publications, Teachers College, Columbia University, 1944). Second printing, 1952.

How to Teach Vocabulary

Dale, Edgar and Joseph O'Rourke. *Techniques of Teaching Vocabulary*. (Field Educational Publications, Inc., 1971).

Dale, Edgar. *The Word Game: Improving Communications*. (Bloomington, IN: Fastback 60, The Phi Delta Kappa Educational Foundation, 1975).

Deighton, Lee C. *Vocabulary Development in the Classroom*. (New York: Teachers College Press, 1959).

ask students to define them only under special circumstances such as writing an essay to define *loyalty* or *courage* or *sportsmanship*.

Miss Fidditch—that symbol of the inflexible English teacher—used to say: "You don't know a word if you can't define it. A word isn't yours until you can use it." By such lofty and unrealistic standards, few students "know" many words. To make reasonably accurate estimates about what students *know* (and that is the teacher's role in life), you must credit even their partial knowledge. For example, students who can read with a great deal of understanding material that uses many of their "threshold words" may not be able to define them or even distinguish an exact meaning among several possibilities; they can use these words in reading but not in writing. Only with respect to words that have moved off the threshold and into the students' meaning vocabulary can Miss Fidditch begin to work at the laudable goal of helping them to use words with precision and recognize when others are doing so.

The Need for Repeated Encounters

It takes time to "learn" words because knowledge grows through repeated uses. I remember *not* learning *jejune*. I came across it in the pages of *The New Yorker* years ago in an article by the political reporter Richard Rovere. I was struck probably by its unusual sound and configuration and the fact that it was used in a context that didn't give me a clue to its meaning. Since I'd been well schooled, I kept a vocabulary notebook into which I dutifully entered *jejune* together with its dictionary definition and a bit of Rovere's context. Years probably went by before I encountered *jejune* again, but when I did I remembered having looked it up and recorded its definition, and I had a clear visual image of the word as it had

BOX 12-3

CAPACITY

Capacity 26 Passengers
      —sign in a bus

Affable, bibulous,
Corpulent, dull,
eager-to-find-a-seat,
formidable,
garrulous, humorous,
icy, jejune,
knockabout, laden-
with-luggage (maroon),
mild-mannered, narrow-necked,
oval-eyed, pert,
querulous, rakish,
seductive, tart, vert-
iginous, willowy,
xanthic (or yellow),
young, zebuesque are my
passengers fellow.
                    —John Updike

SOURCE: *The Carpentered Hen and Other Tame Creatures.* (Random House, 1982).

appeared in the *The New Yorker* column. In fact, I remembered everything about the word except its meaning. Why? Because to learn *jejune* I needed many encounters with it, and *jejune* appears very infrequently, probably less than once in five million words. (Researchers have counted word frequencies and published them in books available to all of us. See Box 12-2.)

A teacher wanting me to master *jejune* would have had to arrange for me to have many more encounters with it. Since *jejune* would not (apparently did not) crop up that frequently in my normal reading, the teacher would have to include the word in reading materials written especially to include it. (Notice its use in Updike's poem in Box 12-3.)

The need for repetition or *redundancy* is an important idea to hold on to in developing vocabulary as well as comprehension. The general vocabulary you select to teach should be geared to a particular group of students and their likely use of those words in reading. Are these word meanings likely to be encountered fairly often by these students? If not, don't teach them. If yes, provide repeated use. Words taught on Monday should have many repetitions before you test on Friday to see if they have been learned.

The principle of redundancy prevents you from overloading students. Obviously, teachers who plan repetitive encounters with words have to choose fewer words. Reducing word lists is more likely to increase vocabulary growth than to stifle it. Overly zealous teachers in secondary schools, aware that SAT's are around the corner, assign lists of words uniformly—say 25 words every week to every student in English 10–B. That practice is wasteful of teachers' time and students', given what we know about the need for repetition and about the range of students' vocabularies. The students who know most of the words in the lists anyway may profit a mite from the weekly reminder that "vocabulary is important if you want to get into the college of your choice." But for average students who normally learn fewer than ten new words a week from all sources, the weekly list does more harm than good. Normally, we don't learn words from lists or from dictionaries anyway. We learn them from repeated encounters in natural contexts.

How Readers Use Context

Let's consider the importance of context. The need in secondary school is to accelerate the natural rate of learning from context. Although students pick up meanings from context without conscious effort, using one or another of the clues in Box 12-4, they do so only if the context itself is very clear and familiar and only, as we said above, if they experience repeated encounters in context. And, of course, as students move into more mature materials, especially content textbooks, the contexts are no longer easy and familiar, and the increase in new terms to be learned is enormous. So teachers help students to become *consciously* aware of the uses and the limitations of context. There are quantities of instructional materials on the market to help you do this. You have only to select wisely.

To remind yourself of the limitations of context, read this sentence: *Adamense gerfloogles the tamen of fliffitries*. You can understand its syntax but you cannot guess at the meaning of even one of the three nouns or the verb because the overload of new "words" is too great. Try these progressively easier sentences. When does the meaning of *tamen* become reasonably clear to you?

> Adamense expands the tamen of fliffitries.
> Experience expands the tamen of fliffitries.
> Experience expands the tamen of adolescents.

Your conclusion? If the text is too difficult, then readers won't get any help from context and they will quit reading for meaning.

To make use of the synonym clue in the sentence below, you must apply what you know about syntax.

"And that solitary meal was a *refection* to be remembered." Knowing that a common use of the verb *to be* is to link the subject and predicate nominative in meaning or identity, you can guess that *refection* is a synonym for *meal*. But many teachers in my classes don't apply their understanding of syntax to this sentence. It is only when I relate *refection* to *refectory*, which some remember from college days as another word for *dining room*, that they connect it with *meal*. Context works best for those most at ease with English syntax, but even they must be reminded to apply knowledge they already have, as of syntax and also of root words.

Can you use context to determine the meaning of *protean* in this sentence?

In form it is protean: the ball and the brick, the cube and the cucumber, the disc and the dumbbell, the melon and the millstone, the bologna and the ostrich egg. . . .

BOX 12-4

CONTEXT CLUES

Unknown word	Context clue	Example
edifice	synonym	Another word in passage means the same as unknown word.
		It is an expanded building which a noted Boston architect described as a "barbarous, miscellaneous *edifice*."
trundles	contrast	The unknown word has a meaning that is opposite to a known word.
		Although it is called the "rapid transit," it *trundles* along at about fifteen miles an hour.
frugality	summary	The unknown word summarizes the ideas that precede or follow it.
		A proper Bostonian never throws anything away. He is likely to save tinfoil, odd lengths of string and twine, scrap paper, empty medicine bottles, twigs and branches for the fireplace. An outstanding characteristic of a true Bostonian is his *frugality*.
conflagration	experience	Life experience tells the reader what the unknown word probably means.
		Fortunately, the fire crews extinguished the minor *conflagration* in the rear cabin.
speleologists	definition	The unfamiliar word is defined in context.
		On July weekends the Science Museum will show a film about *speleologists*, men who explore the silent, sunless underground caves.
obsequious	reflection of a mood or situation	The unknown word fits a mood or situation that has already been established.
		The atmosphere was genteel, the dining room spacious and quietly elegant; hightoned Bostonians sipped their sherry there and ate oysters or soft-shelled crabs secure in the assurance that they were surrounded only by others of their kind who had smiled aristocratically and nodded politely as *obsequious* waiters ushered them to their accustomed tables.

Continued

BOX 12-4 (continued)

CONTEXT CLUES

Unknown word	Context clue	Example
albeit	familiar expression	A word that is unfamiliar in form is readily recognizable in meaning because it fits a natural turn of expression.
		Woolen mufflers, fur neckpieces of great age, and hats that really protect the head, *albeit* with just a touch of ornamentation, are well regarded for routine daytime wear.
antivivisection	no safe clue	Context may be unrevealing or misleading.
		All sorts of causes find champions on the Hill. Earnest ladies in ancient furs flock to teas to promote art galleries and *antivivisection*.

Context in this case includes the colon—and sensing that the colon signals a series of examples of *protean*. But, again, my students respond best when I remind them of Proteus, the god of the sea who had the ability to change shapes.

Context exercises are most effective when the word whose meaning is to be guessed is already partially known. Then students can be required not merely to guess the meaning of the "unknown" word but to show which other words and phrases illuminate its meaning.

Context consists of much more than a phrase or a sentence. To learn a new word from context readers often need to connect a clue coming at the beginning of a paragraph with the "new" word which comes in the last sentence. Chunks of context large enough to illustrate this principle are not found in typical exercises. Therefore, you have to supplement such exercises by guiding students' use of context in content textbooks.

One use of context isn't enough. Before readers can learn a new meaning, they have to check out a first guess again and again.

Readers use context well if they are used to guessing. If teachers have taught them never to guess, they are handicapped as users of context clues. Teaching kids to guess goes against the grain of many conscientious teachers, so perhaps we should say "hypothesize" instead. Even more than *guess, hypothesize* carries the connotation of testing—checking to see whether a hunch works in this and other contexts. It is not wild, unscientific guessing we are promoting, but consistent checking of one's hunches. Eventually, if a reader's guesses from context seem not to be fitting new contexts, he or she seeks the authority of the dictionary. "Eventually" may mean "years." A student said that he had guessed wrong about *chronic* for years. He thought it meant *fatal* because in his experience everyone with a chronic disease had died. It was only when he became aware of *chronic offender* and *chronic liar* that he attached "long-lasting" to his sense of the word.

The student raised the example of *chronic* when we were discussing the merits of studying etymologies, that is, roots and affixes. I was making the point that for most secondary students context is a more powerful tool. He was making the very valuable point that context clues frequently need an assist. The meaning of *chronic* became clear when he saw its relationship to *chronicle, chronology, chronometer.* Students should be taught that context does not always reveal meaning and that guesses must be checked not only with new context but with additional clues like the meanings of parts of words.

What Is a Hard Word?

One measure of a "hard" word is how infrequently it is used. That's a useful measure for test-makers who try to sample in a fifty-item test the thousands of words any student knows. But frequency of use is not a wholly reliable index for teachers, because rare words, from the very fact that they are used infrequently, often retain specific closed meanings. *Antimacassar* is a rare word today but not a difficult one. It has one fixed meaning; an antimacassar is the piece of cloth, usually a doily, that Victorian homemakers pinned on sofas and chairs to keep them from getting soiled. You may consider it a "hard" word if you don't remember its meaning the next time you see it, though chances are the context will make its meaning clear enough. You may remember it better if you know why those pieces of cloth are called *antimacassars.* They protect against (*anti*) *macassar*, a hair oil which was sold in Victorian times under this trade name, derived from a seaport in Indonesia.

Jejune is a hard word not just because of its low frequency but because its present meaning is more metaphorical than literal. It comes from a Latin word that meant "empty as a result of fasting" and referred to an empty stomach. But a writer using *jejune* today means that an idea is empty and lacks nourishment for the mind.

Words that have many meanings and whose meanings change with use are more difficult to learn than rare words. Words that represent concepts which are complex classes of experience are more difficult than words for specific objects and ideas, even uncommon objects and ideas. Common words which become "dead metaphors" are often especially difficult for immature readers. Betsy knows two meanings for *chest*: part of the body and a piece of furniture; she's heard of a hope chest, but a war chest is a whole new idea. Dick knows that grenades and firecrackers explode, but he is not sure what is meant by "knowledge explosion" or "population explosion."

Which words should teachers call attention to, discuss, elaborate on—the hard common words or the easy rare ones? We wish we could answer: "Oh, choose the middle ground, words that are fairly common and not too complex." But that answer is too simple to be helpful. In general, the really hard "common" words which involve complex concepts are "taught" over long periods of time by content teachers. They are not the stuff of vocabulary-building courses.

Unfortunately, high school teachers often spend time on words that are easy and rare—words like *tureen, patina, mendicant, raze, salubrious, eleemosynary*. It would be better to emphasize shades of meaning carried by more ordinary words (such as *miserly, frugal, stingy, parsimonious*) and common words used in unusual ways (*condemn a building, welding a treaty, academic question, rifle a store*).

Influence of School on Students' Vocabularies

To repeat an earlier observation: Family, community, and society influence vocabulary development. Since school is part of students' "society" for five or six hours a day, why does education not have a greater effect upon their learning of vocabulary? Verbal scores on the Scholastic Aptitude Test declined steadily from 1967 to 1977, dropped again in 1979 and 1980, and stabilized in 1981–82.[6] Granted that this decline reflects, in part, the fact that increasing numbers of students from noneducating homes have taken the examinations in these years, we still must ask why the schools have not been more effective in helping these students gain greater verbal facility. Among many answers, we suggest that the teaching of vocabulary falls short in both time and timing. Not enough teachers in secondary schools devote sufficient *time* to vocabulary study—students do not spend enough time in reading and writing. *Timing* is a factor also. Many conscientious secondary teachers, aware of the values of word study, give attention to the vocabulary of a selection only *after* the students have read it. But by then vocabulary instruction is too little and too late. Students need good teaching *before* they read, to alert them to key words and to ensure comprehension. They need discussion of words after reading, too, but for the different purposes of reinforcement and testing. (See Box 12-5 for an English teacher's view that cramming on vocabulary lists doesn't improve SAT scores.)

Because the word factor is so important to comprehension, and because teachers can do so much to stimulate adolescents' interests in vocabulary development, we devote the rest of this chapter to how a departmentalized staff plans a balanced program in this aspect of learning.

Vocabulary Development: A Direct Approach by Reading Teachers

Between grades 5 and 8 and again between grades 9 and 12, all students should have a chance to study vocabulary directly and deliberately. Just how the time for this direct study will fit into students' schedules will vary from one school to another, depending upon its size and budget. If resources are available, we recommend a half year's course in vocabulary development in the junior high school and again in the high school, probably as a cross-grade "elective" to be chosen twice in the six-year span. In schools too small for elective systems to be practical, we suggest at least two extended units on vocabulary development

---

[6]We recommend your study of *On Further Examination*, Report of the Advisory Panel on the Scholastic Aptitude Test Score Decline, College Entrance Examination Board (Box 2814, Princeton, NJ 08540), 1977.

BOX 12-5

AN ENGLISH TEACHER DISCUSSES VOCABULARY BUILDING

High school students and their parents put great pressure on English teachers to help students memorize long lists of big words, supposedly to raise SAT scores. . . . These students have not considered how low the odds are that the few words they study out of a possible 3000 will appear on any one edition of the test. . . .

"My strategy for improving verbal SAT scores is to raise the basic reading level rather than the number of words the student recognizes, for the following reasons: 1) all SATs contain reading comprehension questions; 2) improving the reading level also increases the size of the vocabulary but in a less dangerous manner; and 3) greater speed in reading standardized test questions has apparently helped my students even in math and chemistry tests. . . .

"To prepare students for verbal SATs and adult life, the individual English teacher would do better to teach the basic elements of English, especially reading skills, than just to increase the pre-test hysteria by helping students further into the vocabulary-list quicksand."

SOURCE: Barbara Brown Hillje, "Some Horsesense about Raising SAT Scores," *English Journal* (Sept. 1980): 2–31.

within the English curriculum from 7 to 12, to supplement consistent word study throughout the year in these classes as in all content classes.

While there is no formula for this phase of an all-school language program, we recommend that reading and/or English teachers think of vocabulary development in the much broader context of study of language. The goal should be for students to learn the nature of language and the history of its development from prehistory through the contemporary age of telecommunications. Concurrently with studying the language development of humankind, they should refine their own strategies for learning words. All of this begins in elementary school, of course, and the secondary curricula have much to build upon. One basal reading series, for example, which is developed around a "learning to learn" theme, begins the study of language in grade 4 and includes selections on man's first words and number symbols, Sequoya's invention of an alphabet for the Cherokees, discoveries about the Indo–European language, and many other aspects of communication.

Units of the kind we recommend have long been a substantial part of the English curriculum. If you are a reading teacher, you should not fail to study the English curriculum in your school to learn the substance of such units. If you are an English teacher, you and your colleagues are, no doubt, continuously evaluating your curriculum for grades 7 through 12 to ensure adequate treatment of all aspects of language: its history, semantics, grammar, uses and kinds of dictionaries, dialectology, and etymology. All these elements should be plainly visible and accorded time either as units or separate courses. English classes which neglect language study in favor of literature and composition are out of balance. We realize that English is not content so much as process and that today's schools are under heavy pressure to teach reading and writing, but while applauding emphasis on process, we would argue that much of what students should read and write about is their own and others' use of language.

In units on language a major focus is helping students to become conscious of the strategies they use in developing vocabularies *through* reading and for writing and speaking. We shall discuss three strategies: using context, using word parts, and using the dictionary. In the course of teaching these strategies, you also teach the meanings of many words directly, but the reading teacher's task, unlike the content teacher's, is not to teach words but strategies for learning them.

Word meanings, and concepts, are better learned (and taught) in context. Teachers of content have no shortage of words and concepts to teach, and in doing so they help students apply the strategies refined under your tutelage. But you—as a teacher of process, not content—have less-certain sources of words than your colleagues.

Resources for Word Study

Because words are learned best in context, we urge reading teachers to seek an organizing principle for the reading course as a whole or for units within the course. One such organizing principle might be the history of language; another might be how people communicate. If your whole course is on vocabulary development, you can organize it according to topics. For example, your students' content textbooks can suggest an organization: a unit on the language of science, another on the language of mathematics, a third on the language of history. You can reinforce textbook study methods by showing how to study words before, during, and after reading an assignment. (To avoid repetition, we refer you to the section below on developing vocabulary in content fields.)

But suppose you have organized your reading/study skills class to highlight strategies for learning. In that case, one topic might be understanding the seven types of context clues (Box 12-4), for which you could draw your examples from your students' content textbooks. Another topic might be understanding multiple meanings, and you could tie content fields to this topic by observing how the meanings of words change from one subject to another, as *note* in English, music, business; *influence* in history and science; *energy* in physics, health, and social studies.

For some special reading classes or vocabulary electives, content textbooks are not appropriate. What, then, are your sources of words? Newspapers and television, popular magazines, hobbies—to name a few. Whenever you can, group the words to be learned into categories and relate them to topics of interest.

It is scarcely necessary for reading teachers today to make up their own materials for vocabulary development. The problem is to select judiciously from the deluge of commercial materials available. Ideally, and undoubtedly idealistically, we would recommend that you not order class sets of vocabulary texts, though there are many good ones on the market, including those mentioned in Boxes 12-6 and 12-7. Instead, order six to ten copies of several titles so that you can fit materials to narrower ranges of abilities. For some classes and some

BOX 12-6

VOCABULARY TEXTBOOKS (SERIES)

Essential Skills Series—Vocabulary in Context
(One of six skill areas in the series.) Booklets are arranged on ten reading levels from grade 3 to grade 12. Interest level is grade 6 to adult. Two booklets for each grade level. Each booklet contains an introduction, lesson-passage with questions, answer key, and diagnostic chart. (Jamestown Publishers, P.O. Box 6743, Providence, RI 02940)

McGraw–Hill Vocabulary
Second edition by Gene Stanford. Series of paperback books presents two words or word forms in each of the 120 one-page lessons per book. Each lesson consists of the word, part of speech, pronunciation, origin, definition, meaning in context, synonyms, antonyms, and word variations; practice in recognizing, recalling and using newly learned words. Review words from previous lessons.

Practicing Vocabulary in Context
Seven workbooks for grades 2 through 8. High-interest reading selections include vocabulary words. In each book, 200 words are tested and practiced. (Random House)

Reading Around Words
Designed to "help students learn the skill of analyzing context to determine the meaning and function of an unfamiliar word and to provide repeated encounters with specific vocabulary." Activity books, levels D through M (grades 4 to adult). Cassette tapes available in which *cloze* technique is used in aural presentation of context. (Instructional/Communications Technology, 10 Stepar Place, Huntington Station, NY 11746)

Vocabulary Workshop
Grades 6–12. Each book covers 300–350 words, presented in groups. Analogy and multiple-choice exercises. (Sadlier–Oxford, Division of Wm. H. Sadlier, Inc., 11 Park Place, New York, NY 10007)

Word Clues Series
Seven books, junior and senior high, adult. Each book contains 30 lessons showing students how to use the following context clues: definition, example, compare–contrast, and synonyms. Also practice in analogies. Each lesson teaches 10 new words. Words are taught in the context of stories. (EDL/McGraw-Hill, 1221 Avenue of the Americas, New York, NY 10020)

Wordly Wise
Books 1–9 for grades 4–12. "Thorough and rigorous exercises with crossword puzzles, riddles, word games . . ." (Educators Publishing Service, 75 Moulton Street, Cambridge, MA 02238)

World of Vocabulary Series
Six softcover text–workbooks. Intended for intermediate through high school level. Reading level grades 2–7. For underachievers. Each lesson is built around a short, easy-to-read selection. Placement and mastery tests. (Globe Book Company, 50 West 23rd Street, New York, NY 10010)

---

teachers, we would recommend a collection of individual titles. Avid word collectors (yes, they do exist) will work through books like *Wordly Wise* and *30 Days to a More Powerful Vocabulary* on their own. And you will use them for individual lessons taught to groups and whole classes.

Good vocabulary-building exercises are not easy to devise, and it is better for teachers to select well-made commercial materials than to devote hours to making up exercises that may be inaccurate and misleading. However, pub-

BOX 12-7

LEARNING ABOUT WORDS AND LANGUAGE: A FEW SOURCES FOR STUDENTS AND TEACHERS

Asimov, Isaac. *More Words of Science*. Illus. William Barss (Boston: Houghton Mifflin, 1972). Also by the same author: *Words from the Myths* and *Words of Science and the History Behind Them* (New American Library, 1969); *Words on the Map* (Houghton Mifflin, 1962).

Danner, Horace G. *Words from the Romance Languages* (A Clavis Book, Imprimis Press, 1980).

Dillard, J. L. *American Talk: Where Our Words Came From* (New York: Vintage Books (paperback), Division of Random House, 1977).

Espy, Willard R. *Have a Word on Me* (New York: Simon and Schuster, Inc., 1981). Other titles by Espy: *O Thou Improper, Thou Uncommon Noun* (Crown, 1978); *Say It My Way* (Doubleday, 1980); *Another Almanac of Words at Play* (Potter, 1980).

Farb, Peter. *Word Play: What Happens When People Talk* (New York: Alfred A. Knopf, 1974).

Funk, Charles E. *Hog on Ice and Other Curious Expressions* (New York: Harper and Row, 1948).

Funk, Peter. *It Pays to Increase Your Word Power* (Funk and Wagnalls, 1968), Bantam Books (undated).

Funk, Wilfred, and Norman Lewis. *30 Days to a More Powerful Vocabulary* (Pocket Books, 1975).

Hook, J. N. *The Grand Panjandrum* (New York: Macmillan Publishing Co., 1980).

Horowitz, Edward. *Words Come in Families* (Hart Publishing Co., 1977).

Levine, Harold. *Vocabulary for the College Bound Student* (Amsco Text, 1964). (Grades 9–12).

---

lished materials, after they are carefully chosen, must be used selectively. It is very unlikely that any teacher will find the whole vocabulary text or workbook equally appropriate to all students.

In examining prospective materials, positive answers to the following questions indicate a text worthy of consideration. One or more negative answers tell you to continue the search.

1. Do students encounter words chiefly in context exercises?
2. Are students given opportunities to supply words to fit a given context as well as to simply choose a word from several suggested?
3. Are key words related to each other? Grouped into meaningful categories?
4. Does word study lead to precision in use of words rather than mere recognition of meaning?
5. Are words "exercised" repeatedly?
6. Is the load of new words taught commensurate with most of the students' learning rates?

7. From this text will students learn about word origins in interest-provoking ways?

8. Will I use most of the materials, discarding few that are uninteresting, inadequate, misleading?

9. Does the text emphasize concepts about words that I wish to emphasize in this class, such as semantics, word histories, roots and affixes, or uses of dictionaries?

10. Are the key words not only interesting but likely to prove useful to my students in school and outside?

11. Are the exercises intelligent, lively, and liberally laced with humor?

In addition to these eleven questions, other criteria for selecting materials are implied in the following paragraphs.

Estimating Students' Vocabularies

Judging the level and quality of an adolescent's several vocabularies (reading, writing, speaking, listening) cannot be done with any kind of scientific accuracy. Scores on standardized tests give only partial clues. In addition, you must consider students' formal and informal oral and written language. (In schools that are really concerned about language development, records for every student, accessible to all teachers, include a couple of writing samples from each grade.) The breadth of students' interests and kinds of reading they do will aid your guesses.

Informal testing also helps. What you want to measure is students' potential for learning new words. A test like the one in Box 12-8 requires students to identify words before and after reading the same words in context. Another test measures students' ability to use roots and affixes as clues to meaning. A typical item for this kind of test:

If *ist* means "one who," and "economy" has to do with how nations earn and spend money, what is an *economist*?

You also want to know how alert your students are to unfamiliar words. Have them read a passage you have selected carefully for this purpose, and ask students to underline words whose meanings are unclear in this context. The better readers will find more "unfamiliar" words than the poor readers because the former monitor their intake of meaning and are alert to words that puzzle them. Poor readers, on the other hand, skip the half-known or unknown word and are content with a blurred understanding of the message.

What is difficult, especially for beginning teachers, is deciding what is an "average," "poor," or "superior" vocabulary for a given age or grade. Books in Box 12-2 will give you a rough index of word frequencies and word knowledge. Standardized tests cite norms. But you have to bring your subjective judgment to bear. Students' interest in words is a clue. Ms. Sullivan had been reading to her class from a World War II novel in which the crew of a plane shot down at sea had donned Mae Wests. The students were puzzled, since the actress famous for

BOX 12-8

TESTING STUDENTS' USE OF CONTEXT

Present words selected from the textbook *out of context*. Students may be asked to define or describe or use in a sentence. Or they may simply check a scale indicating how well they think they know (or do not know) the word. Ms. Rorick made up some multiple-choice items for her pretest. Three of the eight words Ms. Rorick used with eleventh graders are given here:

> What is the best definition for each word as it might be used in your history textbook?
>
> 1. *Ideology*—a) study of idols worshipped by ancient peoples; b) a game of chance played by political leaders; c) a set of ideas held by a large group of people; d) study of pictures and symbols used in ancient tombs.
> 2. *Satellite*—a) a small nation that follows the lead of a strong nation; b) an organization of super states; c) a group of scientists who studied with the astronomer Copernicus; d) one of the lower ranks in Hitler's youth movement.
> 3. *Nonaligned*—a) stripped of honors won in battle; b) refusing to take sides with other nations; c) removed from a line of battle; d) having no access to seaports.
>
> When you have turned in Part A of this test, read the section between pages 611 and 621 in your textbook. Then pick up Part B of the test, and again decide on the best definitions for the eight words.

When they read the section referred to, the students found the three words above in the following contexts:

> ✛ These countries all became *satellites* of the Soviet Union. A satellite nation is a small, weak nation that does what a strong nation wants it to do.
> ✛ Because they refused to take sides, they became known as *nonaligned* nations.
> ✛ There were, however, just as there are today, major differences between the U.S. and the Soviet Union. The two nations are based upon different *ideologies*. An ideology is a set of ideas about life and culture—about how people should live.

her curves was unknown to them. Ms. Sullivan explained the origin of the term, tracing Mae's curves in the air. The next day Tim said, "You know, those lifesaving vests won't be called Mae Wests much longer. They'll be called May vests, because that's what they are—vests—and people will think they're called May because their colors are bright like May flowers." Ms. Sullivan had one more reason to feel confident about Tim's vocabulary development.

By the way, students who risk using newly learned words and come up with malapropisms are on their way to stronger vocabularies than students who play it safe and dull. Speaking of malapropisms, Box 12-9 shows how one teacher used Archie Bunker's bloopers to teach a few choice words.

Using Experience to Develop Vocabularies

Since we learn words best in natural settings, teachers make use of such experiences to deepen students' understanding. That doesn't mean that secondary teachers have to set up elaborate field trips and out-of-class experiences

BOX 12-9

A MALAPROPISM EXERCISE

Find and underline the malapropism in each sentence below. Then write the correct word above the underlined word.

1. Whoever sent the flowers obviously wanted to remain unanimous.
2. You're invading the issue.
3. He has some big moves up his sleeve that he can't revulge yet.
4. Don't take everything so liberally.
5. I don't like the insinuendo in your speech.
6. It's a fact that capital punishment is not a detergent to crime.
7. You are in for a shrewd awakening if you don't begin studying.
8. Tampering with the U.S. mail is a federal offense and so is exciting a riot.

Now answer these questions:

1. How did R. B. Sheridan come up with the name Mrs. Malaprop? (Hint: Ask someone who speaks French or check the dictionary.)
2. Which malapropisms given above are a coined combination of two words, either of which could have been used correctly in the sentence?
3. Which malapropisms are the result of substituting a completely different word, but one with a similar sound, for the intended word?
4. Write two malapropisms of your own.

SOURCE: *Classroom Practices in Teaching English* (National Council of Teachers of English, Urbana, IL) 1979–80.

to teach vocabulary. Field trips are more practical for content teachers than reading teachers, in any case. It does mean taking advantage of what's happening outside your classroom, relating today's words to the weekend's football game or this morning's headlines. It means applying new words to class situations and personalities. ("Felix is melancholy and Dolores is vivacious," Ms. Melnik comments, "though his name means happy and hers means sad.") It means dramatizing word meanings (especially good with verbs) and demonstrating more often than defining (making a sound that is *barely audible*, for example). It means using films, filmstrips, pictures, and objects to render the abstractions of words as concrete as possible.

But valuable though real experience is, it's relatively hard to bring into the classroom. Books are easy. So, many persons would say, the best way to improve vocabulary is to encourage wide reading. We agree, with certain reservations. Unless adolescents are alert to words, they skip them; ironically, they may be better motivated toward "building their vocabularies" than toward reading a whole book. So while you encourage wide reading you also plan instructional time for vocabulary development. Weigh one value against the other. A dull lesson on vocabulary is not worth the same amount of time in free reading—even reading "trash."

While planned vocabulary practice is essential, it does not rule out incidental teaching. In fact, a teacher's enthusiasm for words is worth more than any number of workbook pages. The teacher who comes into class and says, apropos of nothing at all, "Say, I've always wondered where that expression 'top seed' comes from, and last night I found out," or "Did you know a *curriculum* in Rome was a race track?" sets the necessary example. You can do this quite deliberately. Get a book like Dillard's *American Words* or Funk's *Hog on Ice*. Keep it to yourself and select an anecdote weekly for class sharing.

Words and Wit   Almost everyone responds to humor, but wit, which depends on word play, works best with bright students. (It's that old IQ syndrome again.) In a secondary reading class, I was introducing palindromes, that old Victorian parlor game, as an example of word play. The students were going to identify the meaning of *palindrome* from the examples. I had no sooner written on the chalkboard "Name no one man" than Larry flashed back with "Able was I ere I saw Elba." Larry knew all about palindromes and could solve them and make up new ones faster than I could collect them. "Of course," he confided one day, "I'm a victim of paronomasia." He relished the blank look I returned and the speed with which I sought the dictionary. What was Larry doing in a special reading class? He'd flunked tenth grade history, but his problem was with self-discipline, not reading skills. Still, he was a joy to have in that class and a special resource for using wit and humor to spark students' interest in words. (See Box 12-10. Reading teachers often use puns to enliven word study.)

Three Strategies to Emphasize

Context, structure, and use of the dictionary are the three strategies to emphasize in reading classes. Use of context is the essential strategy. Children use it from birth to acquire all the language they possess, but when they arrive in secondary school they still need to be made consciously aware of the context clues that reveal meanings in print. Since we insist on the importance of context throughout this text, we move in this section directly to the other two strategies.

Structure   refers here to the structure of words. Linguists refer to meaningful parts of words as *morphemes*. For example, the word *transfers* has three morphemes: *trans* ("across"), *fer* ("carry"), and *-s* (used for plural with nouns or to signify third-person singular with verbs). More often than *morphemes*, we'll use the terms *roots* and *affixes*; and sometimes, as we do with students, to minimize technical terminology we'll refer to "word parts."

Teaching roots and affixes is a trap for many teachers because the most common prefixes and suffixes have the palest and also the most varied meanings. Don't attempt to teach the meanings, per se, of common prefixes and roots. Do use them frequently in groups of words (to be used in context) that permit students to "sense" the common element of meaning still retained by the affix or root. For example, *inconsolable, inaccurate, indestructible* belong together but should not be mixed with *injection, impale, input, inveigh*, all of which use a different meaning of *in-*.

We recommend two general approaches to examining structures of words. Both are related to forming words rather than taking them apart. The first is to

BOX 12-10

HEADLINING PUNS

An epidemic of paronomasia has raced around the world. No longer can the obsession to make puns be xenofobbed off with "paronomasia for the paronomasiatics"; the entire English-speaking world is affected.

"The Pun Never Sets on Britain's Empire" was the headline on a dispatch from London by Alan L. Otten of the *Wall Street Journal*. He reported a rash of puns in the British press:

In the *Sunday Telegraph*, a music reviewer panned a performance as "Haydn Seek," prompting listeners to write asking about "Handel with Care" and "Black Liszt."

The Guardian was not to be outpunned: "Distillery Deal Scotched" was one wry headline, and a story about an economic upturn from Tirana, capital of Albania, was headed "Tirana Boom Today."

Here in the colonies, the grand tradition of *puntiglio*—the Italian word for "word play," source of our "pun"—is growing apace.

The *Washington Star* editorial denounced "Catching Tuna Without Porpoise," while a letter writer objected to "too many kooks spoiling the broth." The *Los Angeles Herald Examiner's* analysis of the impact of the metric system was labeled "Take Us to Your Liter."

SOURCE: Excerpts from an article by William Safire, *New York Times*, 2 July 1980.

---

have students discover the way root words are changed to form different parts of speech. For example students fill in the blanks in charts like this one:

NOUN	VERB	ADJECTIVE	ADVERB
beauty	beautify	beautiful	beautifully
	satisfy		
		rich	
explanation			

Whether as a chalkboard exercise led by a teacher, or as an individual written exercise, filling in the grid should be followed by using the words in context.

In the second kind of exercise, the teacher begins with a common word like *change* (for immature students) and asks for variations to build "a web of relationships"[7]; for example, *exchange, interchange, changeless, unchanging, changeable*. With more mature students, you might extend a Latin root, making

---

[7]Edgar Dale, *The Word Game: Improving Communications* (Bloomington, IN: Fastback 60, The Phi Delta Kappa Educational Foundation, 1975).

sure that they see how the web of relationships works, for example, *aster* (star), *disaster* (beyond the protection of one's lucky star), *astronaut* (sailor among the stars), *astronomical, astronomy, astrology, astrological* (see Figure 12-1). (Another type of web of relationships made up of words related in meaning but not in structure is reproduced in Figure 12-2. This is a valuable variation for "shades of meaning" lessons.)

Obviously, the parts-of-speech grid and the web of relationships can be escalated or eased according to students' abilities. With nonacademic tenth graders, Mr. Webster made *tele* the center of a web. With advanced eleventh graders, Miss Tracy used derivations of *mit/mis* ("to send") and discussed how meanings change.

How valuable is studying word structure? For advanced college-bound students, we recommend emphasis on Latin and Greek roots. We wish more of

FIGURE 12-1

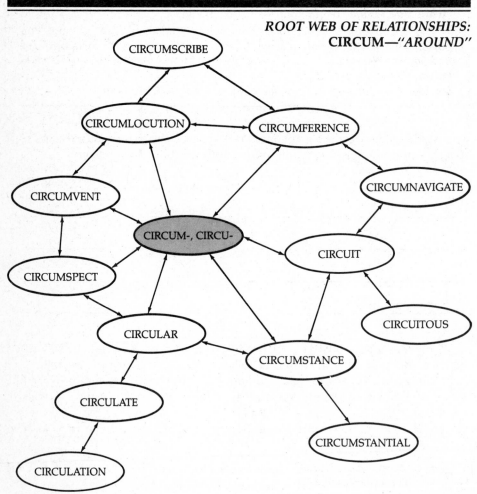

ROOT WEB OF RELATIONSHIPS:
CIRCUM—"AROUND"

these students were taking Latin, but until its study is revived, we recommend for senior high school an elective or a unit on where words come from. However, for immature students, we would go very lightly on word structures, especially those derived from Latin and Greek roots which have undergone considerable changes in meaning and spelling since they first were coined. For these students it is better to stress the word's present-day meanings and forget etymologies. For immature students, focus on coined words, colorful word histories, and contemporary vocabularies. One teacher has her students spin off the names of automobiles and discuss their meanings; for example, *Impala, Dart, Phoenix*. Another teacher develops similar discussions of the names of perfumes.

Using the dictionary   Planned lessons on dictionary usage begin in grade 4 and sometimes before that and can be useless and boring to students in grades 5 to 8. That is not to say, however, that dictionaries should not play a large role in every classroom. Of all reference books, this one should be available in multiple copies. Several *different* dictionaries should be represented. Students should learn that there is not just one good dictionary but many, of different types and qualities for different purposes.

Teachers in grades 5 to 8 should have a variety of levels of dictionaries to send different children to: a primary, intermediate, and advanced level, perhaps picture dictionaries and specialized lexicons. High school English curricula should feature at least one unit on the history and uses of dictionaries, and a wide sampling of modern and early versions should be available from the media center. In addition, every classroom should have on hand half a dozen dictionaries of different levels. Students should use dictionaries to assist them in checking shades of meaning and in verifying their guesses based on context.

Rather than assigning dictionary practice, teachers should see to it that students routinely make use of dictionaries as the need arises. Exceptions are students still in need of refining locational skills and students who need help in fitting dictionary definitions into context. Exercises to aid in developing these and other strategies are plentiful in commercial materials, and those prepared by the editors and publishers of dictionaries are unusually good and usually free for the asking.

If the reading/English teacher does a good job in the direct teaching of these three strategies—use of context, structure, dictionaries—and also brings imagination, enthusiasm and knowledge to awakening students' interest in words, all the rest of the teachers will have a good foundation on which to build further interest and expertise in using the language of their special subjects.

Vocabulary Development in Every Subject

Successful content teachers develop students' understanding of key concepts and the vocabulary that describes them. Developing concepts, attitudes, and values is, after all, the substance of teaching any subject. Therefore, when we talk about every teacher's responsibility for vocabulary development we are only suggesting that teachers improve upon what they are already doing. When students are unsuccessful in learning words and ideas related to history or

FIGURE 12-2

SYNONYMIC WEB OF RELATIONSHIPS: HARD

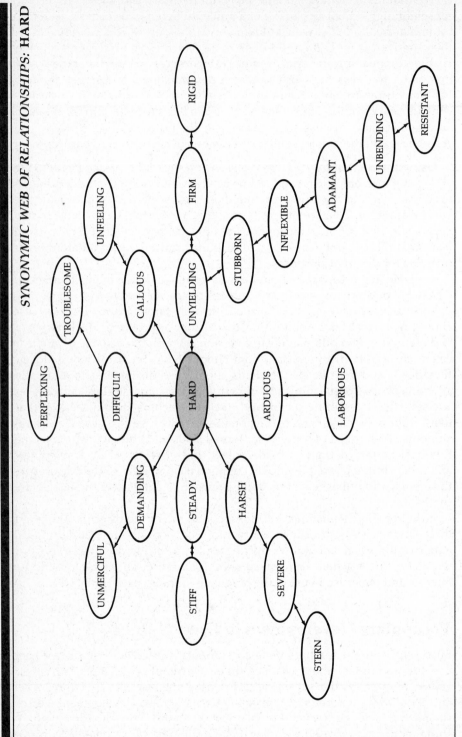

science or any other subject, teachers should ask themselves the following questions:

1. Is the concept load too heavy for these students?
2. Is the burden of technical jargon unnecessarily high? Would familiar words serve as reasonable substitutes for some of the technical terms introduced?
3. Have I reminded students of ways to strengthen their recall of terms?
4. Have I presented key vocabulary as vividly as I can to make these ideas memorable?
5. Do I alert students *before* they read an assignment to words that are essential to understanding?
6. Do I provide additional cues, such as marginal glosses and study guides, to remind students of words worth noting?
7. Given the abilities of the group, am I doing too much for some, too little for others?

Selecting Words for Study

In the 1930s a psychologist made a frequency count of technical vocabulary used in secondary school subjects and found that the average student was expected to learn more new words in these courses than in the first two years of a foreign language. In the years since then, that count can only have increased, given the expansion of information in textbooks. Can teachers cut down on the concepts to be learned and the vocabulary needed to explain them? Clearly, they must. Even teachers who use a single textbook for a whole class can sort out the basic concepts which everyone should acquire and the additional layers to be attained variously by students of different abilities. Since not every student in all four tenth-grade biology classes will be expected to cover the same number of topics, the teacher does not really face the overwhelming task of "covering" all the terms in the glossary.

In most cases, the content teacher does not assign students to a textbook reading until after they understand the major concepts. The textbook is for reinforcement of ideas, not for initial learning. That eases the teacher's task considerably, but while it relegates the text to a supportive role, it does not dispense with reading assignments or the need to preteach vocabulary. The following comments should guide teachers in selecting words to teach.

For any day's assignment, set a limit of 6 or 8 words or phrases. How many such assignments will be made over a week's span? The week's vocabulary load should be nearer to 15 or 20 than to 35 or 40. If your preview of the chapter yielded many times 6 or 8 words which might be new to your students, either the text is too difficult or your word-catching net is too fine.

Sort through the words you have listed. Eliminate any which are clear in context. Save these for discussion *after* reading if they represent important concepts. If students are being taught to use context, they must have opportunities to do so. And your ultimate aim is to have students become independent learners. Eliminate also words which may be unusual but are not essential to understanding the main ideas. In fact, deliberately ignore the esoteric word or phrase except to intrigue exceptional students. If you still have more than 6 or 8 words for any single assignment, arbitrarily choose that many for preteaching and use the others in study guides and marginal glosses.

Teaching Word Meanings

Unlike the reading teacher whose concern is chiefly for vocabulary-building strategies, the content teacher emphasizes the meanings of specific words. What are effective ways of doing this? As we keep saying, stick with context. Write the word or phrase on the chalkboard, pronounce it, and use it in a sentence with the same meaning that it has in the text. This will be a familiar exercise for teachers in grades 5 and 6, who recognize it as part of the directed reading lesson typical of basal reading series. It may be less familiar to teachers in grades 7 and 8, and a whole new idea in grades 9–12.

Many teachers at this point seek to involve students by eliciting what they already know of the words listed on the chalkboard. This is a practice which invites misinformation. Mr. Cassella was getting fifth graders ready to read a selection on the landing of the Pilgrims. *Compact* was one of the words he had chosen to preteach and he asked the wide-open question, "What is a compact?" "A little car" was one answer. "A thing my mother has for powdering her nose" was another. Naturally, none of the children had had any experience of *compact* as an agreement or contract. So Mr. Cassella explained this meaning, went on to the next four or five words on his list, and then assigned the reading. When he raised the key question after the reading, "What was the Mayflower Compact?", the first answer, of course, was "a little ship."

A safer way of eliciting prior knowledge, and one that seems efficient and mature to secondary teachers, is to turn the prereading discussion into a writing exercise in which everyone reacts and no one hears misinformation. For example, the new words may be listed and students asked to fit them into blanks in a *cloze*-type paragraph. Or given a worksheet listing eight words (say) with pronunciations provided through diacritical spellings and page references to the text, students may be asked to find the word in context and indicate on the worksheet whether its meaning is clear.

Prereading discussion is often appropriate, but teachers should be wary of its meandering from the point. One problem is that the point is often a mystery to everyone but the teacher. Much more satisfactory than a game in which everyone guesses what is in the teacher's mind is a brief, clear demonstration or explanation of the term which is unknown to many students, half known by others, and almost completely familiar to a few, who can still profit from a well-conceived presentation.

In deciding how to reinforce the meanings of new words *after* you have presented them in context, you may want to choose among the following:

Demonstrations Especially effective and natural to the sciences, demonstrations can often be used in other subjects, too, when the words represent concrete nouns or demonstrable verbs and adjectives. It is always preferable to show rather than to tell and often downright easier. Who would try to define *capillary action* when you can demonstrate it? Who would explain *chartreuse* when you can show a swatch of the color? In my methods classes I could define *boustrophedon* but I prefer to display on the overhead projector:

> In summertime in Bredon
> nodehportsuob ni etorw I
> Now nobody in Britain
> nettirw evah I tahw dear nac
>
> —R. F. Lister

and let my students figure out what *boustrophedon* means.

Pictures   If you cannot bring an object to class or demonstrate an action, you can substitute a still picture or a series of pictures. If the concept is important and several terms are included in a film, it may be worth the effort to show it. By the way, films are more helpful *before* reading than after. Single-concept film loops are available commercially and easy to show. Effective use of media requires teachers to plan ahead and that's not always practical. And media specialists are not always available. Nevertheless, well-planned use of media is a powerful aid in teaching concepts and vocabulary.

Dramatizations   A variation on the demonstration, dramatizations are more common in history and literature. Mr. Dunleavy often writes a short skit for his tenth graders to perform which dramatizes the meaning of a theme word for the short story they will read. One time it was *reciprocity* that was illustrated, and the variants *reciprocal* and *reciprocate* appeared in the brief dialogue. On other occasions, he makes up a charade, coaches a few students in their lines, and has the class figure out the key word.

Relating the unknown to the known   The students know various meanings of *latitude* and from discussion the teacher leads them to a new use of these meanings in *latitudinarian*. The biology teacher takes her students from *thermometer* to *thermotaxis*; the history teacher takes them from *camera* to *bi-cameral*.

Observing word structure   When appropriate, after deriving meanings from context, teachers reinforce recall of a word by calling attention to roots and affixes. This works especially well in science where so many new terms have been coined from Latin and Greek roots and the meanings have remained stable.

Distinguishing a technical meaning from general meanings   As in the example of *compact*, it may be wise to ignore other meanings and go directly to the specialized meaning. But sometimes it is appropriate to say as one science teacher did: "You all know what *fetch* means when you are asked to fetch something for your mother, but in earth science this word has a completely different meaning. It refers to a long open space of sea where wind causes the waves to travel."

Word histories   Biology students will remember *arachnids* better if they are reminded of the story of Arachne. (By the way, the book by Isaac Asimov in Box 12-7 is a handy source of word histories for science teachers.) Students of U.S. history will have a richer understanding of *filibuster* if their teacher tells them its origin can be traced to the Spanish (*filibustero*), who picked it up from the Dutch word for pirate (*vrijbuter*, which also came into English as *freebooter*). A Congressman who filibusters is stealing, or pirating, the nation's time. (*American Talk* by J. L. Dillard not only enriches the history teacher's vocabulary but tells American history from the perspective of how language has been influenced by ethnic groups.)

Reinforcing Word Learning

Of course, preteaching, important as it is, is only the beginning. Beyond a presentation to a group or a class, teachers meet individual needs by providing glossaries to go with, say, an important chapter in the social studies text. Everyone is supposed to get something out of this chapter but not everyone will read the same sections; so there are different glossaries for different groups. A glossary is simply the teacher's choice of words that certain students may need. The list is cued to the text and gives simpler definitions or explanations than dictionaries usually do. Glossaries are more effective if students must "do" something with the words supplied. Tedious, perhaps, but beneficial is the requirement to make a word card for each glossary word. Another possibility: Jot down the words or phrases that the textbook writer used which shed light on the meaning of this word.

Marginal glosses are a way to nudge the student. If you were sitting beside Laura, tutoring her, you could say: "Look, Laura, the writer put *plebiscite* in italics because it's important. See, there's his definition of it right in the next sentence. Do you find *plebiscite* again at the bottom of the page?" As a surrogate tutor, the marginal gloss adds similar directions to the text. We have used marginal glosses in the textbook study pages of reading texts for grades 4 to 8, and in Figure 12-3 we reproduce a sample. Some teachers make their own glosses to call students' attention to words. On a sheet of paper the same size as the textbook page, they make notes at a spot matched to the place in the text they want the students to notice. These gloss sheets are duplicated and given to the students to insert in the texts at the appropriate pages. This is a cumbersome practice, but it is one way of fitting the text to students' needs, and it works especially well for word study. Of course, you would provide this aid only for students most in need *and* most likely to benefit. Since providing marginal glosses is a time-consuming task for the individual teacher, we suggest it only as a possibility for departments to consider when inservice time and teacher's aides are available.

Follow-up reinforcement of vocabulary is often well provided for in the editorial apparatus of the content textbook. As we said in Chapter 10, make judicious use of these aids. Don't depend on students using them if you do not use them yourself. Indeed, you may find the end-of-chapter notes an ideal source for your oral presentation of words *before* reading.

Putting Vocabulary in Perspective

Finally, content teachers should view vocabulary teaching within the broader framework of the language of their subject area. The teacher's enthusiasm for science or history or mathematics (or any of the school subjects which have

FIGURE 12-3

MARGINAL GLOSSES AID WORD STUDY

How Our Language Grows
Ups and Downs

Just as people change all during their lives, words frequently change in meaning over a period of time.

> These words qualify the main thought of the sentence. They tell you that *words don't change all at once*.

Often these changes are simple alterations of a word's original meaning. *Hospital* once meant a "guest room" or "inn." *Host, hospitality*, and *hospital* still show the meaning.

In the course of change, however, many words have become more dignified. *Nice*, an often overworked compliment today, wasn't always such. It originally meant "foolish or ignorant." *Minister* once meant "servant." The word still carries the meaning that a minister serves the people. However, over the centuries the word has moved up in status. So has *respect*, which at one time meant "to spy."

> These words add information. What do they tell you about the word *nice*?

—Brown, *Language for Daily Use*

evolved from these) extends to enthusiasm for the whole language of science, history, and mathematics. Teachers should call students' attention frequently to the science writer's use of language, not only to technical words but to allusions, figurative comparisons, common expressions, and matters of style. History teachers should consider with their students how historians shape history by the language they use to describe it. Units in semantics and propaganda devices are, of course, the natural province of the social sciences, and reading/English teachers should know where these units appear in the social studies and history curricula. Team teaching or team planning among social sciences and English teachers is an idea that is trendy in one decade, old hat in another. But especially with respect to language development we believe such collaboration is called for.

Words as Physical Entities: Decoding and Spelling

Content teachers in middle, junior, and senior high schools cannot be expected to teach decoding skills even though there will always be a few students in secondary grades who are still in the beginning stages of learning to read. Since we have discussed remedial programs for these students in Chapters 7 and 8, we are not concerned in this section with the decoding skills needed by students who are reading at primary grade levels.

However, many readers in secondary schools who are beyond the beginning reading stage still experience serious difficulties in *applying* their knowledge of letter–sound relationships in identifying new words, especially words of several syllables. It is these students who are the focus of our concern in this section, which is addressed chiefly to reading/English teachers rather than to content teachers.

Problems with Decoding

If test scores and other school records lead you to suppose that a student is misreading words or skipping them, you can check this guess by having the student read aloud and noting the kinds of errors being made. (See also Chapter 7 for more details on this phase of testing.) Oral reading performance is a very

BOX 12-11

POLYSYLLABIC WORDS (FOR TESTING DECODING SKILLS)

anthodium   (ăn thō′ dĭ əm)

multisegmental   (mul′ tə sĕg′ mən′ təl)

molecular   (mə lĕk′ yə lə)

kilocalorie (kĭl′ ə kăl′ ə ri)

reproducibility   (rē′ prə dōōs′ ə bĭlətĭ)

fossiliferous   (fŏs′ ə lĭf′ ər əs)

environmental   (ĕn vī′ rən men′ təl)

deoxygenize   (dē ŏk′ sə jə nīz′)

isomorphic   (ī′ sə môr′ fĭk)

ciliary   (sĭl′ ĭ ĕr ĭ)

Note: Put each word on separate card. Do not syllabicate. Mark primary and secondary accents. Phonetic spellings are your pronunciation guide. Do not show student. Accept minor variations; for example, (ĭ) for first sound of isomorphic or (z) for s in same word.

---

rough indication of how students may read silently. Some oral testing must be individual and is therefore time-consuming. You test only those students who are reading below fifth-grade level although placed in grade 7 or above. Since you don't have time for extensive oral testing, present the student with six or eight carefully chosen words out of context, each word written on a separate card.

Select polysyllabic words that conform to regular English spelling, and are unlikely to be instantly recognized by the student. Words from science texts fill the bill nicely (see the sample in Box 12-11). Mark the accents, explain these markings, and tell the student that the word can be pronounced as it is spelled and that you don't expect him or her to know its meaning. Observe how the student approaches the task. Some will attempt syllabication; many will not try the word at all. Encourage the student to find any part of the word he or she can pronounce. Record the first attempted pronunciation. If the only fault is with stressing the wrong syllable, go on to the next word. If the first attempt is badly mangled, teach the student how to locate the largest element he can recognize (pronounce). For instance, by covering the prefix and suffix of *de•oxygen•ize*, he may recognize *oxygen*.

Some students who read poorly have no trouble at all with these polysyllabic words, and you can assume that their problems with reading lie in comprehension alone.

Students who miss most of the words in your list warrant further observation. Their spelling errors should be analyzed. They should be asked to read aloud passages at and above their presumed reading level so that you can observe what kinds of guesses they make and whether they recognize and correct miscues that make little sense.

Adolescent readers like Philip in grade 7, who can read most material written at about a fifth-grade level, may guess at words from beginning sounds only, reading *summer* for *sunrise*. As you study Philip's other errors (Box 12-12), note that he consistently gets beginnings and endings right but misses the middle. His guesses don't make much sense, indicating that he is not reading for meaning. His mistakes on short common words are not consistent; when his attention is focused on meaning, these errors will not occur.

BOX 12-12

WORD RECOGNITION ERRORS OF A SEVENTH GRADE BOY

Substitutions:
    summer for sunrise
    progress/process
    conducted/constructed
    picture square/picturesque
    lobbed/wobbled
    constant/consistently
    curious/courteous

Also:
    to/for   the/for   where/there

Students like Philip (and they are a sizable group in many junior high schools) are not remedial readers, but they will be severely handicapped in academic learning programs, and unless their word skills improve they will fall farther and farther behind in every subject which requires much reading. Essentially, they lack confidence and, as a result, have developed a hearty dislike for reading. So their teachers move in two directions: (1) they encourage (enforce, if possible) large amounts of interesting reading at or slightly below their estimated reading level (in Philip's case, fifth grade); (2) they build students' confidence in their ability to identify long words quickly and accurately. Neither Philip's reading teachers nor his content teachers will require him to read orally very often. His reading teacher may have him make tapes of his oral reading from time to time so that he can check his own accuracy and measure his own progress. As part of inducing interest in word meanings, his teachers will use many of the suggestions made in the first parts of this chapter.

Reading teachers' direct attack on deficient decoding skills such as Philip has displayed will be subordinate to their emphasis on word meanings and comprehension. It will consist mainly of brief and frequent lessons (say, five to ten minutes three times a week) aimed at developing confidence in identifying polysyllabic words in and out of context. Too difficult for students reading much below grade 5 level and quite unnecessary for good readers, these lessons work best in small group sessions led by the teacher and involving, more often than not, every-pupil response techniques. With students like Philip, independent practice on workbook exercises seldom engages their attention and is largely a waste of time. It would be better for them to work briefly with the teacher and spend independent learning time in reading an interesting book or short article.

Here is a scheme for building students' confidence in identifying polysyllabic words which teachers have found consistently successful in strengthening flabby skills.[8] On the first day, Ms. Craven shows a list of eight to ten compound words drawn from the students' content textbooks. After she and they have pronounced each one, she asks: "What is true about all these words?" Joan says, "They're all compounds," and Ms. Craven makes sure everyone in the group notices that each word is made up of two words. She may comment on the meaning of some, but meaning is not the focal point in this lesson. What is important is her observation, "Many long words that look hard at first are really easy if you notice they are made up of two smaller words." That is the end of the lesson, though Ms. Craven, who keeps a record of the words she "teaches," tries to use several of them in another context later in the week.

On another day Ms. Craven presents a list of polysyllabic words made up of a recognizable root, preferably an English word, plus affixes. Again the words come from the students' content textbooks, and Ms. Craven follows much the same plan as for the compounds, winding up with the observation, "Yes, many long words are easy to identify if you remove the prefixes and suffixes and look

---

[8]Olive Niles described this technique in "Improving General Vocabulary," *High School Journal*, 39: (December 1955): 147–55.

for a word you recognize. You can often make a good guess at its meaning, too. What kind of act is *unsportsmanlike*?''

On a third day, Ms. Craven's list is composed of polysyllabic words that have no easily recognized meaningful parts. This is a much harder list to prepare since most English polysyllables are composed of roots and affixes. I sometimes cheat on lists of this third type by including words that do indeed come from Latin or Greek roots but are not recognized as such by most persons (*mitigate* is an example; so is *anecdote*.) Referring to this list, Ms. Craven asks, after each word has been pronounced, "Are there any compounds in this list? . . . Do you see any words made up of a root and prefixes and suffixes? . . . You can pronounce each of these words syllable by syllable. That's the third way we've discovered this week for dealing with long words that look hard at first."

Those three types account for most of the polysyllabic words in English but not all of them. So on a fourth day Ms. Craven has another list about which she elicits comments. After this discussion, she summarizes: "These words all look pretty strange. Oh, Thelma could pronounce *silhouette* because she knew that word already. But mostly you had to ask me how to pronounce them, and that's how I learned them, too—I asked someone else how to pronounce them, or I looked them up in the dictionary. That's what you'll have to do, too." Then Ms. Craven reminds them of the previous lists, and she notes that these four kinds of words—compounds, root words with affixes, words made up of familiar English syllables or phonograms, and words which aren't pronounced according to English rules because they have been taken over from other languages—account for all the polysyllabic words they will encounter.

Throughout the year these four brief lessons are repeated with variations. On some days Ms. Craven presents a list including all four types, and the students sort them into four categories. At other times she duplicates a newspaper article and asks students to find examples of each type of polysyllable. She posts the original lists and from time to time refers to examples of Type I, II, III, or IV as they turn up in natural contexts. She spreads the word to content teachers who also refer frequently to polysyllabic words of this kind or that.

How Useful Is Syllabication?

Precise knowledge of syllabication is needed only by lexicographers. The typist who wants to break a word at the end of a line saves time by knowing the rules but when in doubt can always look up the word that won't fit within the margins. With the advent of word processors, we may lose those conventions. You've noticed newspapers and magazines splitting the word at whatever letter hits the right-hand margin so that you see peculiarities like *cu/tting*. That practice drives a traditionalist crazy, but it probably won't bother future generations. Instead of hyphenating words, many books and magazines are now printed with ragged right margins, which are a boon to slower readers. So syllabication in writing may soon be unnecessary.

Is it necessary to teach syllabication rules as an aid to reading? No, but it is useful to teach kids to break words they don't recognize instantly into the biggest pronounceable parts, and sometimes the biggest part is a syllable. So I give students practice in identifying the number of syllables in spoken words and words in print. I do not teach rules of syllabication, and I do not fuss over whether the slash should come before or after the consonant or vowel. Most of the time I ask students to tell the number of syllables in a spoken or written word by holding up the appropriate number of fingers. As a variation, with younger adolescents, I show pictures (a *helicopter*, a *telephone*, a *refrigerator*) or flash words on a screen and they write the number of syllables on slips of paper. Eventually, they get the idea that a syllable contains one vowel sound. This practice consumes little time in class, is almost no effort to prepare and can be turned over to an aide, provides variety for the kids, and gives them ear training as well as practice in examining a whole word—both of which contribute to spelling. Inordinate amounts of time are wasted in reading classes on syllabication rules that work only if you know how to pronounce the word in the first place. The vowel–consonant–vowel rule is among the most useless. Is it ro/bin or rob/in? You know only if you recognize *robin*. Is it *con/cū/bine* or *con/cub/ine*? Is the syllable *ain* pronounced ān or ən in a two-syllable word like *fountain* or *maintain*?

Supposedly, any practice which encourages students to look closely at words may sharpen their attention and pay off in both reading and spelling, but many workbook exercises on syllabication are completed without thinking and only induce boredom.

The only real learning I ever observed growing out of a syllabication exercise occurred when a boy questioned his teacher on why she had marked wrong his dividing of *aft/er* in that fashion. She said, "Oh, remember your rule, vccv; you divide between *f* and *t*." So Steve consulted a dictionary and documented his case for *aft/er* (*aft* is root, *-er* is suffix). But the teacher consulted a different dictionary and found support for *af/ter* (root now lost). What both Steve and his teacher learned was far more important than how to syllabicate: Dictionaries don't always agree.

Observing Words

Observing the idiosyncrasies of the English spelling system is likely to interest average-to-superior students, many of whom are or will be wordsmiths. Students will realize that English spellings are related to meaning as well as sound as they consider pairings like these:

> bomb *and* bombardier
> design *and* designate
> phlegm *and* phlegmatic
> picnic *and* picknicking
> mimicking *and* mimicry

Because it contributes practice in drawing inferences (which is worth more than the knowledge itself), I like exercises like this one in which students pronounce familiar words which prepare them to pronounce an unfamiliar one in the same pattern:

1. scene—scepter—science—scissors—scion—scythe
2. scarf—scupper—scone—scurrilous—scarab—scathing

Without wading through tedious workbook pages, students can also draw inferences about the usual patterns of stress in polysyllabic words (strong stress usually on second syllable). A modicum of time and attention in secondary school may prevent an occasional embarrassment as widely read students work newly learned words into their conversation. On the other hand, there is no point in fostering diffidence, and students should be reminded of Professor Strunk's advice to mispronounce with confidence and not make matters worse by mumbling.[9]

Well-educated high school graduates should know enough about the sounds of their language not to make the error of demanding phonics instruction as the only method of teaching reading in the schools which their taxes support. They should have learned also that English is a phonetic language which is least consistent in its oldest, commonest words, especially those derived from Anglo-Saxon, and most regular in its newer Latin-based vocabulary.

Spelling

Since spelling is a convention for writing and is related only tangentially to one's receptive vocabulary, it is not surprising to find that ability in spelling correlates lopsidedly with ability to read. That is, poor readers are usually also poor in spelling, but good readers are not always good spellers. The correlation of IQ with spelling is low, since spelling, like beginning reading, relies more heavily on memory and imagery than on drawing inferences.

Accuracy in spelling depends on attitudes—the students', their teachers', society's. Barring neurological impairments, and given minimal levels of intelligence, anyone can become an accurate speller who wants to give time and attention to the task. In the last several decades, educators have decided that spelling is of less consequence than many other skills, values, attitudes, and knowledge that schools are expected to teach. In this respect, the schools have been in harmony with societal attitudes which place less value on conventions than previous generations did. Casual manners, casual dress, uninhibited language, respect for dialects varying considerably from standard English, a decline in the average person's use of writing—these have been characteristic of the 1960s and 1970s, decades which also furthered casual attitudes toward spelling. Not surprisingly, teachers who are relatively indifferent to the conventions of spelling themselves are not inclined to give the necessary time and attention to spelling in the secondary school curriculum. So, with print all around us, even though personal uses of writing have declined, the chances for identifying misspelled words have greatly increased. We look like a less literate nation than

---

[9] "'If you don't know how to pronounce a word, say it loud!' This comical piece of advice struck me as sound at the time, and I still respect it. Why compound ignorance with inaudibility?" E. B. White in his introduction to the 1972 edition of *The Elements of Style*, by William Strunk, Jr. and E. B. White (Macmillan, 1972).

we used to be. Of course, it's an illusion. Poor spellers abounded fifty years ago, but they were not so likely to be entering college, writing reports, typing letters, teaching school, setting type, editing manuscripts, or doing any of the jobs that add to the drifts of print around us. People brought up in an era when correct spelling was as *de rigueur* as a pocket handkerchief and easily mastered if you were a conforming pupil are constantly assaulted by misspellings even in reputable publications and are convinced that they herald social decay.

Now that conservative and articulate critics of the schools are demanding more rigid standards of correctness, having overcome at least temporarily the opposing views that helped to shape the values of many contemporary teachers who are themselves products of the 1960s, what will happen to spelling instruction? I admit to wishing that pupils who are likely to become teachers, editors, proofreaders, script writers, and secretaries might be trained in decent spelling habits. I don't care about future scientists, lawyers, doctors, statesmen and others who will be able to afford computers and the services of good spellers, if they can find them; and, needless to say, I'm not worried about the spelling of students who will become airplane mechanics, coal miners, waitresses, and truck drivers—or will enter hundreds of other vital but essentially nonverbal occupations. But, of course, it's not that simple to sort out in elementary school who will do what in their long lifetimes, and turning everyone into accurate spellers, the willing and unwilling, those who will use it and those who won't, will be achieved only at the cost of far more valuable elements of the curriculum like literature and the arts, science and history, knowledge about language and self. For spelling, while it is easily taught, requires time for practice, and as we have seen, schools that decide to concentrate on the basics find time for little else, no matter what their goals may state.

Does it have to be this way? No, but when high school teachers join other segments of the public in pressuring the elementary schools to teach the basic skills ("and then we'll be able to do our jobs"), teachers in the lower grades pile on phonics drills, workbook exercises, skills boxes, and computerized spelling games in such deadly earnest that students spend more time trying to acquire the tools than using them. Students arrive in the upper grades less curious about ideas, less informed about life's possibilities, less willing to learn academic subjects, more oriented to means than ends.

Elementary teachers must, of course, set expectations for accuracy and give children the chance to reach them. Everything we have said in this chapter about sustaining children's natural curiosity about words—where they come from, how they got that way, what they do to you and can do for you—leads *toward* better spelling. A moderate amount of attention to spelling patterns, using any of the good spelling programs available today, will show children that there is consistency in the written code of English and interesting reasons for deviations. But this tutelage and drill, however well selected and moderated, will yield paltry results unless children have immediate reasons to value accuracy and to develop responsibility for the reader's comfort. That means kids have to do a lot of writing and have lots of readers to satisfy. So elementary teachers have to weigh practice versus use, accuracy versus fluency, concern for conventions versus concern for ideas. Both sides of the "versus" deserve attention; the question that faculties must decide is how much. The question persists in grades 5 to 12 and is one more reason why the whole school must examine whether or not there is a language policy conceived by the school staff and understood and supported by all teachers and most parents and students.

We have said that spelling is easy to teach. It is, because of all the elements of language use, this is the easiest to investigate. We have mountains of research on spelling to inform us of the factors involved, how to analyze them, and how to correct spelling deficiencies. Your first task is easy: identify your poor spellers. By grade 5 or 8 or 11, plenty of evidence will exist in students' folders to tell you who they are. (They can identify themselves by this time.) You need current samples of misspellings to analyze, and you should collect these from free writing samples and from spelling tests. Take time to collect good samples without giving students the impression that spelling is your number one priority. Analyze the errors which the worst spellers (already identified from school records) made in the first month.

The next task is the hard one: What to do about it? You have sorted out these categories of poor spellers:

1. overdependent on phonics with poor visual memory
2. poor auditory sense, overdependent on visual
3. omits syllables
4. inconsistent pattern, much carelessness.

And you have grouped students by the severity of their problem: (a) extreme difficulties with poor spelling inhibits expression; (b) many errors but little adverse effect on fluency; (c) moderate difficulties with common misspellings. Now you take into consideration the attitudes of individual students—their goals in school and outside, their parents' attitudes, their other pressing learning needs, their and your chances for success. Maybe you decide that for Joe the best thing right now is to get him a secretary—another student who will correct his spelling on all written work before any teacher sees it and will record his errors in Joe's spelling notebook or word box. For Tom, spelling is not so important as firming up his shaky comprehension of fourth-fifth grade reading texts; he needs more wide reading. Bill has a high verbal IQ, aspirations toward the professions, and the conviction that his poor spelling is a charming personality quirk. You decide that a short intensive review of spelling patterns will prove to him that his "handicap" is unnecessary and won't be tolerated. Marie has a few firmly ingrained misspellings that short practice sessions and keeping a notebook will straighten out. Sheila is bright, creative, and afraid of the written word (when she has to produce it); for the time being, you won't nag and you'll let Sheila read her compositions to you whenever possible so that your attitude toward misspellings won't obscure your understanding of her ideas. Kevin has limited auditory skill, but he can train his visual memory to serve him better.

Beyond providing in these various ways for deficient spellers, teachers in grades 5 to 8 continue with a planned commercial program adapted to regular but not excessive practice. This is supplementary to the use of spelling in purposeful writing, which the whole staff has decided is basic. So all teachers agree to provide class time for proofreading and to "take off" for spelling errors in some—not all—assignments.

The basic spelling program, in the hands of the reading/English teacher, aims at developing habits and attitudes and helping students to understand the psychology of spelling. Students should learn why the basic Fernald approach (turn to Box 8-6 for reference) aims at training the eye, ear, and hand. They should realize that understanding how the language works is background information that isn't much help in writing. (If you have to stop to think about the rule, you interrupt your train of thought.) But as the teacher, you should know that *some* of your students—those with logical and analytical minds—can profit from spelling rules.

Mnemonics is a less rational version of spelling by rule. Instead of noting that consonants are doubled to retain a short vowel sound (*stopped*) or preserve a stress (*deferred*), the mnemonic device depends on whimsy ("there's *a rat* in *separate*"). Students should examine the limitations and values of mnemonics.

Since spelling is only for writing, avoid oral spelling practices. If you think the old-fashioned spelling bee is motivational, have students write the words on slips of paper (not the chalkboard), have the written word judged immediately by you or a student, and keep everyone in the game.

By grades 9–12 planned instruction in spelling is likely to taper off to indifference on the part of busy, idea-oriented teachers. That's understandable but unfortunate. We recommend that the whole faculty decide on their responsibilities (chiefly for diagnosis and referral) and that the school support "spelling clinics" of three or four weeks' duration, always in small-group sessions, to which students are referred by any subject-matter teacher for "remediation." A whole school can become spelling-conscious without robbing every student of valuable time. Teachers might well assign *themselves* as students in such clinics to demonstrate that poor spelling is unrelated to high IQ, that it is most frequently a matter of conscience, and yields to therapy.

While spelling is being given its due—regular, unremitting, and relatively minuscule attention in the background—the main thrust is on writing as a means of learning and the study of language as a key to understanding oneself.

Why Isn't All This Good Advice Heeded?

Everything we have said in this chapter about teaching word meanings and the physical properties of words has been said before in a hundred books and articles, many of them, like this one, addressed to those who now or who will soon teach. Why is it that the verbal skills of students who have had the benefits of continuous education in American schools for twelve and more years appear to be less than they are capable of? Without considering the social factors, why are not teaching practices producing better results?

We think the reasons that pertain to quality of instruction are clear. Teachers who are not interested in words themselves cannot sustain children's natural curiosity or revive it when it falters. Too much "practice with words" depends on commercial materials, which can become arid and ineffectual unless teachers select and adapt and infuse them with their own enthusiasm and perceptions.

Aside from the mindless use of exercises—whether dittoed, printed, or computerized—the chief problem is neglect. Teachers in the secondary school must connect ideas with words directly taught as physical entities as well as meanings. (Students learn best when teachers interact with them; on-your-own exercises are insufficient.)

The second major problem is overload—too many words, too fast, for students to assimilate.

While we have separated out "the word factor" from comprehension, because we believe it deserves emphatic attention, we are not done with it. For to separate words from comprehension is an artificial convenience and a temporary one. We shall still be concerned with the word factor in the next three chapters, in which we deal with concept development, comprehension, and responses to reading.

RECAPPING MAIN POINTS

A person's meaning vocabulary consists of words understood in context of print or speech; it is larger than one's expressive vocabulary. The size of a student's meaning vocabulary depends on his or her experiences and environment, intelligence, verbal aptitude, interests, and the quality and amount of planned instruction.

Levels of word knowledge include (1) knowing a word's syntactic function; (2) placing it in a general semantic category; (3) recognizing its meaning in a particular context; (4) identifying an appropriate meaning among several choices; (5) using it correctly in context; (6) giving a precise definition; (7) distinguishing among shades of meaning.

Learning words requires repeated encounters in context. An important aid to vocabulary development is understanding the uses and limitations of context as an aid to learning precise meanings.

In selecting words to teach, it is better to emphasize shades of meaning and the multiple uses of common words than to feature infrequently used words which have concrete references. Students learn easily the labels for many abstract concepts, but real understanding of concepts like *justice* and *democracy* develops slowly with the help of many teachers.

Insufficient time is devoted to vocabulary development in many secondary school curricula. Preteaching key vocabulary before students read a selection is essential.

Reading teachers are responsible for direct instruction in developing vocabulary through using context, word parts, and dictionaries. English and reading teachers also teach the history of language and other phases of linguistic study. Content teachers, in addition to maintaining the application of techniques for vocabulary development, teach directly the meanings of words essential to understanding major concepts. They preteach key vocabulary through discussion of relevant experiences, demonstrations, dramatization, pictures, word structure and etymology, relating new words to known words, and contrasting general and technical meanings.

Some students beyond the reading-acquisition stage will still need help with decoding, especially words of several syllables. Teachers identify students' weaknesses in decoding through informal testing, including oral reading. Planned instruction in decoding at secondary levels aims at building students' self-confidence and interesting them in how the language works.

Normal spelling difficulties are relatively easy to diagnose and correct provided students are motivated and teachers are concerned.

FOR DISCUSSION

1. Why do some persons acquire more extensive vocabularies than others? Why might two students of similar intellectual ability display quite different levels of vocabulary development?

2. Make a list of bad or at least questionable practices related to teaching vocabulary. As you prepare to discuss these, review the comments of the English teacher in Box 12-5. In what ways do you agree or disagree with her views?

3. Consider all the ways that teachers can judge their students' vocabularies. What are the strengths and limitations of each? Include in this evaluation the vocabulary sections of standardized tests.

4. Let each member of your group submit a list of words associated with a topic or field he or she has recently become interested in (such as computers, cooking, economics, tennis). Share each other's lists and from each select a word least known to the group. Let the writer of the list teach the unknown word as effectively as possible. A week later test for how many words are remembered. Repeat the test several weeks later (months if possible). How much forgetting occurred? Why?

5. Debate the question of whether or not secondary teachers should review decoding practices and teach spelling to average students. Does grade level make a difference? Should content teachers "mark down" for spelling errors?

FURTHER READING

Dale, Edgar. *The Word Game: Improving Communications*. (Fastback, Series 60) Bloomington, IN: The Phi Delta Kappa Educational Foundation, 1975.

Dale, Edgar and Joseph O'Rourke. *Techniques of Teaching Vocabulary*. San Francisco, CA: Field Educational Publications, 1971.

Deighton, Lee C. *Vocabulary Development in the Classroom.* New York: Teachers College, Columbia Press, 1959.

This short text remains one of the best discussions of teaching vocabulary in secondary schools.

Johnson, Dale D. and P. David Pearson. *Teaching Reading: Vocabulary.* New York: Holt, Rinehart and Winston, 1978.

Although instructional activities recommended in this 200-page text seem to be slanted toward younger children, the discussion of vocabulary development is relevant and revealing to teachers at every level. A particularly good chapter is on the dictionary and the thesaurus.

13 *Reading as Reasoning*

If it's been a while since you read Chapter 3, "Using Reading to Learn," please review it quickly before you study this chapter and the next two, which discuss what teachers can do to aid the process of comprehension. This chapter focuses on understanding text, especially content textbooks, and Chapter 14 considers ways of remembering and making use of what one reads. While these two chapters emphasize comprehending nonfiction, the final chapter examines a somewhat different phase of the total reading process: responding to imaginative writing. All three chapters are concerned with facets of a single process, of course, so that similar strategies might be discussed in each. To avoid undue repetition, we'll risk the artificial splitting of parts from the whole, hoping that you will bear in mind that this whole book deals with just one process—learning through language—and that these last three chapters get to the heart of the matter: what teachers do when they make reading to learn the primary aim of secondary education.

The title of this chapter comes from an article written in 1917 by the eminent educational psychologist E. L. Thorndike, who describes what a reader must do to make meanings from text:

> Understanding a paragraph is like solving a problem in mathematics. It consists in selecting the right elements of the situation and putting them together in the right relations, and also with the right amount of weight or force for each. The mind is assailed as it were by every word in the paragraph. It must select, repress, soften, emphasize, correlate, and organize, all under the influence of the right *mental set* or *purpose* or *demand*.[1]

The search for meaning at any level of reading, Thorndike is saying, thrusts the reader into reasoning, or drawing conclusions and inferences. In Thorndike's judgment, and in ours, "it is not a small or unworthy task to learn what the book

---

E. L. Thorndike, "Reading as Reasoning: A Study of Mistakes in Paragraph Reading," *Journal of Educational Psychology* 8 (1917): 323–32. An adapted and abridged version of this important article appears in *Research in the Three R's*, a 1958 collection by Hunnicutt and Iverson, published by Harper and Brothers, which may be still obtainable in your library.

says." In this view, all reading might be called "critical" in that it requires the reader to select and evaluate and make decisions in accordance with a purpose or several purposes occurring simultaneously or sequentially in the reader's mind. All reading involves active communication, a dialog between reader and writer, in which the reader subconsciously questions the writer, feels satisfied when questions are answered (he or she comprehends) and talks back to the writer when questions go unanswered. In this chapter we shall consider first how teachers can ensure that readers raise the right and sufficient questions to understand what the writer intends. Then, in a section on "talking back to the author," we shall deal with those aspects of reading which are commonly labeled "critical."

We must emphasize again that reading as reasoning is more than *seeking* meaning. It is *making* meanings. Connecting meanings with words the writer uses, the reader draws on prior knowledge to compose meanings suggested by the text. The closer the writer's intentions and experiences are to the reader's purposes and prior knowledge the more closely the reader's "composed meanings" will match the writer's intended message.

Setting Purposes for Reading

If we are to encourage reading as reasoning, the place to begin is with the setting of purposes. Mature readers in any field set their own purposes; they don't need teachers. Competent readers who may not be so well versed in a particular field get help in defining their purposes from the writers of texts; they need teachers but not live ones, here and now. However, the readers in our classes, who are immature but developing, need live teachers to help in setting purposes. (In Box 13-1, Colin Wilson explains why purpose is essential for all mental acts.)

Students' purposes are like a set of nested boxes. We are not going to deal here with purposes like passing the course, getting a high school diploma,

BOX 13-1

IT'S WHAT THE BRAIN TELLS THE EYE

"Consciousness is 'intentional'—you have to *focus* it or you don't see anything. Everyone is familiar with the experience of glancing at his watch while he is having a conversation, and simply not taking it in. You certainly see the face of the watch and the position of the hands; but you don't see the time. In order to grasp what time it is, you have to make that act of concentrating, of focusing. And this is true of all perception, and in fact, of all mental acts. Our language tends to cover up this obvious fact. We say 'Something *caught* my attention," as if your attention were a mouse walking into a trap; but it isn't. It is much more like a fish, that has to *bite the hook* before it can get "caught." It has to go halfway. We talk about "falling in love," and the phrase is deceptively simple, like "as easy as falling off a log." In fact, it is extremely difficult to fall off a log; you would practically have to fling yourself off. And you have to fling yourself into love, too; you don't fall."

SOURCE: Colin Wilson, *The Philosopher's Stone* (1969). Warner Paperback Library Edition, 1974.

---

earning good grades to win college scholarships, acquiring knowledge necessary for success in college or on the job. Purposes like these—instilled by parents, teachers, and society generally—often stunt or distort the purposes we're really interested in developing: learning to satisfy a personal itch. Although students can set their own purposes for self-selected reading, they have still to learn real reasons for reading assigned texts—reasons beyond earning a grade.

Learning to set real purposes on one's own begins with emulating the purposes which are established by the curriculum and the textbooks and are communicated by teachers. From grade 5 to grade 12 (and into college for that matter), teachers must make clear to students the purpose for reading each time reading is assigned. We can't assume that lessons taught in reading classes will carry over to other classes. Purposes for reading differ from class to class, from teacher to teacher—and from day to day: to preview and plan, to find supporting details, to answer specific questions, to review for an exam are a few of them. Every teacher must provide guidance that gradually moves students from accepting the teacher's purposes to setting their own.

Making sure that students know why they are to read a particular section of the textbook (for instance) is one part of the teacher's effort to assure maximum comprehension. A second part of that effort is clarifying the nature of the text to be read. And the third task, just as vital as the first two, is reviewing how the text is to be read to accomplish the purposes at hand. In actual practice these three parts of the preparation for successful comprehension are interwoven, because purposes are affected by the nature of the text and by the reader's prior knowledge, and both of these influence the reading strategies to be applied. The teacher works with all these elements at once, but we treat them separately here in order to emphasize the importance of each.

Invoking Prior Knowledge and Pointing a Way through the Text

Among his students at Northridge High, the eleventh grade history teacher, Ben Jackson, is known as a talker. His classes are usually dominated by lectures intended to supplement last night's reading assignment. Racing the clock to the warning bell, Ben Jackson barely has time to call out: "Read Chapter 12 for tomorrow and be prepared to discuss it." Students, already packing up their books to get to their next class, may occasionally reflect on the irony of that final exhortation: *Discussion* almost never occurs in Mr. Jackson's class. He does most of the talking, expanding on the text, occasionally directing a few questions to the class and eliciting brief answers, but students' questions, impressions, confusions, or ideas are rarely aired. Later that day when these students open the history text in study hall or at home, they'll face 28 pages of text and vaguely wonder what's important enough to remember just in case discussion should be permitted tomorrow, or what's worse and more likely, Mr. Jackson should spring a quiz.

Without specific directions, most of Mr. Jackson's students will approach the chapter passively, waiting for it to catch their attention, when they should be: (1) thinking about the information being presented; (2) relating it to previous experiences; (3) raising questions about its relevance. This is active reading. It increases students' capacity to differentiate between important and unimportant information, to store information in memory, linking it appropriately to known information, and to retrieve it when needed. But Mr. Jackson's students, unprepared for reading actively, will do badly on the next day's quiz. Some will have read the chapter as a story, grasping a general sense of its contents but with scanty recall of detail. Others, having given equal attention to nearly all the details presented, will recall facts tomorrow but have a vague sense of their relationships.

What could Ben Jackson have done to focus his students' attention properly? He could have provided them with a general idea of what the chapter would be about, helped them to recall what they already know about the topic, and offered specific suggestions for organizing what they would assimilate through reading the assignment. These simple steps would have pointed them toward grasping the message Mr. Jackson views as of prime importance. Without such preparation, an irrelevant or incomplete or distorted message is likely to be the product of even a conscientious completion of the assigned reading.

Ben Jackson needs to recognize that time spent preparing students for the reading experience is at least as important as time spent discussing it the next day. Summarized below are ten strategies he might use to introduce future reading assignments. Over the school year he will try all of them, we hope, selecting those which suit his temperament and work best with differing groups of students. Like any teacher, Ben Jackson needs more than one method not only because variety sparks interest but because different materials demand different approaches: Some lessons are more important than others, students have more or less prior knowledge of particular topics, they grow in their ability to set their own purposes, and time, always a factor, affects Mr. Jackson's preparation.

Lecture Before Reading   A dynamic lecture, tightly organized, thoroughly researched, aimed at an audience that the teacher knows well, is a very efficient way to remind students of concepts they hold vaguely in mind and to prepare them to read about related ideas in the next assignment. There is nothing inherently wrong in using a lecture to review, explain, forecast, arouse curiosity, and otherwise prepare minds to read actively. Lecturing in high school has earned a bad reputation because few teachers have the time to perfect this demanding mode of communication. What passes for a lecture is often a monologue that lulls students into further listlessness.

If, however, Mr. Jackson is knowledgeable and enthusiastic about his subject, if he commands lots of examples, pertinent anecdotes, and illustrations, if he demonstrates as well as explains—in short, if he leavens instruction with drama—he should continue to lecture frequently. Only his timing is off. He should use his talent *before* the assignment. After the reading, the kids should do the talking.

Discussion Before Reading   Most teachers choose to introduce the next chapter by engaging the students in discussion. The purpose is to bring students' prior knowledge to the foreground, so that when they read they will be ready to confirm prior knowledge, add new information to old categories, negate or question any false notions they have held, and establish new categories to accommodate new information. Given an adroit teacher and the right topic, prereading discussion may be the best method of arousing students' interest as well as demonstrating to them (and you) what they already know about a "new" topic in the curriculum. On the chalkboard or overhead projector, the teacher jots down topics, dates, queries, speculations, facts, even misinformation if it is pertinent, and somehow manages to keep the discussion on track and within time limits.

A well-orchestrated discussion informs the teacher and orients the students and is as hard to pull off as a brilliant lecture. But its potential is so great for invoking curiosity and getting students to think that it is worth all those miserable failures that teachers have to endure as they learn along with their students how to manage discussions. The sorriest failures, and they occur frequently, result when teachers ask questions that are too broad. So Ben Jackson's first attempt at a prereading discussion wobbled badly when he started out: "The chapter you're going to read for tomorrow discusses events leading up to U.S. involvement in World War II. What have your grandparents told you about those prewar years? What movies have you seen about World War II?" It is easy for the prereading discussion to become an artificial exercise marred by wild guessing and the pooling of ignorance that kills any interest the students might have had in getting on with the task.

The obvious disadvantage in conducting prereading discussions with a whole class is that many students can "sit this one out." So to prevent students from escaping and to keep discussion on topics coming up in the reading, many teachers look to more structured methods using structured overviews and advance organizers (see below) and dividing classes into small groups. But teacher-led discussions have so much going for them—spontaneity, direction, naturalness—that many teachers simply reduce the numbers of students they have to lead at one time by assigning half or two thirds of the class to read or write while they spend ten minutes first with one part of the class, then the other.

Related Reading as Preparation   If the latest book on artificial intelligence is too advanced for you to understand, you go to the *Reader's Guide* and look for magazine articles that may introduce you to the topic in nontechnical language, or you ask a librarian or a knowledgeable acquaintance to recommend an easier book. The same strategy works with adolescents. Instead of lecturing, teachers may read to the class an easier version of the same topic the textbook presents. Or students may be assigned to read for themselves easier materials leading into the lesson to be assigned.

Another reason for related reading before the assignment is to set the course of a prereading discussion and keep it on track. A newspaper clipping or an excerpt from a magazine article read aloud by the teacher may be the right lead-in.

Mapping the Territory   Partly lecture, partly discussion, aimed at the whole class or a segment of it, this method has the teacher preview the chapter to be read simply by pointing out its organizational features, such as center heads and sideheads, its pictures and other graphics, and its editorial apparatus. Since textbooks are designed to teach, they, too, state purposes usually for each chapter; they, too, provide previews and set prereading questions. But students have to be trained to use these aids; otherwise, they approach textbooks as if they were novels to be read from the first line to the last.

In surveying the chapter, the teacher directs students to the questions at the end since these are also clues to "what to read for." The frequent routine of a teacher-led survey gradually gives way to independent study techniques, which will be discussed in greater detail in Chapter 14. Now, however, is a good time for you to study Box 13-2, which points up the similarities between SQ3R, an independent study technique, and the Directed Reading Lesson, a device common to basal readers, which is useful to content teachers.

For the least mature readers, this preview of the chapter should be made as graphic as possible. Middle school teachers may make visuals of the text pages and project them on the screen, marking them with arrows, asterisks, and glosses as they direct students to important points. Or, instead of whole pages, visuals may contain only the main heads from the chapter, thus highlighting the organization; with these visuals the teacher asks students to anticipate the subtopics before checking their guesses by referring to the texts in their hands.

Finally, teachers may literally map the territory by diagraming the contents of the chapter on a visual or a handout. Chapter 14 discusses this study aid in more detail.

Testing Prior Knowledge   In place of a prereading discussion, or to give structure to discussion, the teacher can make up a quiz related to information in the upcoming chapter. Not to be counted for a grade, this quiz contains objective items (true/false, matching, multiple choice, short answers) that can be quickly corrected in class. This technique saves class time, catches everyone's attention, stirs thinking, and focuses discussion. A sprightly quiz can even entertain students while it stirs up prior knowledge and informs the teacher about their chances for comprehending the text that lies ahead.

Anticipating Issues   Related to the foregoing suggestion, but directed more clearly toward guiding inferential thinking and evaluating ideas, is a prereading exercise made up of statements relating to the major ideas and issues to be encountered in reading. Such an exercise might deal with isolationism in a U.S. history class, predict the results of experiments in a science class, or describe children's rights in a family services course. One English teacher used such an exercise to arouse interest in a short story about Mexican migrant workers. Students were asked to check attitudes toward ethnic minorities with which they agreed or took exception, and they discussed their choices in small groups before reading the story. After reading, students checked the guide again, this time for statements with which the author might agree or disagree. The post-reading check could also be used to show whether their own attitudes were influenced by the story.

Structured Overviews[2]   Some teachers use these devices to focus on vocabulary related to key concepts they wish students to acquire through reading. First

---

[2]Harold Herber credits the coinage of this term to two former doctoral students, Richard Earle and Richard Barron, both of whom used it in doctoral research completed at Syracuse University under Herber's guidance in 1969–70.

BOX 13-2

TEACHER-DIRECTED AND STUDENT-DIRECTED READING

DRL Directed Reading Lesson (teacher directed)	SQ3R An Independent Study Method (student directed)

Preparation for Reading

Teacher sets up connections between text and readers

✤ reminds them of what they already know

✤ previews text; shows how it's organized; reveals its structure

✤ (sets purposes)

Teacher preteaches key vocabulary and relates to concepts

Teacher defines reading task and reviews strategies students will apply

Survey

Student surveys text

✤ sees how it relates to what he/she already knows

✤ looks for structure, clues to organizational patterns

✤ picks up key words and concepts from headings, pictures, preview, summary, boldface, italics, etc.

✤ sets up own connections

Question

Focuses attention and (sets purposes) by raising questions as he/she surveys

✤ turns titles, captions, subheads into questions

Read

Reading guided by teacher through study guides or preposed questions

Read

Reading guided by questions student raised before reading

Continues to raise additional questions during first careful reading

Seeks answers as he/she reads

Discussion

Teacher raises questions and students discuss them in order to

clarify meanings

(reinforce)

extend meanings

Recite

Closes text and recalls aloud what he/she has read

Uses questions as guide, answers them

(*Recite* step may be oral or written recall, for instance, outline, notes or summary from memory.)

Review

Immediately reviews text if he/she cannot answer a question in the preceding step

Later reviews by trying to answer questions originally raised

Uses notes to review

Returns to text only to clarify confused recall

the teacher lists the words and explains the meaning of each. Then students, working in small groups, organize the terms in ways that express what they assume to be the interrelationships among them. They may have the words on cards so that they can try various arrangements, or they may copy them on paper, showing relationships by drawing diagrams. Each group shows its design to the rest of the class and explains its meaning. You can see that this idea is related to mapping, which in turn is a variation on outlining, and that all these ideas emphasize seeing relationships as preparation for reading. The structured overview transfers responsibility for prediction from the teacher to the students. To work well, therefore, it should be introduced after teachers have modeled mapping and outlining. Even then teachers should work closely with students as they construct their overviews. Caution should be exercised, too, in the choice of material subjected to structured overviews. The expected scheme should be pretty obvious. If students stray too far from the relationships that the author is about to present, they may be thwarted in their aim to understand new information or ideas.

Advance Organizers   This is the term applied by an educational psychologist to a summary that a teacher might write and distribute to students when making a reading assignment.[3] Like a prereading lecture the advance organizer shows readers where they are going but it is less likely than a good lecture to arouse readers' interest. It appears to be more useful to older students than to young ones and is most appropriate to texts that contain few structural signals (like captions, main heads, subheads). Obviously, it takes less class time than other strategies described here.

The advance organizer may take the form of a skeleton outline instead of a summary. On such an outline the teacher may fill in all the major topics and leave blank lines for the subtopics, thus cluing students to the number of these which appear in the text and which they must identify. Another kind of skeleton outline asks students to note two kinds of information related to each major concept: what is known prior to reading and what is added by the text. The first part is completed during class discussion prior to reading, the second part during or after the reading.

Preposed Questions   In assigning Chapter 12 to his eleventh graders, Ben Jackson might have drawn three columns on the board and said: "As you read, organize the information under three main points. First, what events were drawing the U.S. into war? List these in the first column. Second, what actions were being taken to keep us out of war? List these in column 2. Why were some of these actions unsuccessful? In column 3, list the consequences of the actions you noted in column 2."

Considerable debate surrounds the value of preposed questions because some research shows that students read to answer these questions only and miss

[3]David Ausubel has studied the effectiveness of advance organizers, reported on their use in several research articles, and stimulated further experimentation by other researchers. One of Ausubel's early articles is "The Use of Advance Organizers in the Learning and Retention of Meaningful Material," *Journal of Educational Psychology*, 51:5 (1960): 273–76.

other important points. The effectiveness of preposed questions in setting purposes depends, of course, on how comprehensive they are and on how teachers advise students to use them. We believe preposed questions can focus concentration on major points. How teachers handle postreading sessions will demonstrate to students whether it's wise to read only for those points or to pay attention also to other significant detail.

Using Skimming to Point Up Purposes   When teachers direct students to find the paragraph that describes the event in the picture on such and such a page or to locate the discussion that explains a particular graph, they call attention to key words, headings, and paragraphs containing important information. Skimming as a prereading warm-up can alert readers to key concepts and lead to additional skills practice. For instance: "On page 324, the authors discuss *detente*. Do they make clear in that section what *detente* means? Who can give a definition or an example?" If reference to the glossary is indicated, students' understanding of the usefulness of that tool will be reinforced.

Using Patterns of Organization as Aids to Understanding

To become proficient readers of text material, students require direct instruction in using common patterns of organization. This instruction begins in primary grades, takes on additional emphasis in middle school, and must be continued into high school as textual materials become increasingly complex. As we said in Chapter 3, comprehension and retention are reciprocal processes and perceiving structure (or following the author's organization) aids both.

Figure 13-1 presents the most common patterns of organization. Materials for teaching reading in grades 5 through 12 are replete with lessons and exercises aimed at the systematic study of these patterns of organization. Especially prevalent in such materials are exercises for finding main ideas in paragraphs and noticing how details are arranged to support those main ideas. However, although the exercises are there in abundance, we really have no concrete evidence as to how widely they are used—or how effective such exercises are. Certainly, content teachers need to examine commercial materials that their students are using in reading or English classes. They should compare the patterns of organization which are taught in these exercises with those found in their content textbooks. Similarities should be evident. Using these, content teachers can help students make the transfer from exercise to "real reading." If content teachers in a particular situation are not ready to do this, then reading teachers must.

Instructional materials from reading classes may indeed prove useful to students who consistently apply the principles to their textbooks. They should be regularly reminded to do so by both their reading and content teachers, who take time to point out patterns of organization in assigned readings. For example, Ms. Toomey, teaching a reading class in grade 6, puts on the chalkboard or overhead projector the main divisions of the article students are about to read. She says: "Skim this article on the Viking Age and tell me the page numbers to put beside each of these topics." She has students predict what details (or

FIGURE 13-1

FIVE COMMON PATTERNS OF ORGANIZATION

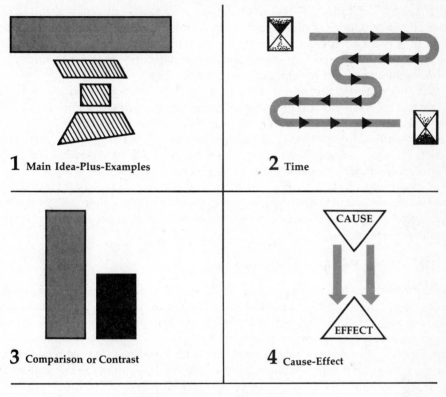

1 Main Idea-Plus-Examples

2 Time

3 Comparison or Contrast

4 Cause-Effect

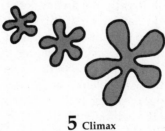

5 Climax

SOURCE: Jewett, Arno, A. H. Lass, and Margaret Early. *Literature for Life*. Boston, MA: Houghton Mifflin, 1958.

subtopics) the author may choose to expand on for the third major topic, The Vikings Ashore. In history class, Mr. Bader does the same thing with the section on pioneer life. These steps take only a few minutes, but they direct students' attention to the fact that *all* writing is organized into some kind of pattern and that recognizing that pattern aids comprehension and retention.

Some kind of pattern—this vague phrase hints at the intricacies and, therefore, the interest of this type of study. For textbook writers and others do not follow consistently the neat patterns laid out by the reading and composition texts. Instead, they combine old patterns and invent new ones. It may well be that we are teaching patterns based upon prose styles that contemporary writers are abandoning. Nevertheless, lessons based on traditional patterns are still useful; after all, many students must learn to read prose written more than fifty years ago. In any case, the lessons are not wasted, for the habit of looking for patterns—new ones, combinations, traditional patterns—stimulates students to think as they read and to remember important ideas.

This pursuit of patterns—or structure—will be reinforced on many fronts. English teachers, who comment regularly on patterns in story and drama, also have students observe patterns in films and television productions of all kinds, not just dramas. In newspaper units, they teach the inverted pyramid pattern, in which the first paragraph of a news item contains all the essential facts, with dispensable, though perhaps interesting, elaboration in subsequent paragraphs. In every subject, teachers point out the patterns characteristic of their fields. Of course, students must use these patterns as well as observe them. Right now our focus is on their using them as aids to comprehension, but they use them, too, in their own writing.

Observing Patterns in Sentences

Identifying patterns in sentences is not necessarily easier than identifying patterns in longer units, and it's more awkward to teach, as you will see from comments that follow. Consequently, in middle school and high school, we give more emphasis to perceiving structure in larger units such as chapters, units, and whole textbooks. For almost all students at these levels, as we noted earlier, we are reviewing principles that have been introduced in the elementary school. By grade 7, if not earlier, we can be sure students will have had much practice in observing patterns in paragraphs, and somewhat less practice in studying how sentences similarly convey relationships such as time order, condition–consequence, cause–effect, and comparison–contrast. Sentences illustrating these types of organization (and others) are presented in Box 13-3 to remind you of some of the challenges to comprehension at the sentence level.

What can you do about these problems? A few students—who have been identified as often failing to get meaning at the sentence level—may profit from instruction and practice with these thought units. Reading and English teachers are chiefly responsible for this kind of practice, which asks students to find equivalent meanings for given sentences, or to express meanings in their own words. Practice sentences are of the kind shown in Box 13-3. Also included in sentence exercises are interpreting ambiguous statements, manipulating clauses and phrases to vary word order while maintaining essentially the same meanings, and teasing out propositions (that is, subject-verb-object statements) contained in both the independent and dependent clauses of complex sentences. English teachers have long been familiar with such exercises, which appear in composition texts under such captions as "Sentence Variety," "Sentence Combining," and "Recognizing Ambiguities." You can infer that they may help in developing prose style. Do they also improve reading comprehension?

BOX 13-3

FIVE COMMON SENTENCE PATTERNS

1. **Main Idea Expanded with Details in No Special Order**
   In the late 1930s, in anticipation of wartime embargoes, the U.S. government had begun stockpiling strategic raw materials such as rubber, silk, tin, aluminum, cork, graphite, and platinum.

2. **Time Order**
   MacArthur flew to Australia to take command of the Southwest Pacific Area *after* he had promised the Filipinos: "I shall return."
   (Inverted time order sometimes confuses the inexpert reader.)

3. **Cause—Effect**
   (a) *Because* the attack was so unexpected, U.S. losses were heavy.
   (b) The manufacture of synthetic rubber in the U.S. and Canada came about *as a result* of Japan's conquest of the Netherlands East Indies, a major source of natural rubber.

4. **Comparison—Contrast**
   Whereas Canadian firms had been manufacturing about 14 planes annually before the war, they were producing 4,000 planes a year by the end of the war.

5. **Condition—Consequence**
   (a) *Had* the United States decided not to use the atomic bomb, invasion of Kyushu *would have* taken place in November, 1945, followed by an assault on the main home island of Japan, Honshu, in March, 1946.

   (b) Commandos destroyed Germany's secret heavy water plant in Norway. The water could have been used with uranium to make atomic bombs. *(When the condition appears in one sentence and the consequence in another, some readers fail to note the relationship.)*

THREE POSSIBILITIES FOR CONFUSION

1. **Double Negative**
   The victory was not unexpected; yet the headquarters staff were surprised by a renewal of confidence.

2. **Ambiguous Sentences**
   Attacking Polish troops on September 1, 1939 thrust Europe into World War II.

3. **Qualification Signals**
   Although, according to some historians, the Russians knew that Germany planned to invade Poland, they signed a nonaggression pact promising to remain neutral in case Germany went to war.

Perhaps. Through working with sentences, both middle school and upper secondary students can become familiar with certain signal words that mark the relationships among ideas. These signal words aid, too, in perceiving patterns of organization in paragraphs and longer units of discourse. Also through exercises students may become more confident and adept in handling the kinds of sentences that most often cause them trouble: inverted time order, inverted syntax (placing the verb before the subject, for instance), long and complex sentences, and sentences which omit connectors so that relationships are implied rather than explicit. These problems of word order and sentence length are often compounded by the presence of unfamiliar words and abstract concepts. Inverted sentences are characteristic of poetry, which presents additional problems of compactness and figurative expression; they appear also in the prose styles of earlier periods, whose written language patterns are no longer familiar to modern speakers and readers. Overly long and complex (sometimes badly written) sentences appear in modern textbooks, too. Whether students will try to work out the meanings of difficult sentences appearing in these contexts depends on how much they want the information or ideas embedded in them.

Exercises that present sentences out of an overall meaningful context operate at a disadvantage. They don't satisfy students' possible interest in information. They are not much better than out-of-context word drills. Just as with words, the meanings of individual sentences are easier to grasp when the reader can connect them with what precedes and follows. In spite of these disadvantages, sentence exercises may still succeed with students who have been persuaded that practice out of context will develop greater ease in coping with sentences in their natural settings. Weighing the odds, we would use sentence exercises sparingly. In reading classes, we would occasionally use them with poor readers whose attention we can focus more easily on short units than on longer ones. For the rest, we prefer to relate sentence exercises to writing rather than to reading, though we have reservations about their usefulness here also. With poor readers as with good ones, comprehension difficulties at the sentence level will diminish with sustained reading from which they demand—and get—meaning.

These reservations are not to be taken as advice to do nothing about sentence comprehension. Content teachers, alert to the kinds of patterns which may cause confusion, can model how they themselves use signal words to perceive relationships, how they seek out the subject-verb-object propositions in complex sentences, and how they tie the meaning which lurks in the selected sentence to the meanings of preceding and subsequent sentences. Science and math teachers have especially good opportunities to call attention to sentences containing qualifiers and negations. (Figure 13-2 is an example of sentence study applied to a mathematics textbook.) Demonstrating how to read a single sentence can be done quickly and should be done frequently. Teachers often call upon a student to read aloud a sentence from a math problem or a science experiment, analyzing the relationships expressed and deciding which words should be emphasized to convey meaning correctly. As you will see in Chapter 15, poetry is an especially good vehicle for developing the power to think through (or reason about) the relationships within sentences.

FIGURE 13-2

RELATING IDEAS IN SENTENCES

Textbook authors often use word clues to signal relationships between ideas. To understand these relationships, you must be able to identify the clues. Read the following textbook excerpt. Refer to the sidenotes. They will help you recognize the relationship of ideas.

Relating Ideas in Sentences in Mathematics

Math at Work

The United States is experiencing an agricultural revolution. As a result, farmers can produce much larger crops than in the past. The rapid growth in production is due to the growth in the size of farms, increased technology, and the development of improved growing and breeding techniques. This has resulted in a huge reduction in the number of hours required to produce most farm commodities. Although the number of opportunities in farming is decreasing, the number of jobs in farm-related industries is increasing.

| These words signal an effect. What is the cause? |
| What kind of relationship do these words show? |
| What two ideas are contrasted in this sentence? |

SOURCE: *Expanding Horizons* (level 8). HBJ Bookmark. Margaret J. Early, editor.

Identifying Meaning in Paragraphs

Teaching how to comprehend is more often applied to paragraphs than to any other unit of discourse. The emphasis from primary grades to senior high school is on "reading to find the main idea," and excellent materials for this purpose are available at every readability level. As with sentence exercises, instruction and practice exercises on paragraphs are removed from larger, meaningful contexts and are therefore tainted with artificiality; nevertheless, we have fewer reservations about their usefulness. For one thing, a paragraph can contain quite a bit of meaningful content, and the paragraphs chosen for an exercise can relate to the same topic, thus offering a respectable amount of useful information. One important reason for examining paragraphs outside of their usual habitat in extended discourse is to provide concentrated practice with paragraphs that do in fact express main ideas. Not all paragraphs do, either explicitly or implicitly. For this reason, as students are learning to identify main ideas in increasingly complex writing—as they must do, grade by grade from first to twelfth—they need an accumulation of clearcut examples rather than the distributed examples found in normal texts. The examples they examine should demonstrate the following:

1. The main idea is stated explicitly in a topic sentence at the beginning of the paragraph.
2. The main idea is stated explicitly in a "clinching sentence" at the end of the paragraph.
3. The explicitly stated main idea appears in both positions—that is, twice.
4. The main idea is embedded in the middle of the paragraph.
5. The main idea is clearly implied but not stated.

Additionally, students should learn through direct instruction as well as through their own perceptions that paragraphs serve other functions than expressing main ideas. Some paragraphs contain only details elaborating on a main idea that appeared in a previous paragraph. Some paragraphs serve as transitions from one idea to another; others summarize and preview, and therefore contain many main ideas. In fact, densely fact-packed content textbooks usually feature paragraphs containing more than one main idea, not only in preview and summary paragraphs but in the body of the text.

Because so much material is available to reading and English teachers for teaching main ideas, we can shorten our discussion of this topic by listing criteria for selecting from the ample supply:

1. Does the instructional material teach the difference between a topic and a main idea? (A topic names; an idea states something of substance about the topic.)
2. Are students taught how to compose main ideas (state them in their own words) and not merely to recognize main ideas or topics?
3. Is there a good balance between explicit and implicit statements of main ideas?
4. Are there sufficient exercises, well spaced, and graduated in difficulty?
5. Do the paragraphs deal with ideas of interest and importance? Are they related in theme?
6. Is the workbook material similar to the kinds of expository prose students are encountering in their content textbooks?
7. Does instruction in main ideas lead to instruction in how details within paragraphs may be arranged in patterns to show relationships?
8. Does the readability level of the paragraphs match the reading ability of the students for whom you are choosing them?

One word more to reading teachers. Although main-idea exercises are profusely available in instructional materials in print, on films, and in computer software, add some of your own making. You can locate (or adapt) articles from magazines, newspapers, and content textbooks that improve on commercial materials by being current and appealing to the students' immediate interests. Such materials will also convince skeptical students that writers *commonly* express meaning through paragraphs based on topic sentences; they also, to avoid dullness, often leave out the explicit statement and depend on readers to draw inferences.

Applications in the Content Fields

Since paragraphs for study of main ideas ought to be carefully chosen examples, should reading and English teachers carry the principal burden for this type of instruction? Yes, probably, in the early secondary grades, but even here they need back-up. In the later secondary years, when most students are unlikely to have direct instruction from reading teachers and when English teachers may be concentrating on imaginative literature more than on informational prose, the content teachers may have almost all the opportunities for this important phase of comprehension. But content textbooks vary in the extent to which they offer good examples. History texts rank high; linguistics texts and math texts, low. Fewer examples occur in texts or manuals centered on directions, but every text probably contains some main-idea paragraphs.

The easiest thing for a content teacher to do is to turn from time to time to a specific paragraph and ask a student to identify its topic and/or state its main idea. Easy but valuable. Our only caution is to make sure that *you* see its main idea, whether it is implied or expressed. If you do not, chances are your students won't. Also ask students from time to time to say whether a paragraph summarizes, elaborates on a previously stated main idea, or acts as a transition between ideas. In addition to working "reading for main ideas" into normal discussions in a content course, teachers also construct study guides for main ideas when the material lends itself to this. An easy guide to construct simply refers students to specific paragraphs and asks them to identify the sentence (from among three or four you have written) which correctly states the main idea, or (even easier for you) have students write their own statements. Of course, workbooks accompanying content textbooks often supply this kind of material. In evaluating these exercises, use the criteria on page 386, which apply as well to content workbooks as to materials for reading instruction.

The important part of instruction in finding main ideas is having students defend their choices. If students do no more than come up with the right answers, they are missing opportunities to learn. Listening to the explanations for right answers is valuable for students who were wrong as well as for students who were right. Discussing wrong answers is sometimes even more valuable. And wrong answers teach you a lot about students' reading strategies. Now and then, when students complete multiple-choice items, have them discuss why the distractors are incorrect. Reading teachers often use wall charts like those shown in Figures 13-3 and 13-4. Reference to these can make discussion and perceptions concrete.

FIGURE 13-3

VISUALIZING CONCEPT OF MAIN IDEA

A main topic or a main idea embraces the details of a paragraph the way the rim of a wheel fits the spokes. Can you supply a main topic that just fits these details?

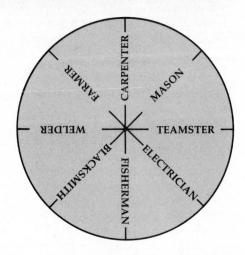

Teaching Patterns of Organization

The ability to perceive patterns of organization is as essential in reading as in reasoning. Patterns occur in word lists, sentences, paragraphs, and longer units of discourse, as we have noted. They also occur in everything else we perceive. Many teachers, therefore, use nonverbal devices as a way to reinforce students' realization that patterns of organization aid both comprehension and recall. One teacher has students test their recall of geometric patterns that are logically organized against those that are haphazardly arranged. Figure 13-5 shows another way to demonstrate the value of perceiving patterns. A perceptive class of sixth graders once showed me they could remember this series of numerals easily if they recognized patterns in it. (Can you identify three or four?)

9 1 8 2 7 3 6 4 5 5 4

We have found the following types of lessons, arranged here more or less in order of difficulty, useful in developing familiarity with patterns of organization. (The lessons can be made easier or harder, of course, by the nature of the content selected in each instance.)

Recognizing Patterns in Pictures   For immature students, collect illustrations from magazines which show groupings of objects (musical instruments, sports equipment, items of clothing, food, vehicles, and so forth) and ask them to suggest an exact title (the main topic) and name the objects (the details). Panels from comic strips, each pasted on a different card, teach time sequence as

FIGURE 13-4

Visualizing Interpretations of Main Ideas:
One Correct and Three Incorrect Interpretations

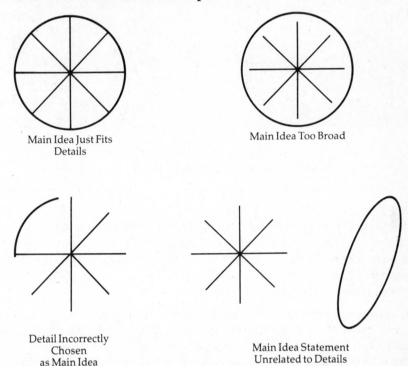

Main Idea Just Fits
Details

Main Idea Too Broad

Detail Incorrectly
Chosen
as Main Idea

Main Idea Statement
Unrelated to Details

Using the analog of the wheel, a teacher helps students to evaluate statements of main ideas or choices of main topics by visualizing whether or not the rim fits the spokes.

students arrange them in the correct order. If the cards are keyed, the student can turn them over for immediate feedback. Look for panels with and without words and at various readability levels. We show a sample in Figure 13-6.

Other patterns of organization can be found in illustrations. Comparison–contrast is easy (old and new, big and little, city and country), and cause–effect somewhat harder to illustrate. Having students contribute to your collection is instructive to them as well as time-saving for you.

Arranging Topics and Subtopics   Print topics and subtopics on strips of index cards and give one pack to each student. Have students arrange the set in outline form on their desks as you check. When finished with a set, one student exchanges with another. Make your packs of topics cards by copying workbook exercises or taking them from the boldface headings of chapters in content textbooks. Of course, you can make them up yourself, and having students make up this simple type of topic outline is a valuable exercise.

FIGURE 13-5

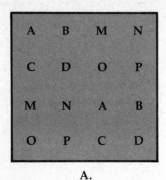
A.

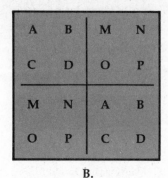
B.

Which chart would be easier for you to reproduce from memory? Why?

Arranging Topics in Patterns   Similar sets of cards can be used to illustrate patterns of organization. For example, a set of cards naming sports and games might be arranged to show contrast (team and individual) or ascending order (numbers of players) or time order (when introduced). Any pattern or combination which student can show the logic of should be accepted.

Observing Patterns in Tables of Contents   Using an overhead projector, show the table of contents of informational trade books as well as content textbooks. Call students' attention to organizational patterns by asking questions like these: "What subtopics come under the second main topic?" "Why did you decide the organization is chiefly sequential?" In introducing content textbooks, be sure to develop at least one lesson on how the text is organized and which patterns predominate in the table of contents.

Arranging Sentences in Patterns   Just as topics can be arranged in patterns, so can sentences. The resulting paragraph made from the list of sentences may begin or end with the topic sentence and the other sentences may be ordered sequentially, or to show cause–effect or comparison–contrast or rising order of importance. Materials may come from published sources, from trade books, or, occasionally, from students' compositions.

Identifying Patterns in Paragraphs   Students may be asked to identify the dominant pattern or patterns in paragraphs selected for that purpose. In supporting their decision, they should point out words and phrases that signal the various patterns. Again workbook exercises are plentiful but should be supplemented with examples from materials the students are reading in content courses (Figure 13-7).

Observing Patterns in Selections and Chapters to Be Read   As Ms. Toomey did in the lesson described earlier, put the main headings of a chapter on the chalkboard or overhead. If no center heads or subheads are given, you might still name them, asking students to skim the text to judge your suggestions.

FIGURE 13-6

Directions: Rearrange the panels of this Beetle Bailey comic strip in sequence. (The correct sequence is 1(1), 2(4), 3(6), 4(8), 5(5), 6(7), 7(2), 8(3), and the numbers should, of course, appear on the back of the panel where the students cannot see them.)

Informal Notes This step follows from the prereading observation of structure. As they read, students should jot down topics and subtopics, completing the partial analysis you had begun in the prereading discussion.

Note-taking from Individual Paragraphs Use workbook paragraphs and well-constructed paragraphs from current articles and textbooks. We suggest mounting suitable paragraphs from all these sources on 5x8 cards (removing all study aids if taken from a workbook), laminating the cards, and sorting them by levels of difficulty (grade-level estimates of readability or simply "easy," "average," "difficult"). Collect these cards over the years and keep them free of directions; then you can sort them for a variety of different uses by attaching special-direction sheets to them. For this current use, your directions are simply: "Jot down on a piece of paper the main topic and subtopics."

With the last two suggestions we have moved close to study skills, which are the subject of the next chapter. Indeed, it is hard to separate active reading from studying, except as we wish to emphasize understanding here and remembering

FIGURE 13-7

USING CONTENT TEXTBOOKS TO TEACH PERCEIVING PATTERNS OF ORGANIZATION

Recognizing Cause-and-Effect Relationships in Science

Information in textbooks is often organized to show cause-and-effect relationships. Causes may be signaled by words like *because* and *since*. Effects may be signaled by *therefore, resulting in,* and *so.* Read the following textbook selection. Use the sidenotes to help you recognize the cause-and-effect relationships.

Avalanches or **landslides** are rapid movements of great blocks or masses of rock. The rock is loosened by weathering but it remains in place. Landslides are sometimes started by earthquake vibrations. But on steep mountains, the spring thaw may start the downward slide of rock mixed with snow. At the foot of the slope lie boulders, bits of rock, and sand. Most landslides are small, but large ones cause great destruction. Much of the destruction of the 1964 Alaskan earthquake was due to landslides.

What two causes of landslides are mentioned in this paragraph?

In Arctic regions, freezing and thawing create a loose rock layer. This surface layer is made up of fragments of many sizes. In the spring, the upper few feet of this layer thaws but the ground below remains frozen. **Water cannot drain downward through the frozen ground** so the surface becomes saturated. Then the pull of gravity starts the mass of rock debris moving, even on gentle slopes. This material may move as a single unit or several units may join in a massive jumbled flow.

What is the effect of this freezing and thawing?

What is the effect of a lack of drainage?

Rivers carry sediment that has fallen, rolled, or slid down the valley walls into the water. Mass movements and runoff work together as major agents of erosion.

—*Focus on Earth Science*
Charles E. Merrill

SOURCE: HBJ Bookman, Eagle Edition. Margaret J. Early, editor.

there. Before shifting the emphasis to remembering, however, we'll examine another aspect of teaching reading as reasoning: the teacher's role in promoting an active dialogue between the reader and writer.

Questioning and Predicting

Our description of the process of comprehension has embraced the notion that all reading is a matter of selecting and connecting. The consciousness of the reader selects from the visual display what he needs to make meaning as he connects new information with what he already knows. Selection implies the examination of alternatives, an act which requires questioning even though questions are not consciously phrased in the usual patterns. Thus, a beginning reader coming in context to the words *winds the watch* subconsciously asks, "Is it *minds* or *winds*? Is it *watch* or *match*?" and decides rightly or wrongly depending on her understanding of what precedes or follows the phrase. An older reader confronts this sentence: "Some historians believe the failure of the League of Nations was largely due to lack of U.S. support" and asks: "What failed? What caused it to fail?" For this one sentence, he raises perhaps a dozen computer-quick decision-demanding questions—and arrives at correct or incorrect answers, achieving "comprehension." No one tells the beginning reader to raise questions and make decisions; she wouldn't be a "reader" unless she had the instinct to search, select, question, decide. The developing reader maintains this acquisitive behavior. But the quality of comprehension depends on how precisely and completely he questions—still subconsciously—and his questions depend on his intentions and his prior knowledge.

We believe teachers can influence the quality of readers' questions by showing them how to set purposes and how to bring to the task at hand pertinent knowledge stored in memory. Earlier sections in this chapter have given detailed examples of teachers working with both these factors, purpose and prior knowledge. Moreover, readers' comprehension is facilitated by knowing where they're going (or where the writer is going), and study of organizational patterns alerts readers to the writer's road signs. By doing as much as we have already described, teachers are influencing the quality of readers' questions.

Is there anything else they can do to develop behavior which is instinctual and gets stronger with use? We think students must be made consciously aware of behaviors they are using instinctively and more or less effectively. Toward this end, teachers can first of all model the asking of good questions. That is what they do in setting purposes, making a good assignment, and preparing study guides which raise questions to be answered while reading. "Questions" on study guides are more often declarative statements to be marked true or false, sentence stems to be completed from several choices, or phrases to be matched. But every item is an implicit question. Study guides simulate the reading behavior of whoever makes them up.

Questions posed after the reading is done are also models. Teachers make sure that students realize that the questions are more important than the answers by having them explain (so far as they are able) the process that led them to an answer. Students are directed also to examine the quality of the questions asked by either the teacher or textbook. What is the purpose of that question? Is it directed at the main idea? Why do these questions focus on details? Are the details significant to our understanding of the author's conclusion?

Another thing teachers can do to raise the quality of students' subconscious questioning-while-reading is to require them to practice it consciously. Thus, teachers shift the act of simulating reading through a study guide to the students themselves. One group in a history class makes up a guide for a section of the chapter which another group later completes. On a simple level, the teacher asks students to write questions instead of answers for a homework assignment, and the next day the questions are evaluated, sometimes in self-directed small groups but frequently under the guidance of the teacher.

What has been said about questioning-while-reading is also true of predicting. You cannot read without predicting. You do it all the time at the word identification level. You predict what a word is from a fleeting glimpse of its shape and surrounding context; as you turn a page, you predict from context alone what the next word or phrase will be. *Cloze* exercises (Box 6-5) are a good way to make students conscious of their skill at predicting.

Predicting how the writer will elaborate on the main topic dramatizes for students how writers and readers collaborate in the making of meaning. We make further suggestions in Chapter 15 that are meant to remind students of what they know intuitively but haven't articulated: good reading is guessing—hypothesizing—and then checking your guesses.

Direct teaching of questioning and predicting, based on modeling and then shifting responsibility to the student, cannot escape aspects of artificiality. Excellent readers obviously practice these strategies, and that's how they've developed them—from practice. But in defense of artificial exercises on questioning and predicting, we emphasize that many average readers can be encouraged to practice them more extensively than they do when only their instincts guide them. We argue, too, that many average teachers neglect to set the stage for practice in questioning and predicting unless they plan deliberately and use artificial lessons when necessary.

Questioning and predicting, which are, of course, integral to drawing inferences and conclusions, distinguishing facts from opinions, sorting the significant from the insignificant, are strengthened in many ways throughout the curriculum by teachers who promote reasoning skills. These skills are often discussed under the rubric of critical reading—the topic we turn to next.

Talking Back to the Author

Students who read nonfiction critically have developed a willingness to disagree. To be sure, they must first comprehend the author's meaning, so that they can be clear as to what they are agreeing or disagreeing with, but once that is accomplished, their responsibility is to question the author's motives, methods, and effects. Questioning of this kind doesn't come easily to adolescents who tend to vacillate between total unthinking acceptance of what the textbook says and equally thoughtless skepticism and distrust of authority.

No one teacher develops attitudes and habits of critical reading, just as no single influence, inside of school or outside, is responsible for a student's development as a critical thinker. But the job that is everybody's needs periodic assessment, and someone must initiate that. Our recommendation is for adolescents to take their own measure as critical readers deliberately and in an organized fashion several times in grades 5 through 12. Accordingly, we discuss critical reading in these pages as it might be practiced and evaluated in an assessment unit—something aside from the constant and regular integration of critical reading/thinking in every part of the curriculum.

A unit in critical reading would be an anomaly. That is why we insist that time set aside is for students' self-assessment of their habits of, skills in, and attitudes toward critical reading. We think a short unit should be scheduled once a year in grades 5 to 8 and a longer period set aside at least every other year in grades 9 to 12. If the whole school staff is involved in the planning, responsibilities might be variously assigned; for example, to reading teachers in grades 5 and 6; to English in grade 7; to social studies in grade 8; to a special elective in the senior high school. Or instead of an elective, self-assessment of critical reading might come in a unit in English in grade 10, in U.S. history in grade 11, or in psychology or family studies in grade 12. This planning for self-assessment units in no way absolves all teachers from paying attention to critical reading in every appropriate textbook assignment and from planning special units such as critical reading in consumer education, propaganda in the social sciences, and semantics in English classes. In what follows, however, we are talking to any teacher whose aim is to remind students of their responsibilities for critical reading.

Self-Awareness: A Requisite for Critical Reading

Begin with examining what a critical or mature reader does. Some teachers rely on films to initiate this discussion.[4] Since you might find useful suggestions in films that you could emulate in your classroom, we recommend them to you for previewing, but you may prefer not to use them with students since active involvement is better than passive viewing for getting adolescents to think. To get started, you might select a short article that is slanted for or against a principle that you know your groups holds dear. Adolescents have strong opinions (and often little information) on topical issues: immigration, law and order, drug control, human rights, parents' responsibilities, ecology, pollution, safety of workers, quality of schools. Local issues may be better understood, and newspaper editorials are likely sources. After the selection is read silently by the class, or aloud by you, you read statements carefully prepared to hit biases which may be inferred from the material and may also be held by the students; students respond by cards signifying "agree," "disagree," "don't know."

So the discussion begins. Out of it you want students to come to an awareness of how readers' biases may result in inaccurate comprehension of what the authors actually have said as well as unwarranted inferences as to what they meant.

To make this point of the need for accurate reading, teachers sometimes also set the task of rapid reading of short statements that contain deliberate inaccuracies which students must circle. (I once read a sign in a taxi as *No charge over $5* when in fact the word was not *charge* but *change*.) From the exercise of spotting inaccuracies should come a discussion of why we misread small details and big important ideas. The mind directs the eye; we read what we want to believe.

---

[4]For example, short films in the Coronet series *Critical Thinking* deal with reading, with listening, and with viewing television. One film, "Making Sure of Facts," stresses importance of checking sources of information and assessing skills and knowledge of the source.

Beyond reading accurately, and indeed in an effort to get the author's ideas straight, the mature reader raises exact and pertinent questions. Again, teachers demonstrate this step with a close reading of informational material on which students are asked to raise questions, paragraph by paragraph. This should not be a new experience to them since all teachers in your school are emphasizing, we hope, that reading is a process of asking and answering questions raised while reading. But the discussion in this unit should focus on the kinds of questions raised. Who asks the best questions—the one who knows most or least about the subject? Can you be critical in an area in which you are uninformed?

The appropriate questions to raise about expository and persuasive writing are these:

✤ Is the information accurate? Is it complete? Is it up to date?

✤ Are opinions offered with good reasons for them? Are they documented?

✤ Does the author draw conclusions from the data presented? Are they similar to or different from conclusions the reader draws?

Clearly, these are not easy questions, and students learn to raise them and seek answers only through years of experience. They are, of course, matters of logical thinking which cannot be taught in units such as we are discussing here. Many schools in this decade, including some elementary schools, are offering courses in logic; to the extent that these courses "work," their results should be seen in students' reading and writing and in their ability to assess their own powers in a unit such as we are discussing here.

Having taken in the author's message accurately, having raised exact and pertinent questions and having followed the author's arguments to her conclusions, readers may or may not be ready to draw their own conclusions. If readers don't have complete information, if they have raised questions for which there are no immediate answers, then mature readers suspend judgment, neither agreeing nor disagreeing with the author. In any case, readers should understand that conclusions about most matters are tentative and subject to change as new data are amassed.

Now these understandings about the process and this awareness of the reader's responsibility are what you want students to derive from the several days spent in discussing how they react to specific reading materials. Your purpose in these experiments is centered not so much on the subject matter of what they read as on the strategies they use. Of course, content is important, too, and you encourage students to relate what they have been learning in their other courses and in previous grades to the materials studied in the current unit. Much will depend on the materials you select, which we will comment on after the following section on the other important factor in critical reading.

Awareness of the Author's Role in Communication

In this age of telecommunications we should be talking about critical viewing and listening as well as reading, but our medium is print and we defend our limited approach on two premises. First, electronic communication originates in language; it is scripted. Second, the medium for teaching critical viewing ought to be television itself rather than classroom teachers. Nevertheless, we resort to a communications model for reminding students that critical reading of nonfiction requires not only awareness of the receiver (self-understanding) but awareness of the sender, even the anonymous author. We use a formula presented by Harold D. Lasswell in the 1930s when communications was becoming a subject to be studied. Lasswell's formula asks:

> Who
> Said What
> To Whom
> Through What Channel
> With What Effect?

Who calls students' attention to finding out everything they can about the writer and his or her motives. *Who* can be illustrated most dramatically with the advertised endorsement, but it must be illustrated, too, with textbook authorship, with local and national newspaper columnists, as well as with well-known authors whose careers can be checked in references like *Who's Who* and *Current Biography.*

Said What emphasizes the need for accurate comprehension of the message.

To Whom invites students to consider how the audience affects the message. The same news stories may be examined in two or more newspapers; the same historical incident may be examined as described by different historians.

Through What Channel refers to the medium, which, for our purposes here, is print and so leads to a study of emotive versus report language. Again this is a subject to which every teacher owes attention directly as well as incidentally, but it is also a part of the study of language to which the English curriculum in grades 7–12 assigns emphasis in units and electives. Here, our purpose is to remind students, through a variety of exercises, of their responsibility to examine an author's use of language to persuade a particular audience or, unwittingly, to display a bias.

With What Effect? reminds students of the need to evaluate exposition and information with the questions we apply also to literature: What did the author intend? How well did she succeed? How worthy was the purpose (according to the reader's values)?

Learning Critical Reading through Writing

An excellent way to learn how to read critically is through writing oneself. Awareness of the uses of language and the effect of audience is much sharper when you yourself are addressing a particular audience for a special purpose. So, in this unit, students test their understanding of the Lasswell formula by applying it. With your help, they determine "who" they will be—what voice to assume in this writing—whom they will address, what language is appropriate, what effect they are striving for. The best test of this kind of writing is a real situation—a candidate to support, an organization to persuade, a proposed school rule to denounce. Students should share their drafts in small groups so that everyone gets a chance to read them critically.

A most practical assignment from the teacher's point of view is to have students in one class write persuasive essays that can become material for reading instruction in other classes.

Materials for Teaching Critical Reading

Whereas twenty years ago, there were few materials published explicitly to teach critical reading, such materials are now in copious supply. They appear in every basal reading series, reading instructional texts or workbooks for secondary schools, and in anthologies and readers for English classes. There are kits on critical reading—*Reading for Understanding* is one that teachers praise[5]—and packets designed for the social sciences. The National Council of Teachers of English publishes materials which are very informative to teachers and students, selected and produced by their Committee on Doublespeak. Periodical publications for students such as the Scholastic newspapers and magazines regularly feature exercises in critical reading. An excellent periodical source for teachers is *Media and Methods*, which every school should subscribe to along with publications from NCTE and IRA (International Reading Association). Two recent paperbacks are *The Pitch* (how to analyze ads) and *The Pep Talk* (the language of politics) by Hugh Rank (Counter-Propaganda Press, 1982 and 1984). Figure 13-8 was reprinted from *The Pitch*.

With a wealth of materials, the teacher faces the usual problems of selection. Students at every level can learn to read critically materials within their readability and experiential range. So readability and topicality become the prime considerations in choosing materials.

Despite the best intentions and efforts of the writers, exercises in critical reading are bound to be artificial. We must accept that disadvantage and use the materials sparingly in such brief assessment units as we have been discussing. The main advantage of "canned materials" is that they may help teachers to plan systematic instruction that may otherwise be omitted entirely. But lessons and units on critical reading based on commercial materials (or teacher-made lessons, for that matter) are inconsequential unless critical reading is continuously at the forefront of teachers' and students' minds as they read everyday material in school and outside. So the best materials are content textbooks, newspapers, magazines, and television scripts—including the advertisements.

For many years, advertisements seemed to be the *sole* medium for teaching critical reading. Understandably so, since they are available, colorful, dramatic, and fair game. But an occasional series of lessons on advertisements doesn't fulfill a school's obligation to teach critical reading. Youngsters reared on television are capable of quite sophisticated analysis of advertisements; what is curious is that they are both knowledgeable and indifferent. In a consumer society,

[5]Thelma Gwinn Thurstone, *Reading for Understanding 3* (grades 7–12), Science Research Associates, 1978.

FIGURE 13-8

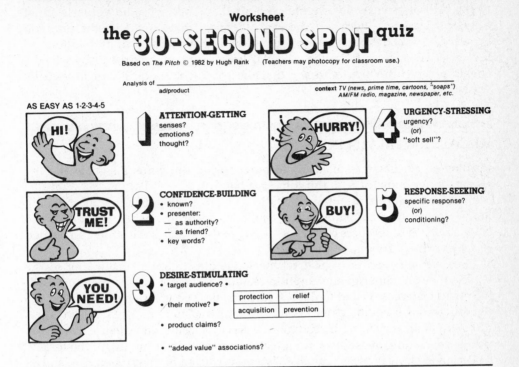

Worksheet
the **30-SECOND SPOT** quiz

Based on *The Pitch* © 1982 by Hugh Rank   (Teachers may photocopy for classroom use.)

Analysis of _____
ad/product

context *TV (news, prime time, cartoons, "soaps")*
AM/FM radio, magazine, newspaper, etc.

AS EASY AS 1-2-3-4-5

1 ATTENTION-GETTING
senses?
emotions?
thought?

2 CONFIDENCE-BUILDING
• known?
• presenter:
— as authority?
— as friend?
• key words?

3 DESIRE-STIMULATING
• target audience? •
• their motive? ►

protection	relief
acquisition	prevention

• product claims?
• "added value" associations?

4 URGENCY-STRESSING
urgency?
(or)
"soft sell"?

5 RESPONSE-SEEKING
specific response?
(or)
conditioning?

they enjoy the hard sell, the soft sell, planned obsolescence, and conspicuous spending. Reading teachers should probably leave the important study of advertising to consumer education and the social sciences and concentrate in reading and language classes on other parts of the news media and on books.

As a final word, we reiterate that teaching youngsters how to think, much less *to* think, is probably not possible. The best we can do is to work on habits and attitudes, to set up situations in which thinking is required at levels students are capable of, and to encourage them to observe their own processes occasionally. As part of schoolwide language development, teachers and administrators should examine where in grades 5 to 8 and 9 to 12 those opportunities are planned, so that, for example, the English teacher knows what the science teacher sets up.

And don't be discouraged with adolescents' slow and uneven growth, nor evaluate too harshly the seeming ineffectiveness of lessons in critical reading. An incident with ninth graders crystallized for me the artificiality of the planned lesson on critical reading. It was a good lesson, systematically developed, using well-conceived materials targeted to the students' abilities and interests. Such fallacies as begging the question, false attribution, and generalizing from too little evidence were carefully examined and applied in fresh exercises, one of which had to do with drafting 18-year-olds. Mark recognized the false premises and illogical reasoning advanced in the passage and selected the "right" answer for the question posed. "But," he added in the face of all the logic he had noted, "I still believe 18-year-olds should be drafted." "Then why did you select that answer?" I asked. "Because," he said, "I knew that would be the one you expected." I was discouraged, of course, until I realized that Mark had learned the expected answer from the artificial lesson and might still learn why he should accept it. Which is to say that the contrived lesson is not necessarily wasted effort.

RECAPPING MAIN POINTS

Reading as reasoning is making meanings, using the writer's signals and the reader's prior knowledge of the subject at hand.

Comprehension is intentional. Students learn to set purposes by imitating models set by the curriculum, the textbook, and the teacher. In addition to setting purposes, teachers clarify the nature of the text and the strategies needed to achieve the purposes.

Here are ten ways in which teachers can direct students' thinking to the subject they are about to encounter in reading: lecturing, discussing, and reading aloud materials related to the text about to be read; mapping the selection to be read; testing students' prior knowledge; tapping students' opinions on issues to be studied; presenting a structured overview; using an advance organizer; posing prereading questions; and directing a survey, or scanning, of the text.

Perceiving how prose is organized is a powerful aid to comprehension, and all teachers should reinforce and extend this skill that elementary teachers have introduced and reading teachers continue to stress. Patterns of organization in sentences, paragraphs, and longer units of discourse including chapters and whole books must be taught repeatedly in grades 5 to 12 both directly and incidentally.

The paragraph as a complete unit, if it contains a main idea expressed or implied, is widely used to teach comprehension. To be useful, paragraph comprehension exercises must be carefully selected and reinforced by study of paragraphs in "real" settings such as content textbooks and other books and articles.

Paragraphs serve other purposes in addition to presenting a single major idea. Topical arrangements, which present main ideas elaborated by details, are only one kind of organization. Instruction should emphasize other patterns as well (such as sequential ordering, comparison–contrast, cause–effect, order of climax), and students should discover combinations of these and analyze their uses. Studying patterns of organization in reading is supported by note-taking, which reinforces retention of ideas. It also teaches students to use these patterns in expressing their own ideas.

Reading is a matter of selecting and connecting. Although readers do this subconsciously, teachers can help them to improve the quality of their comprehension by making them aware of questioning and predicting. Teachers model questioning-while-reading by the questions they pose before and after reading; they also provide for students to monitor their own questioning and predicting behaviors.

Often discussed as "critical reading," skills such as drawing inferences, distinguishing facts from opinions, and sorting the significant from the insignificant are specific applications of questioning and predicting behaviors. Since critical reading is an important phase of comprehension (a catch-all term), it cannot be separated out from the whole for purposes of instruction. It should permeate all reading and learning. However, special attention can be given in units in which students examine their development as critical thinkers. Awareness of one's own biases is essential. So is awareness of writers' purposes, devices, and effects.

Materials for instruction in critical reading should go beyond advertisements and news media and include content textbooks.

FOR DISCUSSION

1. Review the ten suggestions for introducing a reading selection in a content course. Discuss those you have tried, giving details of your lessons. Suggest variations on the ten enumerated.
2. Using the criteria on pages 385–86 present an evaluation of one or more published exercises for teaching main ideas.
3. Analyze a chapter from a content textbook at a grade level of your choice. Examine paragraphs in the first and last section and at least one middle section. Numbering paragraphs consecutively, say whether the paragraph states a main idea, contains a topic sentence, illustrates a main idea introduced previously, contains more than one main idea, or summarizes a preceding section. Comment on the clarity of organization of the chapter, and discuss any comprehension problems it may pose for the students to whom it is assigned.
4. Prepare (and if possible teach to your colleagues) a lesson that shows how perceiving organizational patterns aids both comprehension and retention. For the amount of time allotted, you may have to select a narrow segment of a text. Explain in general terms what should precede and follow your lesson.
5. From a local newspaper or national news weekly, select an article (perhaps on education) which you treat in the manner described on page 00, that is, consciously phrasing "exact and pertinent" questions that a critical reader should raise. Discuss whether questions raised are answerable. Is there a need to suspend judgment? Can you draw tentative conclusions?

FURTHER READING

Dieterich, Daniel. *Teaching about Doublespeak*. Urbana, IL: National Council of Teachers of English, 1976.

Estes, Thomas and Joseph Vaughan. *Reading and Learning in the Content Classroom*. Boston: Allyn and Bacon, 1978.

Herber, Harold L. *Teaching Reading in Content Areas*. 2d ed. Englewood Cliffs, NJ: Prentice-Hall, 1978.
  Copious examples of study guides throughout this text and in nearly 50 pages of appendix.

Weil, Marsha, and Bruce Joyce. *Information Processing Models of Teaching*. Englewood Cliffs, NJ: Prentice-Hall, 1978.
  All three models (concept attainment, inquiry training, and advance organizer) have implications for teaching comprehension in content classes.

14 *Studying = Reading + Writing*

"Oh, I can read all right," Phil says. "The thing is, I can't remember all that stuff they ask about on exams."

"I can read," says Laverne, "but I have a hard time getting ideas down on paper."

"With me," says Charlie, "it's a matter of time. If I spent enough time on history, I could make B's, too."

"I can't concentrate," Esther says. "Pretty soon my eyes get tired and I get a headache."

In their own way, these tenth graders are telling us that in grades 5 to 8 and 9 to 12 the chief learning task for most students is not simply how to read but how to absorb ideas and make them their own. (The proof that you "own" an idea is that you can share it with others.) Phil and Laverne hit directly on two of the major topics of this chapter: *reading to remember* and *writing to learn*. Explicit in Charlie's complaint is the crucial issue of *time*, which we deal with in the section on rate and schedule. When Charlie complains about not having enough time, he may be hinting at another vital issue, *motivation*, which we'll skirt in this chapter because there is no need to repeat what we've already said about it. Esther, too, is probably masking motivational deficiencies when she raises the issue of concentration.

Finally, in this chapter, we tackle the perennial question of teachers in a departmentalized situation: Who does what and when do we find the time anyway?

Writing as a Way of Learning

Every good reading teacher has to be as much concerned with production as with reception. How do you judge students' intake except by their output? "Oh, by having them check, circle, underline, match, and fill in blanks," says the harried teacher, unable to react to stacks of freely written responses. "Or," another rationalizes (not unreasonably), "these kids are inhibited by poor writing skills. I've got to give them a chance to show quickly and easily what they know." These reasons for using recognition exercises instead of requiring freely written responses make sense when our concern is only for less able students. However, they ignore the possibility that some of the less able students may become more able if they can practice putting into words ideas they glean from reading.

Unfortunately, most students, even those who can profit from practice in ordering and expressing ideas, spend more time filling in blanks than in answering questions freely. Reading teachers are not the only ones who have misused objective tests and study exercises, of course; content teachers also generally assume that writing or composing will be learned in English classes and practiced sufficiently there. And English teachers, unwilling to assign papers they haven't time to read, can be expected to cut back on assignments when their loads exceed a hundred students.

A fortunate consequence of the outcry in the 1980s for higher standards of literacy has been a lively movement to enlist content teachers in teaching writing as well as reading. At the same time, recent investigations into the teaching of writing have begun to bear fruit. Although we know less about writing as a process than we do about reading, and much less about teaching writing than teaching reading, we know—and have known for a long time—that they are closely related abilities. Good teaching of one leads to improvement of the other. As with reading, merely requiring students to write is insufficient. And also, as with reading, the more you do of it the easier it becomes.

Writing skills deteriorate without continuous critical attention. Twenty years after Albert Kitzhaber showed that the writing performance of Dartmouth seniors was inferior to their performance in freshman composition,[1] college faculties are beginning to realize that continuous attention to writing can be achieved only if professors outside the college writing programs give serious attention to how students express ideas in writing. At one major university, for example, the curriculum reform undertaken in the late 1970s permits students to earn credits in advanced composition by writing at least four papers totaling 4,000 words in philosophy, history, the sciences, and other content courses. Action like this on the part of colleges will undoubtedly drift down to the high schools at the same time that the "language across the curriculum" movement pushes up from the early grades through the middle school and junior high.

For teachers to accept the responsibility for assigning moderately extensive writing in content courses, we believe the following conditions must prevail:

1. Teachers must assign more writing than they can meticulously "correct."

2. Since the reason people write is to be read, administrators must help teachers to find additional readers. Some of these must be paid professional assistants. Others can be parents, students, and volunteers.

---

[1]Alfred R. Kitzhaber, *Themes, Theories and Therapy: Teaching of Writing in College.* The Report of the Dartmouth Study of Student Writing (McGraw-Hill, 1963).

3. Administrators and teachers have to do more writing themselves so that they can experience what it feels like to get words on paper.

4. In developing a language policy for their schools, faculties must think through why people write and why writing in the school program serves not only purposes of communication but also of thinking and learning.

Let's examine each of these statements in more detail:

Assign More Writing   Learning through writing and learning to write require that students write freely in every class; but few secondary teachers, English or content teachers, require from their students even one piece of sustained writing each week. With more than a hundred students, careful evaluation of even one piece of free writing per week is a burden that most teachers avoid—understandably, since they have so many other demands upon them and quicker means of evaluation are available. None of the quicker means, however, provide students with the necessary practice in recalling ideas, arranging them in an effective order, choosing precise vocabulary, making decisions about what is pertinent, seeking examples to prove a point—in short, thinking clearly about ideas and information they are acquiring.

A compromise—not the whole solution, of course—is for teachers to accept that they do not have to evaluate every paper but can keep students on their toes by selecting papers of individuals and groups at random for careful grading and by filing all papers in students' folders for periodic reviews. Teachers should try to *read* most papers for ideas and should train themselves to react to ideas, often orally with individual students, often by jotting a quick question or observation on the pages.

Add Readers to Staff   If every content teacher as well as every English teacher is to be responsible for the literacy of all students, then administrators and faculty will have to come up with imaginative plans for handling the paper load. English teachers without budgets have learned to widen the readership of their student writers by ingenious means (for example, see Peter Elbow's *Writing without Teachers* included in the list in Box 14-1), but school boards must face the fact that there is a price tag on lifting the levels of literacy. Probably the surest way to get teachers to assign sufficient writing so that all students have a chance to learn to express meaning is to provide teachers with the necessary support. English teachers and all content teachers need professional paid assistance in evaluating students' writing.

Faculty Must Also Write   Across the country in the last several years teachers have enrolled in summer writing courses which have encouraged participants to write themselves, to share ideas about both process and teaching methods, and to continue inservice workshops in their regions patterned after their first summer's experience. Any faculty examining its language policy can emulate these projects simply by assigning themselves to write (perhaps professional articles, curriculum guides and reports, or the same writing assignments they require of their students) and submitting them for reactions from their colleagues as well perhaps as from outside consultants.

BOX 14-1

A FEW BOOKS ON WRITING FOR YOU AND YOUR STUDENTS

Elbow, Peter. *Writing without Teachers*. New York: Oxford University Press, 1973.
> See also his newer book *Writing with Power*, Oxford, 1981.

Hirsch, E. D., Jr. *The Philosophy of Composition*. Chicago: University of Chicago Press, 1977.
> As the title implies, this is a thoughtful book for teachers, not secondary students. Chapters on readability contain new insights for reading teachers.

Kirby, Dan and Tom Liner. *Inside Out: Developmental Strategies for Teaching Writing*. Rochelle Park, N.J.: Hayden Book Co., 1980.

Macrorie, Ken. *Telling Writing*. New York: Hayden Book Co., 1970.

Murray, Donald M. *A Writer Teaches Writing*. Boston: Houghton Mifflin, 1968.

Strunk, William, Jr., and E. B. White. *The Elements of Style*. 2d ed. New York: Macmillan, 1972.

Zinsser, William. *On Writing Well*. 2d ed. New York: Harper and Row, 1980.

A different approach was taken in Greenwich, Connecticut, where an enterprising language arts coordinator persuaded writer William Zinsser to give a course on writing to the administrative staff. Not only did the administrators learn to write memoranda to staff and letters to parents in simple and precise language, they also developed a deeper understanding of how students learn to write and how teachers can assist.

Is the School's Emphasis on Writing Practical?   Why do we deplore the low priority on writing in schools when the way to communicate, as Ma Bell tells us, is to "reach out and touch someone"? While the volume of daily mail has increased enormously, the proportion of personal mail has dropped to ten percent, including greeting cards. However, although most people write less frequently than ever before for social purposes, the production of print has expanded enormously. Writing for print or the electronic media has become a major occupation of many employees of the "information industry," a $500 billion yearly enterprise that embraces more than half our work force, according to the U.S. Department of Commerce.

Nevertheless, the primary reasons for writing in the school have little to do with learning to communicate. That is of *secondary* importance. The first reason for practicing writing in school is to learn how to order thoughts and express feelings. As whole school faculties come to realize that writing is a necessary means of learning, they will be better able to define their roles in developing writing as well as reading among their students.

In the rest of this chapter we shall look at ways to develop reading/writing strategies for learning, and we shall refer to these strategies by the more familiar term "study skills." We begin with practices that all students in the grade span from 5 to 12 should be engaged in, and we end with those advanced practices which only the more mature students in secondary schools can use profitably in academic learning.

The Journal as an Instrument for Learning

The French boy learns to write, Rollo Brown told American educators in 1915, by writing.[2] The least-likely-to-succeed nonreaders in ghetto junior high schools learn to *read*, Daniel Fader told us in 1962, through filling two pages daily, copying if necessary but writing words.[3] Children in English schools, a thousand American educators discovered in the 1960s, still keep notebooks or journals as did any of their forebears in the eighteenth and nineteenth centuries who were lucky enough to get a formal education. So the journal has been revived by many American teachers, and a good practice it is, too, though like any other practice it is subject to misuse and to parental criticism. (Some parents object that personal journals are *too* personal and encourage narcissism in children and nosiness in teachers.) We believe the personal journal contributes effectively to children's fluency in writing, which is a major goal in language development in elementary grades, and that it gives teachers an insight into children's thinking. Through keeping a journal, or diary, children can learn about themselves. The time spent in this kind of writing is more wisely invested than time spent on workbook exercises. The personal journal is a useful device for teachers in self-contained classrooms and for English teachers in departmentalized programs.

The journal for learning in content subjects is a different matter. In middle schools where team planning operates, all teachers might agree that one learning journal should serve all subjects. Thus, students making daily entries might record a science experiment one day, another day a reaction to a math concept, and on still another day a comment on the treatment of native peoples. The learning journal, unlike a diary or personal journal, is not private. Teachers in a middle school might take turns in reading and responding to a week's entries, thus keeping up with a student's entire school learning experiences, noting, for example, that Henry is using the words he learned in English class to comment on his math lesson. Another group of teachers might decide that each subject should have its own notebook, one that will remain in the classroom so that a teacher can always refer to a student's work in preparation for a conference with the student or with parents.

Notebooks are standard equipment for secondary classes, and a journal is simply a special kind of notebook. What distinguishes the journal in its return engagement in American education is that it is more informal and personal than the notebook and much more demanding upon the students' ability to express whole thoughts. Notebooks tend to be dependent on teachers' dictated notes, outlines of the textbooks, and answers to questions set by the text, workbook, or laboratory manual. The learning journal transfers responsibility for learning to the student. It still depends for its structure on the textbook and teacher, but the aim is gradually to reduce this dependence. For example, compare the journal

---

[2]Rollo Walter Brown, *How the French Boy Learns to Write*, special edition for the National Council of Teachers of English, 1963, by arrangement with Harvard University Press, which published the first edition in 1915.
[3]Daniel Fader and Elton McNeil. *Hooked on Books: Program and Proof* (G. P. Putnam's Sons, 1966).

entry Jeanne made in Ms. Kravitz's science class this year with Dick's lab page for the comparable unit last year (Box 14-2). Whereas Dick simply entered findings from the experiment in the designated boxes, Jeanne had to think through the answers to Ms. Kravitz's questions: What concept did you learn? How can you be sure you're right? These are questions she answers in her journal nearly every day.

The learning journal is a natural way of establishing with students that they know whether (and how much) they've learned if they can write about it in sentences that others understand. Putting an idea into words reinforces our grasp of it. "How do I know what I think until I hear what I say?" asked the astute fifth grader, echoing E. M. Forster. The question implies what every psychologist knows from studying relationships between thought and language.

The informality of the journal serves another purpose: to aid the transition from expressive or personal writing to expository and transactional writing. The writing of mature students is often unnatural and inaccurate because they have been forced into attempting abstractions before they really understand them. Therefore, they "borrow" phrases, paragraphs, and much more sometimes. The journal encourages them to use personal pronouns and avoid passive verbs that conceal the agent and therefore the responsibility for the action. They can move from this journal style into writing for others in similarly personal, direct, and honest styles.

Of course, not every entry in the learning journal needs to be in declarative sentences. Entries will vary with the subjects and with students' learning styles. Informal notes, partial outlines, and "mappings" (see below) will appear frequently. So, too, should questions, which are the essence of learning through reading.

One very great advantage to the learning journal, as contrasted with study guides, workbooks, and more formal notebooks, is the insight it gives teachers into individual learning styles. We still have much to learn about how students process information, and journals are a window on the process. From them we may learn something about how students arrive at ideas they consider worth remembering.

Patterns of Organization and Recall

As we said in the previous chapter, instruction that alerts students to the writer's structure or pattern of organization aids retention of ideas as well as initial understanding. For that reason, we might have included the examples of paragraph patterns in this chapter as well. Especially pertinent to our topic here is the suggestion made in Chapter 13 that teachers should demonstrate with some such device as the one shown in Figure 13-5 *why* it is easier to recall a clearly defined pattern whether it is visual or verbal than a loosely structured one. Often students are able to use the writer's organization, especially the organization of textbooks, to aid recall, and their outlines or notes or summaries should reproduce the organization as they perceive it. But sometimes the student has to impose a clearer organization on the material to be remembered than the text offered. Reproducing the author's pattern will not be as effective an aid to recall

BOX 14-2

JEANNE'S JOURNAL ENTRY

What did you see?

I looked at a hydra under the microscope. It had a long body with 6 tentacles. My hydra was not very active. It seemed to float in one spot. However, it did stretch out and pull itself into a ball. It did this three times. Also, its tentacles kept moving. When I touched one tentacle with a needle, it contracted. The body and other tentacles contracted at the same time. When I tapped the watch glass, my hydra coiled into a tight ball.

What did you learn?

The hydra reacts to touch by contracting. Since other parts of the body react to touching one tentacle, its nerve and sensory cells must be connected throughout the body.

DICK'S LAB PAGE

1. Wait until the hydra is fully extended, then touch one tentacle with a needle. What happens?

the tentacle contracts

2. How do the other parts of the body respond to touching one tentacle?

they contract

3. Which parts of the hydra are most sensitive to touch?

tentacles

4. Does the hydra react equally to a weak and strong touch at the same point?

no

as reorganizing the information and ideas in a new, sharper structure. While instructional materials offer much practice in outlining well-organized writing, teachers must also give students direction in reorganizing ideas into patterns they can handle more easily than the writer's.

Taking Notes to Aid Recall

Good books on how to study have been readily available to teachers and students for fifty years or more. To cite just three examples: *Better Work Habits* by Rachel Salisbury, an excellent workbook for the early secondary grades, was first published in 1932; W. H. Armstrong's *Study Is Hard Work*, a text for high school students, was published in 1930; and F. P. Robinson's *Effective Study*, which introduced SQ3R, first appeared in 1937. Through fifty years the importance of study skills has been emphasized in school texts, professional journals, research, and methods courses. Yet we hear repeatedly the charge that high school students cannot read and write well enough to learn the content of high school courses; that is, they are deficient in study skills.

Of course, the criticisms are exaggerated. Even in recent decades a good number of students have been learning how to study in high school and earlier. They have learned sufficiently well to succeed in college and graduate school and become noted researchers, teachers, and scholars in dozens of new fields as well as traditional ones. True, many of these successful students have taught themselves how to study. Noting only that they might have done so more efficiently with the aid of teachers and texts like those mentioned above, we can turn our attention away from this relatively small group and ask what we can do for the much larger group of average students who are expected also to apply study skills in content courses but are not sufficiently skilled or motivated to teach themselves. Why is it that so many high school graduates are lacking in study skills even though we have known for many years what kinds of instruction and practice they need and even though good instructional materials have long been available?

The answer lies, we believe, in the inconsistency of teachers' effort and the frailty of students' motivation. Repetitive though it sounds, using patterns of organization must be taught from grade 5 through grade 12, not just once each year but continually and directly in reading and writing classes, and incidentally in all content fields. (Indeed, these patterns are introduced in first grade and should receive attention right through college.) And this consistent practice must be turned to immediate use. The fundamental reason why students fail to remember as much as they are able to is that they see no real need for recall.

So every lesson aimed at reading to remember must contain a reminder of why one should bother. Two immediate reasons for recalling ideas are (1) to pass tests and (2) to report information to others. (Of course, the real reason for making ideas your own is to become a more interesting and interested person, to enrich your life and contribute to the society you live in and those that will follow, but students have to have end-of-the-week reasons, and these reasons are tests and reports.) The workbook exercises are like learning to hold the racquet; the game is still to be played. As reading teachers, we tend to stop with the warm-up exercises. As content teachers, we often fail to check on how students are helping themselves to remember. Both reading and content teachers must fill in the gap between the warm-up exercises and the tournament. It isn't enough for the reading teacher to provide only the skills exercises and the content teacher only the reasons for them. Working together, content teachers and a reading teacher can show students how to apply study skills to serve real purposes.

Reviewing for Examinations

Students in grades 5 to 8 should begin to take notes in order to strengthen their recall of information which they are expected to learn whether for teachers' tests or for school-wide evaluations. Good students in these grades should be able to organize responses to essay questions in social studies, English, and science courses.Usually, they should have open-book tests so that they can refer to a text for details, but this privilege is a boon only to students who are thoroughly familiar with the material. Even when examinations are of the objective type, with or without open books, students should learn that recall of major ideas is aided by note-taking.

We are not talking about note-taking for all students. For poor readers in middle school/junior high we advise that examinations call for limited writing, presenting objective items rather than free-response questions. For students who are seriously disabled in reading, the exams on content should be oral, and for these students especially, easy response patterns are desirable. They should learn a few concepts so well through repeated exercises and practice with simple study guides that the development of independent study skills, which is beyond them, is also unnecessary.

Let's return to the students for whom note-taking is practical. All the steps in perceiving organization lead to informal note-taking and eventually to more formal textbook study methods. In grades 5 to 8, we recommend emphasizing informal note-taking and postponing formal outlining until senior high school—even though most basal readers and other instructional materials introduce formal outlining as early as grade 4. These exercises, based for the most part on quite artificially structured prose, probably do not do any great harm, however, and if carefully guided by the reading teacher, they can reinforce students' ability to see relationships between major and minor ideas. But often the textbook lessons on outlining are merely assigned and not discussed, and they constitute mindless activity for most students. Even with guidance, the lessons often focus on the conventions of the formal outline, taking time away from the real reason: noticing the coordination and subordination of ideas.

Asking middle school students to make formal outlines based on content textbooks often presents them with a task beyond their present abilities because the writer has not followed an organizational plan that conforms to the formal outline. In order to produce a formal outline, the student would have to reorganize the author's ideas, and that is much too demanding a task for students who are still at the stage of concrete thinking and not yet at ease with abstract logical relationships. These students are much better off following the author's organization, whatever it is, using the text's boldface headings to guide their note-taking.

Informal note-taking encourages students to concentrate on ideas rather than form. The only formal requirement is to indent minor ideas under major ideas. Since textbook headings are usually reliable clues to major ideas, the first step in note-taking is simply to survey the text and write down the major ideas, leaving space for adding the details which will be noted in a careful reading. In doing this students are merely continuing on their own what teachers have been doing in the prereading steps of a directed reading lesson.

One trouble with vertical note-taking is that students don't know how much space to leave, and the finished notes are not as handy for reviewing as they might be. A better device, suggested by Donald D. Durrell nearly thirty years ago (in *Improving Reading Instruction*, Harcourt Brace Jovanovich, 1956), is the Idea Line. The student counts up the number of major ideas in the passage and turning a sheet of paper sidewise blocks out three, four, or more columns. At the top of each column goes the main idea, and the details are filled in below (see Box 14-3). The Idea Line can be used to test one's recall by folding it horizontally just below the main ideas. With only the main ideas exposed, students attempt to recall the details. Or with only the details in view, they tell what the main ideas are.

The Idea Line demonstrates to students one way of using notes. In showing students this way (or any other) teachers should discuss the psychology of note-taking. Why do people make notes? Do they always refer to them? Is it more valuable to try to put down notes from memory after the initial reading, or is it better to keep referring to the text for accuracy? How often should you review notes?

Other types of note-taking for mature readers will be discussed in a later section of this chapter.

Taking Notes for a Report

Examinations are artificial devices which more often evaluate teaching than learning. A more natural reason for taking notes is to share information with others. Content teachers can provide real purposes for investigating topics and sharing one's findings, and reading/English teachers can take advantage of out-of-school topics in which students are interested.

Reports related to the unit under study, when the reporters are given sufficient time for preparation and presentation, can stimulate real learning among both listeners and reporters. Yet how often the report turns out to be a badly garbled rendition of an encyclopedia entry only tangentially related to the topic at hand.

To prevent students from confusing copying and note-taking, consider how to work into your long-range teaching plans the following ideas:

✣ Discuss with a small group how to reduce to manageable chunks a general topic they have selected from those suggested at the end of the chapter. When you and the students have listed questions of interest, have them

BOX 14-3

AN IDEA LINE
(Made by student to aid study of eighth grade social studies text)

A. Growth of U.S. between 1877 and 1914	B. Immigrants discriminated against in the cities	C. 1890s—immigrants being excluded from U.S.
1) 15 million immigrants between 1860–1900	1) Had to live in urban ghettos	1) Blamed for labor violence, unemployment, slums
2) Until late 1870s, most from western and northern Europe	2) Got poor jobs—long hours, low pay	2) Groups called for quota systems and literacy tests
3) By 1890—more than half from southern and eastern Europe ("new immigrants")	3) Many employers prejudiced	3) 1882—Congress passed Chinese Exclusion Act
4) Also—Chinese, Japanese, and Mexican		

identify the key words they will look for in the index and table of contents of trade and textbooks and in encyclopedias and other reference books.

✤ Anticipate the outcome of the above step by selecting beforehand a limited number of sources. Of course, the media specialist should be part of planning and executing this assignment. Sources should be informational books on the topic rather than encyclopedia entries only.

✤ Show students how to use an index and table of contents to lead them to possibly appropriate pages. Then show them how to skim materials until they find relevant sections.

✤ Demonstrate making notes on different cards or slips of paper for each subtopic of the report you are to make (see Figure 14-1).

✤ Remind the students that since the purpose of notes is to jog the memory, their notes should consist of topics—not complete sentences—and should contain different amounts and kinds of information depending on how much cuing is needed.

✤ Help individuals decide how they are going to organize their report. This step can serve both an oral and written report. Let them decide which pattern of organization they will use, since reading has made them familiar with many patterns.

Since these steps take time and attention to individuals, you cannot teach note-taking effectively with whole classes. Therefore, whether you are a content teacher or a reading teacher, you stagger report assignments so that you never have a whole class working on reports at the same time. You enlist all the aid you can. For example, the content teacher might work with one group and ask the

FIGURE 14-1

SAMPLE NOTE CARDS

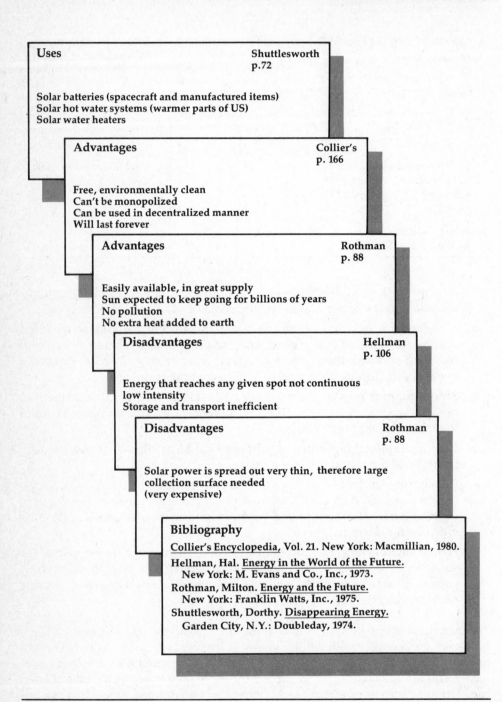

Uses   Shuttlesworth
                              p.72

Solar batteries (spacecraft and manufactured items)
Solar hot water systems (warmer parts of US)
Solar water heaters

Advantages   Collier's
                              p. 166

Free, environmentally clean
Can't be monopolized
Can be used in decentralized manner
Will last forever

Advantages   Rothman
                              p. 88

Easily available, in great supply
Sun expected to keep going for billions of years
No pollution
No extra heat added to earth

Disadvantages   Hellman
                              p. 106

Energy that reaches any given spot not continuous
low intensity
Storage and transport inefficient

Disadvantages   Rothman
                              p. 88

Solar power is spread out very thin, therefore large
collection surface needed
(very expensive)

Bibliography

Collier's Encyclopedia, Vol. 21. New York: Macmillian, 1980.

Hellman, Hal. Energy in the World of the Future.
    New York: M. Evans and Co., Inc., 1973.

Rothman, Milton. Energy and the Future.
    New York: Franklin Watts, Inc., 1975.

Shuttlesworth, Dorthy. Disappearing Energy.
    Garden City, N.Y.: Doubleday, 1974.

reading teacher and the media specialist to work with two others. Another possibility in some situations is to use the trained professional who regularly aids content teachers with writing assignments. Team teaching, even when it means a combined class of forty or more for the two teachers, permits frequent note-taking and reporting sessions that can be carefully monitored. Of course, when one group has been taken carefully through the note-taking sequence once (with good results), the next time they can be given much more freedom to pursue the steps on their own.

You don't have access to the aides mentioned? Then you must plan even more carefully who is to be given reporting assignments. At first you may want the full-scale assignment to go only to your most able students, the ones you guess will profit most from your guidance. Then, on the next round, let these students serve as aides to others. Meanwhile, you have been leading up to the major assignment by teaching parts of it. For example, Ms. Benson gets her seventh graders ready for reporting by showing an informational film. She prepares for the film in the same way that she prepares for a reading assignment, that is, by building background, discussing key concepts and vocabulary, and suggesting the organizational pattern of the film. After the film, the group decides on the major points and subtopics they would highlight in reporting the film's content to others. This warm-up exercise ends with the completion of the outline; no report is written.

Instead of assigning the least proficient readers and writers to a full-scale report, Mr. Goodman assigns them to quite specific pages of books they can read (related to the unit theme) and asks them to write a different fact on each of three or more note cards. They contribute these ideas in informal small-group discussions.

Increasing Independence in Study

A principal difference in the ways you work with the most able and the least able students is that you push the former toward early independence. But you make very sure you know who the "most able" students in your subject are. At one time or another every one of us has been an immature student in some subject. The fact that Emily did a fine report on the Spanish settlements in the Southwest when she was in seventh grade doesn't guarantee that she can now in tenth grade write a research paper on the development of rockets. But she can make many decisions on her own, including when to ask for help.

Ben, on the other hand, will always need to have content teachers make very clear what is worth remembering and show him informal ways of aiding his memory. The least able students will do most of their note-taking in personal, even idiosyncratic, journals, because these youngsters need to use immediately whatever information they acquire. The information they have to share with others is almost never of the academic sort that Emily and other able students must learn to absorb, call their own, and adapt to new purposes.

Emily and Ben are on the opposite ends of a continuum of abilities related to academic learning. Coming between Ben and Emily are all those students who have varying degress of abilities, more than the Bens and less than the Emilys.

Moreover, over the years, Ben may move a step or two towards Emily's position. Emily, who developed from an eager reader into a *willing student* in the early secondary years, will continue in the process of becoming a *mature* student for as long as she continues to learn, probably for the rest of her life.

So far, Emily and her peers have learned how to use study strategies for learning from texts in the lower ranges of readability, and now they must learn to apply these strategies to more complex and varied kinds of reading. At lower ranges of accomplishment they have learned:

+ to keep a learning journal
+ to perceive structure in text that informs, explains, argues, describes, and persuades as well as tells stories
+ to use different patterns of organization in taking notes and making reports
+ to respond accurately to study guides that are composed chiefly of objective items
+ to explain their choices on such guides
+ to use writing for transactional purposes such as answering free-response questions, reporting to others, describing an event or procedure, explaining a process, or making an argument

They have learned to do all these mostly under guidance. Increasingly now, they must learn to apply these strategies to the more demanding assignments of the subjects they take in grades 9 to 12—and beyond. They still need guidance, but increasingly their teachers' aim is to transfer to them the major responsibility for selecting what is to be remembered, devising ways to remember, and making new uses of newly acquired concepts. To the list above, these students must add the following:

+ writing essay answers to questions posed on examinations and take-home assignments
+ developing more formal strategies for studying textbooks, such as
  formal outlining
  mapping
  SQ3R
+ using their learning journals as sources for writing which will be read by others
+ writing research reports

All of this develoment takes time and the collaborative efforts of teachers over a span of eight years or more.

Writing Essay Answers

To get good answers from students we have first to pose good questions. Very often content teachers can adapt questions from the editorial apparatus of their textbooks. Ms. Palmer, an eleventh-grade history teacher, duplicated for her class the following questions:

1. The United States was a better place to live in 1860 than it was in 1790. Cite evidence to support this statement.

2. Compare abolitionism with other reform movements such as those to eliminate child labor and to gain women's rights.

3. Describe the attitude towards slavery that would be typical of (a) a southern plantation owner; (b) a New England cotton mill owner; (c) a northern clergyman; (d) a poor farmer in Tennessee.

She discussed with them the key words and the patterns of organization suggested by each question. Then she let her students choose one of three questions to answer in an essay begun in class and finished at home, as an "open book" test. The next day students worked in groups of three to four to critique each other's papers.

Ms. O'Hara, a tenth-grade biology teacher, enlisted the help of Mr. Coltrane, the reading teacher, after her class did less well than she had expected on a free-response question included in the end-of-term test. Deciding that the students' problems were probably related as much to their misreading of the question as to any real lack of information, they began to develop a file of good questions (see Box 14-4), and Mr. Coltrane spent time with Ms. O'Hara's students in his reading classes discussing the meanings of the emphasized words in these questions.

In another school, the history teachers became concerned with the quality of students' explanations of historical events. They decided to require an essay answer to the same question for all students taking Anthropology I. Then all the history teachers in a departmental meeting evaluated the papers (names removed) using the holistic evaluation procedures described by Cooper (Box

BOX 14-4

SAMPLES FROM MS. O'HARA'S FILE OF TEST QUESTIONS

#1.   *Compare* the ways in which division of labor is seen in modern society with the ways in which it is seen in a metazoan.
(First, on scrap paper, make two lists. Then note likenesses. Begin your answer: Division of labor in a metazoan is similar in many ways to division of labor in a modern society. For example, _____)*

#13. Biologists theorize that certain bacteria were among the first forms of life on earth. What *evidence* can you cite *to support* this *theory*?
(What is a theory? Underline the theory part of the first sentence. Check textbook for evidence. What is evidence?)*

#23. In guinea pigs, black is *dominant* over white. When a *heterozygous* black guinea pig was crossed with a white one, the offspring produced were three white guinea pigs and one black. How do you *interpret* these results?
(You are expected to know what dominant means. Is it important in understanding this experiment? What about heterozygous? Interpret means to explain why the offspring were three white, one black.)*

*Mr. Coltrane's questions and advice.

14-5). From this procedure emerged plans for improving the questions and teaching students how to respond (as Ms. Palmer and Mr. Coltrane had done).

Teaching students how to write an essay in answer to an examination question is not very much different from teaching writing as English teachers have been developing the process over the years. The advantage the content teacher has over the English teacher is that previous class work has been building up to this essay. Students have completed study guides and discussed them; they have taken notes on the topic. Exam questions are a further means to help them generate ideas—that is, have something to say. Students need help in ordering or arranging their ideas, and the suggestions imbedded in a good question help them to do that. They need to consider style and diction. The work on vocabulary before and after reading assignments in the text will contribute to their writing style and choice of words.

BOX 14-5

HOLISTIC EVALUATION OF WRITING

"Holistic evaluation is a guided procedure for sorting or ranking written pieces. The rater takes a piece of writing and either (1) matches it with another piece in a graded series of pieces or (2) scores it for the prominence of certain features important to that kind of writing or (3) assigns it a letter or number grade. The placing, scoring, or grading occurs quickly, impressionistically, after the rater has practiced the procedure with other raters. The rater does not make corrections or revisions on the paper. Each paper in the lot will be rated by two, three, or more readers."*

When a group of content teachers rate an essay, they may create a scale of three to five answers (if the writing is in response to an examination question) representative of quality from *excellent* to *failing*. Or they may make an analytic scale assigning points for content (major concepts and relevant details) and delivery (organization, wording, mechanics). Or most simply, they may sort the essays into three categories: good, fair, poor. Whether they use guides worked out in advance or simply discuss sample papers at some length before and during the rating, teachers who rate papers together with some regularity over a period of time find their judgments becoming increasingly similar (reliability improves).

Comparing ratings with others' and having a broader sample of students to judge provides insights that you may miss in grading papers on your own. Moreoever, you gain confidence from knowing that multiple ratings based on holistic evaluations provide valid measures of student performance. Students profit too: group scoring develops explicit criteria and assures them that response to their writing has been reasonably comprehensive and concerned with substantive matters.

Holistic rating procedures permit teachers to read papers fast. The procedures don't save teachers' time since they must read more than their usual stint. The trade-off is the gain in reliable measurement.

*Charles R. Cooper, "Holistic Evaluation of Writing." In *Evaluating Writing: Describing, Measuring, Judging*, Charles R. Cooper and Lee Odell, eds. (National Council of Teachers of English, 1977): 3.

Perhaps the best opportunities for improving writing in the content fields come with the evaluation of these short essays, which should be assigned as in-class and take-home exercises as well as more formal examinations. Have students in groups of three or four evaluate each other's progress, providing them first with a checklist of ideas that should be included. Have them consider different ways of expressing these ideas so that they can evaluate answers with reference to style and form as well as substance.

Essay answers are a microcosm of the research papers to be discussed below. In many situations the frequent inclusion of essay answers carefully evaluated by the students themselves, their teachers, the department (on occasion), and professional writing assistants (where available) is the main contribution to the development of writing that content teachers can make. They need not be concerned with writing exercises (such as sentence-combining). Content teachers should focus on ideas, not exercises. As specialists enthusiastic about their subject, content teachers are in a fortunate position for stimulating ideas and thus serving the student writer's first need—having something to say. One way a content teacher communicates enthusiasm is to read to students tantalizing bits from nontextbook sources and to encourage them to pursue these leads. Informal discussion of ideas, formal debates, role-playing, and dramatization of events are worth a hundred lessons in sentence-combining. Students find ways to combine sentences when they have something of interest to say to a sympathetic audience.

By the way, many essay answers should be written in the students' journals and not graded. Wherever possible, teachers who are serious about improving youngsters' writing refrain from grading a paper until they have given students a chance to act on the advice of their editors—that is, their teacher and peers.

Three Strategies for Studying Textbooks

Study guides are crutches—very necessary to beginners in any subject whether they are new to seventh grade social studies or twelfth grade psychology. But the support of study guides must be gradually withdrawn and independent methods substituted for them. Let's consider formal and informal methods by which students aid their retention of important ideas.

Outlining   Students who are well taught in observing relationships between major and minor ideas and taking informal notes have little or no trouble moving to formal outline patterns. Along the way they should have had practice in translating running discourse into outline topics. The best way to teach this aspect of outlining is to provide numerous models, proceeding as follows:

+ Select a well-organized segment of a content textbook—about a thousand words.
+ Outline it yourself, making judicious use of typographic aids provided by the editor.
+ From your outline make a skeleton for students to fill in after they have read the whole section all the way through and decide which of the author's headings to use, which to discard. They fill in the outline.

✤ Follow up with similar lessons on the same textbook, or other content textbooks your students are using.

✤ Ask students to outline a section on their own which they later compare with one you have done on the same section. Be sure to discuss reasons why outlines vary from one person to another.

Conscientious students include too much in their outlines, thus defeating the purpose. Sometimes not-so-conscientious students include too much because they copy sentences from the text rather than thinking how to state them as topics. Other outlines are too thin to be real aids to memory. The usefulness of outlines, of course, must always be demonstrated immediately for most students. So have them recall the outlined section orally to a partner or write a resumé, referring only to the outline, not the text. Let them experiment with recalling for a quiz a passage they have outlined and a comparable one they have not.

When I went to school, outlining was in vogue. In seventh grade we were required to outline all of *Treasure Island*. It was a good twenty years later before I discovered Stevenson had written a great story. In eleventh grade Mr. Bottomley dictated a segment of an outline of U.S. history every day and somehow managed to keep most of us in that class excited about the events that the Muzzeys were describing in that well-worn and respected text. In twelfth grade we were required to outline on our own a whole history of English literature, which served me in good stead in later college classes. Of course, I was an academic student in college preparatory classes in a most traditional New England high school. I never knew what the kids in the other tracks were required to do, or how they felt about it.

I would have thought no teacher today would repeat Ms. Soule's sin against seventh graders and Robert Louis Stevenson, but, alas, I keep running into students and parents who report that English teachers are still requiring outlines of short stories, novels, and plays. So I feel obliged to proclaim the obvious: Formal outlining is appropriate only to informational text—history, philosophy, the sciences—and not to all examples of text in these fields.

Mapping   As a technique for figuring out the author's organization and making it visual, mapping is a powerful aid to comprehension. As an aid to memory, it serves some students better than outlining or SQ3R, and it fits many modern texts far better than outlining.

"A map is a graphic representation of the intellectual territory traveled . . . via reading. . . . It is a verbal picture of ideas which are organized and symbolized by the reader," says M. Buckley Hanf, illustrating her definition with the map of a selection on black widow spiders reproduced in Figure 14-2.[4] Hanf asserts that mapping improves the memory because in designing this structured pattern, the reader proves that he comprehends all that he needs to remember. Categorizing

---

[4]M. Buckley Hanf, "Mapping: A Technique for Translating Reading into Thinking," *Journal of Reading* 14:4 (January, 1971).

FIGURE 14-2

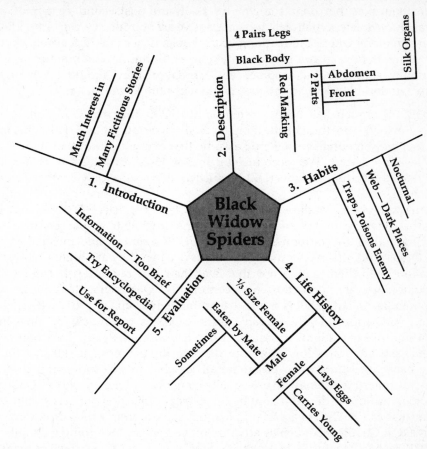

SOURCE: M. Buckley Hanf, "Mapping: A Technique for Translating Reading into Thinking," *Journal of Reading* 14:4 (January 1971) 228.

details in a map (as in an outline or idea line) and giving labels to the category supplies the reader with a trigger for all the information stored in the mind under that label. Hanf finds support for mapping in these words of psychologist George Miller: "Our memories are limited by the number of units or symbols we must master, and not by the amount of information that these symbols represent. Thus it is helpful to organize the material intelligently before we try to memorize it. The process of organization enables us to package the same total amount of information into far fewer symbols, and so eases the task of remembering."[5]

An important function served by mapping (as with all textbook study aids) is

---

[5]George Miller, "Information and Memory," *Scientific American* (August, 1956). (Quoted by Hanf in the article referred to in footnote 4.)

to remind students that studying should never be attempted passively. Reading textbooks requires at least a ballpoint and scratchpad. When students own their own textbooks, as they do in some high schools and postsecondary institutions, they fall into what is sometimes the semipassive act of underscoring or highlighting. In situations where the marking of textbooks is permitted, teachers should show students how to combine note-taking, outlining, and summarizing with underlining so that recall is practiced. Moreover, they should teach highly selective underlining and annotating to highlight the key ideas only.

SQ3R   So much has been written about SQ3R (Survey–Question–Read–Recite–Review), a method of studying textbooks introduced by F. P. Robinson in 1937, that we sometimes mistakenly assume that everyone knows and loves the formula—and uses it. We reproduced it in Box 13-2, showing how it parallels the Directed Reading Lesson (DRL) which is used so widely in the elementary school.

Upper and postsecondary school students tend to resist SQ3R, in part because they have by this time acquired sloppier study habits, in part because they haven't acquired the component skills that SQ3R requires, and mostly because SQ3R helps students master a demanding text when they are highly motivated but cannot help them with a text that is at their frustration level. The implicit assumption of every instructor who recommends SQ3R is that students can *read* the content texts, but SQ3R is an aid to learning only from texts that are *readable*.

Even with appropriately readable texts, SQ3R is too much for most high school and college students to assimilate in a few lessons. Reading teachers must be persistent advocates for SQ3R and develop the component skills gradually before expecting students to put them all together in this independent study strategy. Content teachers who are equally convinced of the merits of SQ3R can, of course, further the development by consistent application of parts of it to each lesson. Just as the DRL is a variant of SQ3R, so are other prereading methods discussed in Chapter 13, such as advance organizers and mapping techniques.

SQ3R is hard to teach because it requires not only the development of component skills but the replacement of old habits. Consider that most students—even the best of them—turn to the first page of a chapter and begin at the first word. It's the student in a hurry, sometimes the less conscientious one, who is sensible enough to turn first to the questions at the end to see what the authors consider important. The survey step requires skimming and scanning, which many students, again the better ones, shun. So teachers from grade 5 on have to patiently establish the habit of surveying or previewing *every* nonfiction selection. Much of this can be done in separate skimming lessons as described below.

The raising of questions is the key step. When I teach SQ3R, I begin by turning titles and subheads into questions. Many editors do that for readers these days; so I use newspaper and magazine articles as well as textbooks for practicing the questioning-while-surveying step. We jot down the questions raised during the survey, then add others during and after careful reading.

We begin with short segments of text, gradually extending to a chapter's length. We practice the *Recite* step in class. Frequently, I use paired practice for

BOX 14-6

HOW ONE HIGH SCHOOL TEACHES SQ3R

The teachers in Fayetteville-Manlius High School (New York) prepared *Skills for Learning: A Guide to Academic Success*, a 22-page pamphlet which they mail home to every student when school opens in September. This is how they present SQ3R:

Reading a textbook is different from the kind of reading you do in your leisure time for personal enjoyment. It also differs from the kind of reading you do when you are asked to do a research paper. Each kind of reading requires its own special techniques. The method presented here for reading a textbook more efficiently is called the SQ3R Method. The letters stand for *Survey, Question, Read, Recite,* and *Review*. Many high school students have found this method to be extremely helpful.

A. SURVEY

The purpose of this step is to acquaint you with the general ideas in the reading assignment and to help you learn the key vocabulary words.

1. Read all titles and subtitles in the assignment.
2. Look at all the pictures, cartoons, and drawings.
3. Read the introduction and summary if they exist.
4. Develop a vocabulary list with definitions for all italicized words, boldface words, and words that come before a parenthesis. Use the glossary, context clues, and a dictionary as necessary for the definitions.

B. QUESTION

The questioning step accomplishes two things: first, it causes you to think about the reading assignment; and, second, it provides a good reading-study guide for you to follow as you read.

1. Read the questions at the end of the chapter.
2. Read any questions handed out by the teacher.
3. Restate the above questions in your own words.
4. Make up questions from the titles and subtitles using the six indicators of information (who, what, where, when, why, and how). Then write these questions.

C. READ

The third step in SQ3R is to read.

1. Read one section at a time.
2. As you read, try to answer the questions you raised in the questioning step.

D. RECITE

The purpose of this step is to actually write the answers to the questions you have been trying to answer by reading.

1. Write the answers to the questions you developed or identified for Part B, one section at a time.

Continued

BOX 14-6 (continued)

HOW ONE HIGH SCHOOL TEACHES SQ3R

2. Study your vocabulary list.
3. Open your book and check your answers against the reading for accuracy and completeness.
4. Correct your answers as necessary.
5. Organize your questions and answers according to the 2-6-2 format of the Cornell Method of note taking, and include them in your notebook.
6. Read the next section of your reading assignment and repeat all of Part D until all sections are completed.

E. REVIEW

The review step entails what is usually meant by the term "study." If carefully done, it should reduce the time spent getting ready for a test.

1. Put the book away. Do not reread the chapter.
2. Read the questions and try to answer them without looking at your answers.
3. Check your answers with your notes to see if you are correct.
4. Repeat Steps 2 and 3 until you answer each question accurately three times in a row.
5. Picture the questions and answers in your mind. Try to visualize all that goes together in each part.
6. Ask yourself what the main points of the assignment were and what evidence was provided. Check your memory by referring to the notes generated from your questions.

this, one partner reciting, the other using the questions as a kind of check list. Just as often I use the second R to stand for *Write* and have students write summaries of their recall. Finally, after several days, we return to the questions and again, working in pairs, see which can be answered from memory and which require *Review* of the text.

You can see that conscientious development of SQ3R could take a full semester study skills course in grade 11 or 12. I think that for certain students it is worth that much time and effort, for it is an omnibus strategy that puts together component skills and furthers students' real purposes in academic learning. When content textbooks are well matched to students' reading development, SQ3R can serve well the whole range of students bound for postsecondary education, which may be as high as 80 to 100 percent in some schools, suggesting a wide gamut of learning styles in some of these classes. For first-generation college-students-to-be, for other youngsters who are just beginning, in their phrase, to get themselves together, I can think of no more important service that high schools can render.

Writing a Research Paper

Even though students may have had many assignments between grades 5 and 10 which required them to consult reference texts and other sources, to take notes, and to report their findings orally or in writing, they usually do not face a major research paper until grade 11 or 12. When such an assignment is made in English, history, or science classes, teachers cannot assume that reference skills supposedly learned earlier are still in good working condition. So both teachers and students approach the research paper warily. Renewing reference skills, motivating students for a task that requires sustained attention, stimulating thinking about the content to be researched, helping students through several drafts from note-taking to final manuscript—the dimensions of the assignment are such that many teachers as well as students quail before it. In fact, among English teachers, the wisdom of assigning a research paper in secondary school has long been the subject of debate.

In this debate we join with proponents who marshal the following arguments on behalf of this assignment:

1. Students continuing beyond high school will be expected to produce research papers; they probably won't be taught how to do so by the professors who make the assignment.

2. The research paper involves skills that students have begun to develop in early grades and which deserve to be pulled together and used in combination for an important purpose.

3. Students need practice in sustaining effort and attention on a worthwhile academic task.

4. Students by the end of high school should have at least one product they can be proud of which is crafted of language and made to last.

Nevertheless, we believe this assignment should not be made lightly or by the decision of an individual teacher. All the faculty in grades 11 and 12 should come together to deliberate such issues as these:

1. Which students should be expected to write a major research paper? How shall we identify them?

2. What assignments should be included in the curriculum for grades 11 and 12 that lead up to the major research paper? Should these contributory assignments be directed to all students anticipating postsecondary education even though the paper itself may be required only of the most able?

3. Is one such paper in the last two years of high school sufficient?

4. What are the dimensions of a "major research paper"?

5. What criteria will we apply in evaluating these papers?

6. If one research paper is sufficient, should a team of teachers be responsible for it? (For example, teachers of English, science, and history and a media specialist might constitute a team for students whose topics relate to the effects on society of a scientific advancement, the education of scientists during a particular period of a nation's development, or the role of women in science during the mid-twentieth century.)

7. What research tools should juniors and seniors use? (Computer terminals and microfiche readers should not be foreign to them.)

8. What kind of publication of these papers is appropriate? (For example, should papers which meet certain standards be added to the library?)

9. Should excellent papers receive public recognition?

If we were part of a faculty discussing these questions, we would favor the requirement of a single research paper of between 500 and 1,000 words in either the eleventh or the twelfth grade for all students contemplating enrollment in four-year colleges. This paper might originate in any of the students' academic courses, but it should contribute to the requirements for an English marking period as well and might earn a grade in more than one content subject also. For "academic" students who are recognizably weak in reading and writing, modifications might include shorter papers derived from fewer sources, or one or more of the several steps in the process but not the final product.

A faculty taking a team approach would have to decide which general topics would be acceptable and how these topics would be scheduled so that the media specialist can predict which materials will be needed at what times during the year. Successful learning depends to a great extent on how willing the staff is to add to their other responsibilities the guidance of students' research. So the scheduling of student and faculty time is an essential step.

Once general topics have been agreed upon, teachers can work with students on how to define researchable topics in these general areas. Box 14-7 shows the topics that one group of teachers decided on, and we have chosen one of

BOX 14-7

TOPICS FOR INDIVIDUAL AND GROUP RESEARCH

This is part of the list of topics compiled by a faculty team in a senior high school that had agreed to work together with students writing research reports. Some of the topics cut across subject areas; some are more clearly aligned with one area than another; but each requires at least two consultants: the English or reading teacher and a content teacher.

1. Immigration into the United States: Its Problems and Benefits

2. Endangered Species in North America

3. Effects of Climate, Natural Resources, and Occupation on Single-Family Dwellings Typical of Four Regions in the United States

4. The Thirties: Styles in Architecture, Furniture, and Clothing

5. Environmentalist Organizations in the United States Today

6. Volcanic Eruptions in This Century: Chronology and Consequence

7. The Peacetime Uses of Nuclear Energy

8. The History and Potential of Personal Computers

these—*Immigration into the United States: Its Problems and Benefits*—to illustrate the process of narrowing a topic.

Working with a group of students who are interested in some aspect of this topic, Mr. Henry, the history teacher, suggests that the topic can be limited chronologically and geographically, but he recommends putting these options aside until the students have brainstormed the whole topic. As their questions go onto the chalkboard or screen, it becomes apparent that the students are interested in political and social effects of immigration in their section of the country and that some are particularly concerned with problems of illegal entry in the last two decades. Some of the questions which emerge are:

a. What immigrant groups have settled in this region?
b. What attracts them? What jobs do they fill?
c. What political rights do immigrants have?
d. How many immigrants become citizens? How soon?
e. Are first-generation Americans today different from those of the decades between 1890 and 1910?
f. What measures have been taken by the U.S. Immigration Service to prevent illegal entry?
g. What is the guest worker program? Where has it been tried? With what effects?

The students see that some of these questions go together and could constitute sections of one research paper (for example, questions *a–d*). Others, like *e* constitute a main topic and can be further broken down. The last two might each be treated as the central question to be answered in a research paper, and each would need further refining and delimiting.

Ms. Bennett from the science department works with the group as well, and some students decide to investigate the contributions of immigrant scientists in the 1940s and 1950s. From the English department, Mr. Rafaela makes the suggestion that some students investigate the contributions of immigrants to cultural changes between the first and second World Wars. He takes aside interested students and they break this topic into subtopics: films, fiction, graphic arts, and so forth.

In all these discussions, teachers and students work toward defining the parameters of a particular research report. Will it survey several aspects of a delimited but still appropriately broad topic such as *a* to *d* might suggest? Or will it focus on a single issue and gain depth by the number of examples it records?

After discussions such as the above, which demonstrate how to define a suitable topic, the next step is to consider sources. Now the media specialist joins the group and discusses sources in the school and public libraries and shows how interlibrary loans can be arranged. She demonstrates electronic search tools if these are available, and brings appropriate reference works and trade books to the group. Students begin to test the appropriateness of their questions. Teachers lead the discussion so that students can learn from shared experiences how to test the relevance of information to the questions raised.

A lesson is devoted to documentation. An appropriate form for references and footnotes is introduced (one that the faculty have all approved), and questions are answered as to when quotations are needed, how much excerpting is appropriate, when paraphrasing is preferred and how credit is given to sources of information and ideas. The "ownership" of ideas is discussed. Should students interject their own opinions? Yes—and they should differentiate their opinions from those of their sources. They should make clear whose opinions they agree with, and say why they agree.

Before students begin to work on their own, teachers present at least one group lesson on how to take notes on cards. A later group lesson, timed for when students have collected most if not all their notes, is directed at how to use notes to make an outline of the emerging research paper.

But these teachers are anxious to avoid a common problem in "research papers"—the stringing together of excerpts from sources which have not been thoroughly digested or related to students' questions and experiences. So from the beginning, they have directed students to keep their questions in focus and to look for a point of view to emerge from their reading which they can support. Because teachers are aware that students resort to plagiarism most often when they are trying to cope with topics that are over their heads, these teachers try to guide individual students into topics that interest them and that they can comprehend with as much stretching as they are capable of.

Long before the students are ready to write, they have begun to consider the audience they are addressing. We hope that audience can be a real one—for instance, future students in Mr. Henry's history classes or Ms. Bennett's science course, students who will use the library that will accession the best of these research reports, citizens of the community, or readers of a specific journal to which the paper may be submitted. But even if the audience is only the faculty committee which will evaluate the paper, students should define a real or fictitious audience to whom they are addressing their report. Their concept of audience will help them to decide on a pattern of organization for their ideas, the depth of detail they will need, and the style of writing. Many teachers propose that students strive for a particular level of readability suitable for, say, tenth graders or college freshmen or readers of *Atlantic Monthly*.

Of course, not all research papers need be of an academic nature. Many students are eager to search out practical information on fields they might enter, business enterprises they might start, regions of the world they might explore; or to follow their avocational interests in sports, films, fashions, cars, or airplanes. Such interests provide the same kind of practice in narrowing the topic, identifying a bibliography, using research tools, taking notes, ordering ideas around the problem to be solved, and addressing an audience.

In the above discussion we have assumed that a faculty in grades 11 and 12 have decided that they will be responsible for assigning research reports, or parts thereof, in their regular courses. An alternative approach would be a special course in report writing to which students are assigned in either of the two grades. However, this "extra class" would not eliminate the need for a faculty committee to determine assignments and to participate in the evaluation of research papers. It is simply a way of scheduling the necessary instruction.

Adjusting Rate of Reading and Making a Study Schedule

The Need for Rapid Reading

Reading as rapidly as one can comprehend the message is an asset to busy junior and senior high students, not just those bound for college where required reading threatens to wipe out all extracurricular activities for the plodding student. The pressures are almost as great in the secondary years when adolescents develop expensive social habits that must be supported by part-time jobs. Not only adolescents from poor families feel economic pressures these days; increasingly, middle-class youngsters are spending more time earning and spending money than reading books. Even when strong ambitions draw them toward high school diplomas and college entrance, they skimp on study time and therefore desperately need fluent reading skills. That is why we urge attention to rate of reading as soon as readers can comprehend at fifth and sixth grade levels.

Everything recommended to this point that improves comprehension—wide reading, reading to answer questions raised by oneself and others, guided reading in all content fields, note-taking, SQ3R—all these will lead to fluency. But more is needed. Very often good readers in fifth grade are slower than they need to be because too zealous a concern for accuracy in the primary program has dissuaded them from taking chances in decoding words. Rapid reading, so long as the materials being read are within the realm of the half-known and partly familiar, can be trained by specific techniques and sustained practice.

Reading experts tend to be stuffy about rate of reading, deploring expenditures on machines and crying "Charlatan!" at every commercial venture that promises increases in rate. However, schools continue to buy expensive equipment and parents continue to enroll their offspring in out-of-school speed-reading courses because the need for rapid reading in a print-saturated culture is very apparent. We would rather see school systems invest the money they are budgeting for reading machines in better libraries, services to teachers, and staff development. In fact, one service to teachers would be a course in speed reading for them. Not only do teachers need to read more rapidly in order to cope with paper work, keep up with their fields, and become more interesting people, but they can also learn a great deal about teaching reading through taking such a course.

Reading experts who turn thumbs down on rate-improvement programs employing films, tachistoscopes, and various types of rate controllers are not moss-backed curmudgeons. Most research studies fail to support lasting gains for average participants in rate-improvement programs that ignore differences in individuals' purposes and in the kinds of materials they will read after the external pressures of controller, stopwatch, or coach have been removed. Nevertheless, there have been notable exceptions, and many individuals attest to benefits they have earned from assiduous practice in courses they found through advertisements in newspapers and magazines.

What can reading and content teachers do to help students to increase their rate of reading generally but also to vary their rates according to purpose and the kinds of materials being read? If machines are already part of your equipment, use them sparingly, chiefly for motivational purposes. Your whole purpose is to move students away from the support of external pressures toward the establishment of an inner drive for fluency.

Provide consistent timed practice in reading under natural conditions. The success of the *McCall Crabbs Standard Test Lessons in Reading* (New York: Teachers College Press, Columbia University) since the 1920s has been based on the fact that these three-minute daily exercises (including questions) can be scored immediately and charted so that students always know what progress they are making.

Some teachers have found consistent use of *cloze* exercises results in improved rate of comprehension. For example, daily or several times a week, Ms. Jenkins had students in her efficiency reading elective read as rapidly as possible under timed conditions passages of 500 words taken from various reading workbooks. Immediately thereafter students read *cloze* versions of the same passage (duplicated with every fifth word deleted), restored the words, and scored their papers. These were easy exercises for Ms. Jenkins to prepare, and used over several months they netted real gains for many students.

Students should figure out their "normal" reading rates in each subject textbook they are asked to read and report these estimates to their content teachers. The least that secondary teachers of content can do for the reading program is to figure out how long it will take the fastest, the slowest, and average readers in a class to complete a typical assignment—and let this knowledge influence their expectations of their students and themselves.

How much a reading teacher can do for reading rate depends on the nature of the classes. Developmental classes in grades 5 to 8 can include attention to rate for students reading at or above grade level. But students whose needs in reading and writing are more fundamental won't have time for rate improvement. In senior high schools, electives in speed reading permit the kind of concentrated and sustained practice which is demanded if bad habits are to be replaced. We strongly recommend this elective for senior high schools and suggest that in most situations it be given higher priority than so-called remedial classes which are often too little and too late at these grade levels.

Commercial materials for improving rate are abundant and should be selected carefully for ease and interest. Their readability levels should be below the independent reading levels of the students who are to use them. Reading teachers can easily manage daily rate practice with differentiated materials adjusted to individual needs, since students reading at different rates can all finish different exercises in about the same amount of time.

In addition to standard rate practice, teachers should teach when and how to skim for specific information or to scan for general impressions. Commercial materials are plentiful, but use of content textbooks and materials related to content makes more sense. Skimming sessions should be short, snappy, and fun. Begin with easily found items: capitalized and *italicized* words, dates, and figures. Use every-pupil response techniques; for example, asking everyone in a small group to put an index finger on the right spot on the page. Answers can be vocal or not. Skimming should, of course, be related to the use of the index in textbooks and to finding information in reference books.

One teacher-made device which is easy to prepare and provides challenging material for scanning consists of two short articles from the same magazine or anthology cut into paragraphs, each paragraph pasted on an index card. Both sets of paragraphs go into the same envelope and the student is directed to sort out the two articles as rapidly as possible. To make self-checking easy, key each card on the reverse side. The same cards can be used for practice in arranging ideas in a logical pattern as a follow-up to arranging topic cards. A set of thirty envelopes of this kind provides useful differentiated practice for thirty sessions or more depending on the size of groups. (Each student works on a different envelope each time.)

Teachers in business courses have devised similar sorting games using collections of letters to be categorized in various ways, such as Immediate Reply Necessary, Refer to Sales, Discard.

Scheduling Study Time

Most students need help in budgeting their time. Reading teachers and English teachers sometimes invite guidance personnel to share this brief segment of a study skills course, recognizing that general advice such as that contained in textbooks and films must be followed up by conferences with individual students if it is to mean anything. Student-to-student discussions about how to budget time, especially those that mingle high school with middle school students or bring in graduates who are now in college are often worth the effort even though results are not immediately visible.

Preparing individual schedules is a logical follow-up to study-habits inventories. (See the unit Learning about Ourselves as Learners between Chapters 6 and 7.)

Scheduling Direct Instruction in Study Skills

There should be no need to raise the issue of where to find time to teach study skills—and who will do it. Of course, every content teacher declares as a top priority teaching students how to learn. And if learning through reading and writing is consistently taught from primary grades through high school graduation, students going on to postsecondary education in this decade will have developed the study skills and habits they need for continued successful learning.

That is an "if" which must be explored school by school. None of the generalizations we are about to offer will fit all secondary schools, which are as various in students' needs as they are in size. In studying whether or not your particular school is preparing students well for continuing their education, you can invite recent graduates to tell your faculty and students what successes or failures they are experiencing in college that are directly related to what they learned, or failed to learn, in high school. Such information should be shared with faculty all the way back to kindergarten because preparation for college begins there, and not in the last two years of high school, as the present discussion may unwittingly suggest.

Periodic self-study by a high school faculty is valuable at any time but it is vital in these times when new populations are seeking postsecondary education. We can no longer depend on family and peer influences to make up for whatever the schools neglected in developing independent study habits.

Even in schools that are moving toward improved learning programs— through staff development and strong administrative leadership—we believe that some students in eleventh and twelfth grade need another chance to take stock of their study skills and evaluate their chances for success in college. They need the "prepping" that well-to-do parents buy for their children at private schools and skills centers. Perhaps 25 percent of the graduates in most high schools could profit from an extra class in study skills. This 25 percent would *not* include excellent learners but would be made up of the least able college-bound students, those in the middle quartiles of achievement test scores. In many schools where these numbers might not be sufficient to warrant a regularly scheduled class, special arrangements can be made for an extra elective. In other schools, the study skills elective is a well-established feature which has proved its usefulness.

We hope that few schools have to choose between proficiency classes for underdeveloped eleventh and twelfth graders or a study course for the college-bound. Where this hard choice does present itself, however, logic suggests that the study-skills elective will yield more dividends for the college-bound students immediately and for society eventually. This course should spend a period or two in evaluating students' present habits, and the balance of the time on two goals: (1) daily practice in improving rate of reading; (2) refinement of at least one independent textbook study method. For that one method I would choose SQ3R and work every day either on one aspect of it or on the whole technique applied to textbooks students are using currently. You might choose a variant method that you have had personal success with and can be enthusiastic about. The point is that by college entrance these students must be freed from dependence on teacher-made study guides. They are unlikely to find them in college. They must learn to substitute their own study aids.

Big high schools can afford a variety of reading/writing electives for the upper grades: speed reading *or* study skills *or* advanced report writing *or* vocabulary development. Students can be guided into beneficial choices. But the preceding paragraph is addressed to schools with limited resources that cannot offer a range of reading/writing electives to all students, the exceptionally able as well as the disabled. Accordingly, we focus on the students just above the median and below the top quartile.

For the very able students, we hope that somewhere in the eleventh or twelfth grade a seminar series can be offered which centers on *how to read a book* (the title of a text by Mortimer Adler and Charles Van Doren that we might recommend to able seniors). These students may have learned how to learn from textbooks that are equipped with study aids, but some encounter college texts and other sources in history, science, philosophy, the social sciences, and imaginative literature that are not especially edited for students. Adler and Van Doren present practical advice in readable English on how to read all kinds of text. This paperback is worth having students buy for future rereading in college, but right now they need to discuss the ideas among themselves under your intelligent guidance. If you have a Great Books Seminar in your high school, *How to Read a Book* might be included there, or a regular senior English course might include a unit featuring this text.

RECAPPING MAIN POINTS

The principal means we have of judging students' comprehension of ideas is how they express them. Accordingly, teaching to read also requires teaching to write.

Under present conditions, teachers are more likely to evaluate reading comprehension by having students respond to objective test items. To enable teachers to assign more writing, administrators should keep classes small, hire lay readers, and persuade teachers that they need not "correct" all papers but should respond to them; administrators should also provide in-service means for faculty to improve their own writing, and they should develop with staff a schoolwide language policy.

Even though many people don't use writing to communicate these days, a renewed emphasis in schools on writing is eminently practical because writing is a principal means of learning. Having students keep a learning journal reinforces their understanding of information-processing, keeps teachers informed as to how and if students are learning, practices writing skills, and reinforces learning from text.

Perceiving patterns of organization aids comprehension and recall through providing the reader with the structure for note-taking and summarizing. Lessons aimed at reading to remember must contain explicit reasons that are meaningful to students, such as succeeding on examinations and making reports.

Younger students should take notes following the organization of the content textbook they are studying. However, mature students must sometimes reorganize the writer's presentation to make it more logical and memorable.

To prevent mindless copying when the assignment is to take notes from several sources, teachers should instruct students in how to select a manageable topic, identify key words in order to use indexes and references, assemble sources including informational books at many levels of readability, and demonstrate how to take notes on each subtopic on cards that can be organized easily for the final report.

As good readers become good students, they need instruction in how to write essay answers on examinations, how to select and apply textbook study methods congenial to their learning styles and the nature of the text, and how to use learning journals as sources of essays and research reports.

Three textbook study methods that must be taught with care by reading and content teachers are outlining, mapping, and SQ3R. Since each requires skills previously taught but perhaps not mastered, teachers must review component skills and show how to combine them. SQ3R also requires the replacement of old habits with new ones that may seem at first to be time-consuming but that are eventually efficient.

Writing a research paper in grades 11 or 12 is a major assignment that a team of teachers should direct from beginning to end: The process includes exploring a topic to understand its ramifications, narrowing the general topic to a specific one, learning to use resources, documenting sources, developing a point of view, writing for an identified audience, and revising. The whole faculty should deliberate the worth of such an assignment and identify which students should undertake it.

A much-needed aid to study is rapid reading. External pressures on rate must give way to practice that stimulates students to vary rate according to the text and purpose. Related to saving time by improving rate is scheduling study time. Most high schools need to schedule how-to-study courses for at least the lower half of those bound for college.

FOR DISCUSSION

1. Describe the skills that a good reader in grade 5 to 8 learns in becoming a good student during these years. What does this student need to add to these skills in senior high school in order to become a self-starter, ready for college?

2. It is easy to understand the need that capable readers have for developing study skills. What ought to be done for not-so-good readers who are nevertheless capable of average performance? What about dyslexic students who have college aspirations? Describe those students who should *not* have instruction in how to study. Explain.

3. If writing is one way of learning, should not *all* students be required to write freely and frequently? Discuss the issues.

4. With your colleagues discuss your own study habits. How did you acquire them? Do you consider yourself an efficient learner? Why or why not? How will your own experiences in developing study habits influence what you teach your students?

5. Discuss the uses of study guides in content subjects. (Be sure you are familiar with several types of study guides. You or your instructor should obtain samples as a basis for this discussion.) What types of students profit most from them? Under what circumstances might study guides prove deleterious to learning of certain kinds? What kinds?

FURTHER READING

Devine, Thomas G. *Teaching Study Skills*. Boston: Allyn and Bacon, Inc. 1981.

Elbow, Peter. *Writing with Power*. New York: Oxford University Press, 1981.
  Like *Writing without Teachers*, this book speaks directly to beginning writers, not to

students through teachers. Therefore, it is first of all for you as a writer; its force may also affect your teaching.

Fulwiler, Toby, and Art Young, eds. *Language Connections: Writing and Reading Across the Curriculum*. Urbana, IL: National Council of Teachers of English, 1982.
Fulwiler's essay, "The Personal Connection: Journal Writing Across the Curriculum," is particularly useful. Recommended also is Elizabeth Flynn, "Reconciling Readers and Texts."

Kahn, Norma. *More Learning in Less Time*. Upper Montclair, NJ: Boynton/Cook Publishers, Inc. 1979.
This "guide to effective study for university students" contains useful information for you as student and as teacher.

Note: See also the references for students and teachers in the unit "Learning about Ourselves as Learners."

15 Responding to Imaginative Writing

In the last two chapters we have been concerned with how readers absorb information and ideas from nonfiction through a lively process of asking and answering questions, making predictions and checking hunches, and using outlines and diagrams to make relationships graphic and memorable. Although we considered readers' critical reactions to nonfiction in the last section of Chapter 13, our emphasis to this point has been rather more on comprehending than on responding and much more on informational than on imaginative writing. Now in this chapter we focus wholly on imaginative writing, which calls on the reader not only to receive but to respond.

You may wonder why we devote a whole chapter to imaginative writing in a book that is addressed to improving students' abilities to learn through reading, which presumably will be done mostly through content textbooks. Our reasons are practical. First, imaginative writing is a good vehicle for illustrating many higher-order reading skills, such as drawing inferences, understanding metaphor, predicting outcomes, and sensing the author's tone and intent. Second, it appears that students who exhibit skill in reading-as-reasoning read widely in fiction as well as nonfiction and presumably apply many of the same strategies (depending on their purposes) in reading both kinds of materials. Third, in spite of certain similarities, the two modes of writing are sufficiently different that teachers cannot use them interchangeably in teaching how to read.

Up to this point, we have been addressing you as a reading teacher or as an English teacher who is taking the lead in teaching strategies for learning through reading. Now we need to address English teachers, not as teachers of reading and writing or the processes of language, and not as content teachers either but as teachers of literature. We argue that the teacher of literature is not a teacher of content any more than the art or music teacher, for like them the English teacher aims primarily at developing habits of turning to art for personal gratification rather than mastering specific works of literature.

Teaching literature, then, calls for a rather different set of ends and means from teaching reading-to-learn. It complicates curriculum planning that language is the medium for literature as well as for science and philosophy, that it is the medium we use to teach and inform as well as to entertain and delight. The complications must be recognized in order to be straightened out, but they need straightening out only in instances where the effectiveness of teaching is threatened. For example, care must be taken not to apply content-reading strategies to the reading of literature. We shall point out specific instances of how strategies for literature and the content subjects converge with, and depart from, each other as we develop two main topics in this chapter: (1) differences in responding to imaginative literature and text;[1] and (2) encouraging responses to literature.

Differences between Imaginative Literature and Informative Text

As we noted in Chapter 11, story and poetry satisfy deep-seated psychological needs. One reflection of this is the presence of the same stories in what appear to be widely divergent cultures; for example, scholars have identified more than four hundred variations of the Cinderella story, ranging from an Algonquin Indian version to a Siamese tale. We learn from stories as we learn from life not information primarily, though experiences of both kinds do indeed inform. To put it metaphorically, stories inform the heart rather than the mind. They tell us truths about human beings by describing that which is more likely to happen rather than that which has actually happened. Many of the oldest stories tell about human nature by invoking the supernatural. And the language of story, especially of poetry, strikes at the hearer's subconscious by indirection and connotation, by symbols and images. Yet the language of poetry is also, in some degree, the language of exposition. So it is quite natural for reading teachers to begin by using the language of story and to continue to apply the same teaching strategies to both imaginative literature and informational text even though readers bring different purposes to each and should respond differently to each.

Story is a natural human response, as natural as language itself, perhaps more natural since stories can be nonverbal, as in films and dreams. Because this is true, it is easier to read most stories than most text. But paradoxically, it is easier to respond verbally to text you understand than to stories and poetry you understand. The reason for this, as Adler and Van Doren remind us, is that the purpose of imaginative literature is to please, not to teach. "It is much easier," they say, "to be pleased than taught, but much harder to know *why* one is pleased. Beauty is harder to analyze than truth."[2]

Harder but not impossible. After readers have had many, many chances to be delighted by literature, they can begin to articulate what there is about the story or poem that pleases them. This attempt to say *why* begins long before children reach middle school and it is not in any way an analytical approach. Rather,

---

[1]We use *text* in this chapter for all writing except fiction, poetry, and drama. We assume two kinds of writing: imaginative literature and text, which is everything else.

[2]Mortimer Adler and Charles Van Doren, *How to Read a Book*, rev. ed. (Simon and Schuster, 1972).

teachers are pleased to notice such signs of incipient critical awareness as, "That story reminds me of . . ." or "Read us another story by. . ." or "I like *Danny the Detective* better than *Pippi Longstocking*" or "I know how Jason felt when his mother told him to leave." By the many means we shall describe in the next section, teachers gradually prevail upon students to extend such comments and to examine why they feel as they do. To be aware of one's feelings, to articulate them, and to explore how a writer plays upon them—this is all part of the larger development of fluency in language which is the aim of all education.

In reading expository and persuasive prose, the reader who is raising questions and making predictions carries on an active dialogue with the writer, even with the faceless authors of school textbooks. With imaginative literature the dialogue between writer and reader seldom surfaces during reading. A reader who "talks back" during the reading of imaginative literature is more likely to be arguing or pleading with, advising or encouraging, characters in the story rather than addressing the writer who created them. The dialogue with the author comes later, after the novel or short story or poem has had its effect upon the reader. The reader begins: "You made me feel thus and so about Scout and Atticus. How did you do it?" Or the reader says: "You wanted me to feel sorry for Miss Boo, but I thought she was a fool." Or: "The story didn't end the way it would have in real life, and you didn't prepare me for the surprise at the end." Comments like these, simple though they may seem to an artful reader of literature, do not spring spontaneously to the minds of innocent readers. These kinds of questions, and much more sophisticated ones, are the results of years of learning to listen to stories and to read them and to react to them openly and freely along with like-minded persons who share the experience.

The delayed dialogue with the author of imaginative literature (as compared with concurrent dialogue with the writer of nonfiction) reflects the different purposes of the two genres. The author of the novel, especially the contemporary novel, creates a world, invites you into it, and remains out of sight. The point of view of this author we say is *omniscient*. Even when the author writes in the first person, the reader interacts with the character of the "I," not with the author, who as a real person is hidden still. Writers of nonfiction, on the other hand, are always present, explaining, describing, arguing, persuading from their point of view. These writers want you to be aware of them, if only to be persuaded of their objectivity. The intent of writers of nonfiction is to persuade you of the accuracy, objectivity, credibility of their statements. Writers of imaginative fiction ask, instead, that you enter a believable world they have created for you even though you must for the moment suspend your disbelief.

That "willing suspension of disbelief" means that you should read a novel, short story, or poem as quickly as possible, as passionately and uncritically as you can. You cannot begin to question the author about how this happened and why this resulted until you have heard the whole story. Good readers of nonfiction raise critical questions at every step because they want to get the author's message straight. Good readers of poetry and fiction subject themselves to the will of the poet and storyteller, opening themselves to feeling. Only later, looking back, will the good reader think about those feelings.

This demand of imaginative literature to be taken whole, to be read at one gulp if possible, presents problems to the teacher of reading, who wants to ensure comprehension every step of the way. Slow, unsteady readers cannot read very much "in one gulp"; even good readers get lost in the details and misunderstand crucial incidents because they have overlooked foreshadowings. So literature teachers effect compromises. For example, they select short novels in preference to long ones. They are careful to set up points of connection between the reader and the work *before* reading in the hope that the connection will be sustained even through an extended reading experience. For less mature readers they choose not only short novels, poems, plays, but less complex ones. And when students must read a long and complex work (and mature students in middle and senior high school should have this experience under the guidance of a sensitive reader of literature), then teachers divide the work into segments that can be discussed before proceeding. Segmenting a long work should be done by episodes, according to the structure of the plot, not by so many chapters or pages evenly divided for weekly or daily assignments. Whenever possible, however, good teachers remember that the reading of imaginative literature should be uninterrupted.

The differences between imaginative literature and expository prose are chiefly in aim (the contrasting effects desired), but because purpose dictates form, there are differences, too, in structure and style. Fortunately, students who are learning to look for structure in everything they read and see are prepared also to make use of the structures they find in imaginative literature. The uses are different, however, because the important aims of the reader of imaginative literature, paralleling the aims of the writer, are *not* to remember information and *not* to apply newly learned concepts to new problems.

Not to remember what happened in a novel or short story? No. What good readers remember over the years is the effect of such reading, the pleasurable re-creation of feeling. The details fade. I've long ago forgotten why Maggie Tulliver was swept away in the flood or why the tears were streaming down my cheeks as I hurried to finish *Mill on the Floss* the night before the exam in my senior year in high school. More recently, I've forgotten the details of Will Stanton's meetings with the Old One but not the atmosphere of that Christmas season in contemporary England in Susan Cooper's *The Dark Is Rising*, nor the foreboding of evil or the steadfastness of Merriman.

But teachers depend on students' remembering incidents and characters well enough to discuss them intelligently, you say. True, and the discussion itself should reinforce both the recall of details and the pleasurable effects of the whole reading. However, students need to remember details only long enough to serve their understanding of the whole work. What is important in reading literature is to *enjoy* detail while reading, and later, if it's necessary, to be able to refresh one's memory easily. So responding to literature, whether through discussion or writing, should always permit going back to the text.

There should be no closed-book tests of literary reading. How will students be able, then, to write an intelligent essay on Hamlet's moral dilemmas, which they may be asked to do without reference to the text as part of their evaluation for college entrance? Their classroom experiences in responding to *Hamlet* with chances to refer to the play will help to stamp the incidents on their memories; their thought-through feelings will remain with them because they approached the reading of the play in the first place prepared to sympathize, if not empathize, with the characters. But the question itself is unfair because, in almost every test situation, they will be permitted to select those works that they can intelligently draw upon for examples to prove a general proposition.

Because it is important to notice details *while reading* in order to feel the effects described by the author, this is one of the skills literature teachers emphasize, and they do so in relation to structure. For example, in the novel and short story, readers learn by years of experience preceding the adolescent period that the teller of tales sets the scene and develops the plot through a series of incidents leading to a climax and followed by a denouement, or outcome. The concepts of *setting, plot, incident, narration, dialogue, climax* and *denouement* are entirely familiar to students in grades 5 to 8, though they may not know these names for these concepts (see Figure 15-1).

To accept a fiction writer's invitation to enter the world he is creating and to meet and come to know the characters, the reader must become familiar with the setting and note details about characters. Many inexperienced readers of fiction fail to observe and to use details. We can, however, train them to do so, though their comprehension of details will depend on how well they can combine what they already know (that "theory of the world in their heads") with the clues provided by the author. Training in combining information on the page with information in the head—specifically in relation to details of setting, for example—can develop the habit, which will be used subconsciously in future reading. To do so we propose exercises of the kind shown in Box 15-1 because we do not want to interrupt the reading of a whole work of fiction, the first reading of which must be fluent and pleasurable.

Similar attention to clues to character, sometimes in exercises such as the one in Box 15-2, come *after* the reading of a work and build habits for the reading of each subsequent work.

So also, after having read through the whole story, short novel, or segment of a novel, students can go back and examine how incident relates to incident and builds toward the climax.

As we have said, students are probably aided by their long-time exposure to television and movies in developing a sense of structure for imaginative literature. From time to time, however, they need to have this internalized coding brought to the surface and examined in relation to written literature. For the structures of imaginative literature are changing, and mature students should be able to discuss the episodic plots of the great epics and early novels and compare them to the classic unity of the "new" form—the short story—and its counterparts in contemporary TV dramas. Similarly, they should be observing the changes in structure in recent fiction and the emergence of new crossbreeds of fiction and nonfiction in which real incidents may be reported in the literary manner of fiction and offered as "faction."

We are not recommending labeling as such, except for mature college-bound students. We nevertheless believe that students from grade 5 on should recognize different forms of literature and note, for example, that the shape of a poem, even a narrative poem, is different from the shape of a short story. We would have young people look at the shape of a poem on the page while

FIGURE 15-1

READING AND DISCUSSING SHANE

Below is a fascimile page from a school edition of *Shane*, showing questions which middle school students discuss to strengthen such concepts as *conflict, incident, character.**

3. The source of conflict in *Shane* is the historical struggle between the ranchers and the homesteaders, and the author realizes there is something to be said for both sides. He is careful to show good and bad, strong and weak, on both sides of the struggle. Is this statement true? Explain.

4. Think of some of the Westerns you have seen or read. What types, or characters, in many of them are missing in *Shane*? What big scenes are typical of Westerns? Which ones appear in *Shane*? Which ones are missing?

5. *Shane* is a compact novel. There are no unnecessary scenes, no wasted words. Three incidents set the background. Then the action soars to a climax and suddenly concludes. We could diagram the plot this way, with each square representing an important scene that carries the action forward.

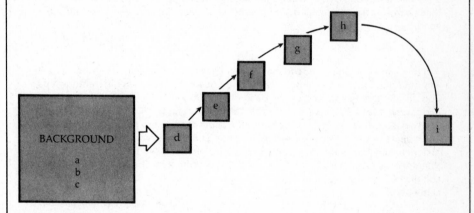

On your paper, write the letters *a* through *i*. Beside each write the number of the phrase below that belongs with that letter in the diagram.

1. Shane whips Chris
2. The stump scene
3. Fletcher makes his offer
4. Shane strikes Joe
5. Scene with the peddler

6. Shane fights Wilson and Fletcher
7. The Starretts decide to stay
8. Shane and Joe fight Fletcher's men
9. Wilson kills the farmer

6. Was the ending satisfactory? Realistic? What had Shane learned about life? What had each of the Starretts learned?

*From *Shane*, Jack Schaefer, edited with an introduction and reading aids by Margaret Early, Houghton Mifflin, 1964.

BOX 15-1

DRAWING INFERENCES ABOUT SETTING

Here are the opening paragraphs of several short stories. Underscore the words and phrases which help you to make a guess about where and when the story will take place. Write your guess in the space provided.

A

They came over the Pass one day in one big wagon—all ten of them—man and woman and hired girl and seven big boy children, from the nine-year-old who walked by the team to the baby in arms. Or so the story runs—it was in the early days of settlement and the town had never heard of the Sobbin' Women then. But it opened its eyes one day, and there were the Pontipees.

—Stephen Vincent Benet, "The Sobbin' Women"

B

The cooling afternoon rain had come over the valley, touching the corn in the tilled mountain fields, tapping on the dry grass roof of the hut. In the rainy darkness the woman ground corn between cakes of lava rock, working steadily. In the wet lightness, somewhere, a baby cried.

Hernando stood waiting for the rain to cease so he might take the wooden plow into the field again. Below, the river boiled brown and thickened in its course. The concrete highway, another river, did not flow at all; it lay shining, empty. A car had not come along it in an hour. This was, in itself, of unusual interest. Over the years there had not been an hour when a car had not pulled up, someone shouting, "Hey there, can we take your picture?" Someone with a box that clicked, and a coin in his hand.

—Ray Bradbury, "The Highway"

C

I'm an archaeologist, and Men are my business. Just the same, I wonder if we'll ever find out about Men—I mean really find out what made Men different from us Robots—by digging around on the dead planets. You see, I lived with a Man once, and I know it isn't as simple as they told us back in school.

We have a few records, of course, and Robots like me are filling in some of the gaps, but I think now that we aren't really getting anywhere. We know, or at least the historians say we know, that Men came from a planet called Earth. We know, too, that they rode out bravely from star to star; and wherever they stopped, they left colonies—Men, Robots, and sometimes both—against their return. But they never came back.

—Alan Bloch, "Men Are Different"

D

Remember? I can still smell it. I met her in the Aldwych Underground Station, at half past six in the morning, when people were busily rolling up their bedding and climbing out to see how much of the street was left standing. There were no lavatories down there, and with houses going down like ninepins every night, there was a shortage of baths in London just then, and the stench of the Underground was appalling.

—Jill Paton Walsh, *Fireweed*

listening to its sound as the best reader in the class (usually the teacher) reads it aloud. Without asking or giving definitions of poetry (except perhaps as an able junior or senior chooses to do so in a personal essay or journal entry), we would show poems printed as prose and as the poet wrote them, tying all this to contemporary forms like concrete poetry, but remembering that the form of

BOX 15-2

DRAWING INFERENCES FROM WHAT CHARACTERS SAY

One of the ways in which we judge people in life is by what they say. So also characters in novels reveal their emotions, moods, and traits through what they say. Here are some quotations from the characters in Charles Dickens's *A Tale of Two Cities*. After reading each speech, circle the word that you think indicates most exactly the emotion, mood, or trait shown by the speaker. Use your dictionary if you are unsure of meanings of choices.

1

"Here! Your mother's a nice woman, young Jerry, going a-praying agin your father's prosperity. You've got a dutiful mother, you have, my son. You've got a religious mother, you have, my boy; going and flopping herself down, and praying that the bread and butter may be snatched out of the mouth of her only child."

Does Jerry Cruncher's speech show sarcasm? amazement? indignation? fear?

2

"It is extraordinary to me," said he, "that you people cannot take care of yourselves and your children. One or the other of you is forever in the way. How do I know what injury you have done my horse?"

What emotion does the speaker display?   fear? regret? pity? anger?

3

"I have had unformed ideas of striving afresh, beginning anew, shaking off sloth and sensuality, and fighting out the abandoned fight. A dream, all a dream, that ends in nothing, and leaves the sleeper where he lay down, but I wish you to know that you inspired it."

Is the speaker cheerful? angry? despairing? penitent?

---

traditional poetry, if not the language, is easier for students than are modern forms.

The aim of the reader of imaginative literature is to grasp first what it *is* (a short story? a sketch? a satire? an allegory? a lesson? a lyric?)—which is, in a sense, recognizing the author's intention (to persuade through humor? to entertain through a heightening of suspense? to extend our experience of human nature? to create beautiful sounds or images?). Secondly, the reader aims at grasping the unity of the work as a whole. Thirdly, the reader tests whether or not he or she has done so by reducing the whole to its simplest unit—to a skeleton.[3]

What does this mean for teaching literature? What reading methods apply and don't apply? It is immediately obvious that SQ3R does not apply, nor do advance organizers. The directed-reading activity fits only in part. As a literature teacher, you cannot spoil the suspense by summarizing, and while you may set

---

[3]This is the term used by Stephen Dunning in his excellent short book, *Teaching Literature to Adolescents: Poetry* (Scott, Foresman, 1966). See also the companion text by Dunning, *Teaching Literature to Adolescents: Short Stories* (Scott, Foresman, 1968).

background, you are very careful, in most cases, to let the authors spring their own surprises.

Reducing the unity of the whole to its simplest statement implies paraphrasing or summarizing, but the terms are not exactly synonymous. The summary of a nonfiction piece condenses the original into fewer words and, *as a summary*, compares favorably with the original. However, the simplest statement of the unity of a work of literature is not the original condensed or synopsized. It is, in fact, a skeleton, the barest essentials, which if fleshed out by another artist might result in a wholly different work of art. A skeleton is nearer to what the reading teacher calls a main or central idea, but *skeleton* is a better term than "main idea," for it may be applied to a poem or prose sketch that captures a sensory image rather than a concept or idea.

Many teachers have avoided asking students to put the unity of a poem or story into their own words in the mistaken notion that this somehow desecrates literature. On the contrary, the prose statement of the poem's idea or of the story's plot sharpens the student's realization that literature transforms ideas into experiences that are to be felt as well as understood. Should the teacher judge whether a student's statement is right or wrong? That judgment should be made but not by the teacher directly or alone. The student should be able to defend the statement by returning to the text.

Which brings us to the question of interpretation of literature, especially of poetry. Because most imaginative literature is created out of a writer's personal needs, not to inform others, perhaps not even to touch others' senses, the readers' responses to literature are similarly personal, since it is their individual experiences, emotions, and senses which are being touched. When readers say that they like or dislike a work, and go on to say why, they are probably telling more about themselves than about the work. But gradually as they explore what the author did to make them feel that way, to invoke a particular memory, for instance, or an emotion, they begin to understand literary devices and to arrive at standards for judging. All this is a very gradual process that teachers can assist chiefly by creating an atmosphere in which students are willing to test out their own reactions and to listen to their peers'. But eventually students must come to a sense of their responsibility for interpreting literature not simply by personal whim but with respect for the meanings of language.

So teachers, while encouraging more latitude in the interpretation of literature than of nonfiction, nevertheless urge students toward interpretations which are defensible. Interpretations of poetry, says Laurence Perrine, can be better or poorer, not right or wrong. A better interpretation is one that accounts for more of the details in a poem and does so most economically, that is, without having to add ideas from the reader's experience that are not actually experienced by the poet.[4]

The structure of literature presents less of a problem to readers than do style and diction. When the writer's purpose is to inform, she looks for the least

---

[4]Laurence Perrine, "The Nature of Proof in the Interpretation of Poetry." *English Journal*, LI (May 1962): 393–98.

ambiguous language and the simplest, most direct style to convey ideas. But when the writer's aim is to remind readers of other times, places, experiences that will evoke certain moods, and feelings, she uses allusive language and words with many connotations. Moreover, the writer compresses much meaning into the fewest possible words. For instance, in a simple poem, Herbert Asquith describes birds' eggs, which have been blown for a boy's collection, as the "tombstones of the spring," suggesting with just one word a whole vision of gloom, death, and destruction, contrasted ironically with life-bringing spring.

Let's summarize the differences between imaginative literature and informational prose with respect to aim, effect, composition, and expected response. Since imaginative literature frequently appeals to the subconscious and to the emotions as often as to the intellect, it is harder for the reader to explain its effects. Informational prose, on the other hand, aims at the reader's active consciousness and is, therefore, more easily analyzed and explained. A good reader of imaginative literature submits to the author's will; on the other hand, a good reader of exposition carries on a lively dialogue with the writer whose intent is to inform or persuade. Marked differences in structure, diction and style characterize the two genres and are reacted to differently by good readers of both genres. For instance, noticing details is essential to the enjoyment of literature, but details are not to be remembered in the same way or for the same reason that ideas in expository prose enter the reader's knowledge. One reader's interpretation of imaginative literature may be better than another's, but interpretations are less likely to be judged right or wrong than are conclusions drawn from reading exposition.

The rest of this chapter deals with various responses that young readers can make to imaginative writing and suggests ways in which teachers can help them to give articulate verbal expression to thought-about feelings.

Developing Responses to Literature

Responding to Fiction

In the last several decades the teacher's role in getting youngsters to respond to literature has changed dramatically. We no longer view response to literature as the answering of teachers' questions but rather as developing readers' sensibilities toward the life fiction creates, identifying the feelings aroused, thinking about them, and expressing them. Beyond the expression of the readers' own feelings is the aim of refining readers' judgments of fiction and, accordingly, their tastes. In short, teachers aim to help students enjoy literature—that is, experience it fully—and to select literature which offers the fullest and truest enjoyment. Those goals, which are so easy to state and subscribe to, are also easy to miss, if we are to judge by how infrequently adults choose to read the great literature of the past or even contemporary fiction if it is serious rather than escapist.

Nevertheless, the teachers of this decade know a lot more about the teaching of literature than did our teachers, who may have known more about literature but less about helping average students to respond sensitively. The problem then and now has been getting youth to read in the first place, to read with comprehension and sensitivity. The reason for much of the question–answer sessions that used to masquerade as "discussion" was that teachers were checking to see if the reading had been done. So teachers, who are really not interested in grilling students as if they were defendants in a lawsuit, are looking for ways to ensure that students read a selection with interest and enjoyment, and that they understand the story well enough to be able to discuss its implications. To satisfy the first requisite, teachers choose very carefully any stories or novels to be read in common and make sure that they set up points of connection between reader and author before reading, using variations of some of the techniques for introducing a selection which are described in Chapter 13. To ensure understanding before discussion, teachers use guides and glosses, about which we shall say a few more words below.

To be a good teacher of literature today as in the past you must know literature. You must be a sensitive reader yourself. To teach good literature well, you may get by with a rather narrow repertoire, a relatively few short stories, novels, and plays that you love and can bring to life for adolescents. But you won't succeed beyond the class periods devoted to your performances, and maybe not even that far, unless your students come to your teaching of literature already enjoying reading. To develop their pleasure in reading widely, you have to know more than a few good works of literature. You have to read widely yourself in all the kinds of fiction, including junior novels, that immature readers can enjoy (see Box 15-3).

The literature teacher ought to read widely and well because the first big job is wise selection. You have lots of aids to selection but no one can read a novel for you. The novels you have been learning how to read in college and in the upper years of high school have taught you how to analyze fiction, but they are not appropriate for immature students. You have to apply your skills of critical analysis to the reading of a whole body of fiction with which you may not be familiar at all upon completing a degree in English or American literature. (For one thing, you will be expected to teach multicultural literature in many junior and senior high schools today.) So you will have a lot of reading to do every year you teach: the books you need to know at least superficially in order to encourage wide reading, the works from which you will choose new selections for in-common reading, and, of course, the writing of your students in response to *their* reading.

Use of Study Guides

You also have to read very critically the teaching materials—the study guides—which you will use with the works you select for in-common and independent reading. Because you need all the time you can spare for reading, we do *not* recommend that you yourself prepare study guides for all the materials you teach. You should not have to do so because so much good material is available to you commercially. (See the sources listed in Box 15-4.) You may have to adapt some of these materials to the needs of a specific group of students, but you should never have to begin from scratch unless you are teaching a novel that

BOX 15-3

TO CATCH UP

Donelson, Kenneth L. and Alleen Pace Nilsen. *Literature for Today's Young Adults*. Scott, Foresman and Company, 1980. 484 pp.

> Up to date, comprehensive, this text will give you a running start on the fiction and nonfiction titles you should become acquainted with if you are going to promote reading for personal satisfaction.

Sebesta, Sam Leaton and William J. Iverson. *Literature for Thursday's Child*. Science Research Associates, 1975. 565 pp.

> From many fine books on children's literature, we select this one for teachers of adolescents because it is especially strong on works of fiction and nonfiction for the upper elementary grades that can also be used to advantage with young adults. It is a readable text that offers excellent advice on how to help readers to articulate their responses to literature.

Chambers, Aidan. *The Reluctant Reader*. Pergamon Press, 1969.

> Donelson and Nilsen (above) count this as one of the great books on young adult literature.

Carlsen, G. Robert. *Books and the Teen-Age Reader*. rev. ed. Harper and Row, 1980.

> Long respected for its insights into adolescents' reasons for reading (or not), this text has been revised to include new examples while it retains valid principles for stimulating and guiding their reading.

Burton, Dwight L. *Literature Study in the High Schools*. 3d ed. Holt, 1970.

> This text on how to teach literature has valuable insights for teachers of reading as well as English teachers.

TO KEEP CURRENT

English Journal. National Council of Teachers of English, 1111 Kenyon Road, Urbana, IL 61801.

> Monthly issues contain reviews, articles about young adult literature in the classroom, interviews with authors, and an annual poll of what young adults are reading.

The Horn Book Magazine. Park Square Building, 31 St. James Avenue, Boston, MA 02116.

> Published since 1924, this bimonthly is found in every public library (ask the children's librarian if it isn't in the open stacks). Adolescent novels are reviewed in every issue as well as current adult books of interest to high school readers.

Journal of Reading. International Reading Association, 6 Tyre Avenue, Newark, DE 19711.

> Many articles on reading interests and literature (as well as the teaching of reading generally) and reviews of recent books with appeal for adolescents.

Media and Methods. North American Publishing Co., 401 N. American Building, 491 North Broad Street, Philadelphia, PA 19108.

> Frequent articles on promoting books for adolescents in the classroom, annotated list of Young Adult Reading each issue, and an annual listing of the best new paperbacks.

no one has taught before (and that might be an unwise choice). It may be harder to find study guides for short stories, but composing these guides is less time-consuming. Even so, begin with the editorial apparatus included in the school edition; find the teacher's manual that accompanies it; and if you make a new

BOX 15-4

STUDY GUIDES YOU CAN BUY

Study guides related to young adult novels on their list are available from the following publishers:

Sundance Publishers and Distributors of Educational Materials, Newtown Road, Littleton, MA 01460
These paperback distributors publish Novel Ideas Packets (teacher's guides and student activity sheets) to accompany novels widely read in junior and senior high schools.

Bantam Publishers
Study guides are available for many classic and contemporary novels on this paperback publisher's list.

Scholastic Books
Scholastic Units, on the market for at least two decades and revised yearly, are made up of multiple copies as well as single titles of novels and short fiction illustrating themes of interest to adolescents. Units contain guides for students and teachers.

National Council of Teachers of English, 1111 Kenyon Road, Urbana, IL 61801
Various publications contain study guides and teaching units. Send for current catalogue. We note the following:

Using Junior Novels to Develop Language and Thought (Five Integrative Study Guides), Constance Weaver, ed. For use in middle school, guides are for Blume's *Tales of a Fourth Grade Nothing*, O'Brien's *Mrs. Frisby and the Rats of NIMH*, Hunt's *Across Five Aprils*, and Lewis's *The Lion, The Witch and the Wardrobe*.

Thematic Units in Teaching English and the Humanities by Sylvia Spann and Mary Beth Culp. Fifteen units. Three supplements have been published adding fourteen more units on such topics as the Exodus theme in Black literature, divorce, male/female roles, mysteries, the Jewish experience in American literature. The third supplement is aimed at "underachievers and reluctant readers."

Teaching Fiction: Short Stories and Novels, Kenneth Donelson, ed. Teachers' ideas include ways for individualizing so that students move through books at their own pace.

guide, or adapt an old one, contribute it to the English department's files. Of course, in a well-managed department, there will be files of guides on every selection that has ever been taught in that school. If there isn't such a file, that's the English department's top priority for staff development. The sources of guides for the department file are (1) publishers, (2) teachers, (3) students. Student-made guides are one way of responding to literature that we shall note below.

In order to learn what constitutes a good study guide you will be asked to construct one or more in preservice and inservice courses. A good study guide begins with your sensitive reading of the short story or short novel. You read seeking the unity of the work as a whole. What is this story essentially about? There will be a surface answer to this question and probably a deeper one which not all students will reach. What details will students need to observe if they are to arrive as you did at this unity of the whole? (In Box 15-5 we reproduce part of a study guide for a short story by John Updike.)

In most cases, we would use guides chiefly to focus attention on details that must be observed in order to draw inferences. We would design items that lead to the making of inferences, allowing also for students to make justifiable inferences that we may have missed. Ordinarily, we would not go beyond understanding and appreciating the story in a study guide, leaving matters of judgment and application to come in other ways. The study guide in literature is primarily a device for preparing students for personal reactions, coming later, which will be fluent and thoughtful because of the initial preparation. Work-books that accompany anthologies and the literary selections included in basal readers for grades 5 to 8 often serve the same purpose as study guides. Many of these you can use as study guides without further adaptation.

Study guides serve useful purposes in teaching literature. A study by Sanders showed that tenth graders who had read six short stories with well-made guides responded more fluently and thoughtfully to two additional stories than did comparable tenth graders who did not have the benefits of the guides.[5] But study guides that focus on unnecessary details, that are too long and miss the unity of the work, or that are glib and tangential and reflect only the teacher's reading may not only kill enjoyment of reading but distort the students' under-standing of literature generally. And those, you remember, are the goals: to contribute to students' pleasure in literature (not just this particular work) and their understanding of why literature (not just this particular work) is created and what it does for readers.

Especially to be avoided are guides that query readers' "application" of ideas by presenting often cryptic statements of a "theme" or message and asking students to choose and defend one or two that suit their interpretations of the work. Some guides, for instance, suggest proverbs that are often related only very tangentially to the meanings of the story. This is a bad practice for two reasons. In the first place, we should not imply that reading fiction is message-hunting. Stories have meanings, of course, but few stories outside of Aesop's and Montaigne's fables are reducible to morals or proverbs. In the second place, the applications of literature are personal, indirect, and often untraceable. It is almost impossible to make up "applications" that genuinely fit other readers. Forced to choose, students do so and their real reactions may be stifled.

It is more sensible to reserve the "third level" of the study guide for matters of

---

[5] Peter Sanders, "The Effects of Instruction in the Interpretation of Literature on the Responses of Adolescents to Selected Short Stories." *Research in Reading in the Content Areas: The Third Report*, Harold L. Herber and Richard T. Vacca, eds. (Syracuse University Reading and Language Arts Center, 1977).

BOX 15-5

A STUDY GUIDE FOR USE WITH "A & P,"
A SHORT STORY BY JOHN UPDIKE

Teacher sets up points of connection between the students and the short story perhaps by asking a question (What have you done to try to impress someone?) or by comparing the situation in the story to be read with one just completed. Students read the story and complete the study guide, referring to the story as necessary. Then they are ready to discuss their reactions in small groups. Teacher may sit in on one or more small group discussions and then lead a brief discussion in which the whole class participates.

While this study guide focuses on characterization, as does the short story itself, the exercises in Section A help the reader to affirm where and when the story takes place and what happens. Note that #1 and #2 refer to setting. The student is to decide whether the statement is true or false and to check the details from the story listed below each statement, which support the decision. Exercise #3 asks students to draw inferences from details in the plot. It sends readers back to the story for evidence to support the inferences they select.

A. What Happened?

1. Sammy works at the checkout counter at an A & P in a town on the coast north of Boston. (Put T beside details that helped you decide the statement is *true*. Or put F beside details that helped you decide it is *false*.)

_____ third checkout slot   _____ over in Salem
_____ rouge on her cheeks   _____ in nothing but bathing suits
_____ the title   _____ not as if we're on the cape

2. The story takes place in the 1980s. (Put T beside details that support *true*. Or put F beside details that support *false*.)

_____ powder blue Falcon   _____ bathing suit styles
_____ price of herring (49¢)   _____ Mr. Lengel's attitude toward
_____ floor plan of supermarket   girls
                                                     _____ Tony Martin Sings

3. Write A beside statements with which you agree. Write D beside those with which you disagree. Find a sentence or paragraph in the story that supports your answer.

_____ Sammy feels sorry for Queenie because she seems to be poor.
_____ Sammy is respectful of most of the A & P customers.
_____ Stokes, a married man, ignores the whole incident.
_____ Sammy quits in order to impress the girls.
_____ No one is impressed by Sammy's gesture.

Continued

BOX 15-5 *(continued)*

A STUDY GUIDE FOR USE WITH "A & P,"
A SHORT STORY BY JOHN UPDIKE

_____ Sammy regrets his act almost immediately.

_____ Sammy works at the A & P for the fun of it, not because he needs the money.

_____ Mr. Lengel is glad to have Sammy quit.

The first exercise in B requires readers to accept or reject brief descriptions of Sammy. When readers' opinions vary, they should discuss disagreements. The second question requires them to put into their own words their interpretation of the story's key sentence.

B. Interpreting Character

1. Check the words and phrases below which accurately describe Sammy.

_____ show-off   _____ cynical
_____ sense of humor   _____ tough but tender
_____ conceited   _____ male chauvinist
_____ mean   _____ insensitive
_____ idealist   _____ too sensitive for his own
_____ street smart   good
_____ he knows the score   _____ dishonest
_____ foolish   _____ chivalrous

2. What do you think Sammy means when he says at the end, "I felt how hard the world was going to be to me hereafter"?

Section C asks students to make judgments about the author's point of view and to articulate their reactions to the story. The responses they check should be starting points for discussion.

C. What Do You Think?

Check any of the statements below with which you agree. Be prepared to say why you agree.

_____ 1. This is an amusing story but it doesn't say anything important about life.

_____ 2. Although humorous, this story describes a crucial point in the passage from youth to adulthood.

_____ 3. Updike is making fun of puritanical fussbudgets like Mr. Lengel.

_____ 4. Updike is making fun of adolescents like Sammy.

_____ 5. This story perpetuates stereotypes of males and females and therefore should not be included in high school anthologies.

Continued

BOX 15-5 *(continued)*

> ### *A STUDY GUIDE FOR USE WITH "A & P,"*
> ### *A SHORT STORY BY JOHN UPDIKE*
>
> **After discussion growing out of the study guide, many teachers elect to use the story as a springboard for personal expression, either oral or written. If the suggestions below are used for role-playing, everyone who has read the story plays one or more parts. All the improvisations would go on at once; no group performs for the rest of the class. Some teachers might end the lesson with role playing. Others might direct their class to choose one of the topics as a writing exercise.**
>
> #### D. Suggestions For Role-playing or Writing
>
> A. Mr. Lengel describes the incident to his wife.
> B. Stokesie tell his wife what happened.
> C. Sammy explains to his mother and father that he has no job.
> D. "Queenie" tells her parents what happened.
> E. The three girls discuss the incident.
> F. Big Tall Goony-Goony describes the incident.

judgment than to strive for personal application. If this can be articulated at all, it comes best in free responses such as those described later in this chapter.

The objective-test items of study guides present opportunities for every-pupil response techniques. In fact, that is what a study guide is: a device for getting every student to respond. It is also the glue which holds students' attention to the discussion when small-group methods are used. As such, the study guide is a great help when both teachers and students are beginners in small-group discussions. An alternative arrangement, which should be used frequently, is for the teacher to lead a small group of students while the rest of the class is writing or reading. The teacher learns to do more listening than leading in this type of discussion but remains a key participant, guiding the talk in profitable directions and helping students to raise their own valuable questions. Recent research studies hint that this kind of teacher-led discussion results in improved learning probably because a teacher can take advantage of students' insights, which may be lost in students' independent discussions of responses to study guides—or never invoked by cut-and-dried objective questions.

Teacher-Led Objective Questioning

A variation on the study guide is a set of multiple-choice questions to which students respond individually immediately after reading a selection.[6] In class the teacher calls for every student to respond by flashing a different colored card for *a*, *b*, *c*, or *d*; or by holding up one to four fingers for each choice. When there is complete agreement, there is no need for discussion. When there is disagree-

---

[6]Paul Diederich used this technique with freshmen at the University of Chicago, as he explains in the preface to *Critical Thinking in Reading and Writing* (Holt, Rinehart, and Winston, 1955).

ment, students defend their answers by referring to the text. This technique works equally well with nonfiction but is useful also for beginning a discussion of imaginative literature and for fostering accurate, close reading. Of course, the effectiveness of such a lesson depends entirely upon the quality of the multiple-choice questions. Sometimes you can find good questions in workbooks and teachers' manuals and in materials created by other teachers which can be purchased.

Programmed Instruction in Literature?

In the 1960s when we were sure that computer-aided instruction would take over, a few persons began to consider programming the study of literature. This seems a particularly effective approach to the close reading of poetry and an excellent way to help students "unpeel" a poem. The poet John Ciardi collaborated with two teachers to produce one slim volume which programmed the reading of "Stopping by Woods" and a few other well-known poems.[7]

Note that the heading of this section questions programmed instruction. We do so because many teachers are aghast at what they look upon as a mechanical analysis of literature. We disagree. For students who are ready for the *study* of literature (having already read widely) this is an excellent way to teach close reading. It is excellent because it provides immediate feedback, leading students from answers to questions, and it demonstrates how one good reader—not all readers—responds to a particular work. Try it for yourself with Hopkins' "Spring and Fall" (Box 15-6). If you are convinced that you were led to insights not apparent to you on other readings of this poem, look for exercises that you can adapt to programming. Or write your own programs—and plan to publish them—because teachers need your help.

Responding through Role-Playing

An entirely different approach from study guides, one that must receive just as much emphasis, is role-playing. In fact, study guides simply prepare the way for role-playing; both techniques will be used for the same work on many occasions, though on others you might stop with the study guide or start with role-playing. The purpose of role-playing is to help students identify with characters. It may be done orally or in writing. When it is done orally, an English teacher like Ms. Martinez, who does a lot of work with improvisation, sets up a situation in which the author's characters appear in an incident not described in the original story. For instance, after reading "A & P," she may say to three students: "You are Sammy, you're his mother, you're his father. He's just come home after quitting his job. What do you say to each other?" Everyone who has read the story is one of the three characters and all improvisations go on simultaneously. There is no audience. Much later in the year students may be

---

[7]James M. Reid, John Ciardi, and Laurence Perrine, *Poetry: A Closer Look*, Programmed Instruction with Selected Poems (Harcourt Brace Jovanovich, 1963).

BOX 15-6

PROGRAMMED INSTRUCTION FOR A POEM

Test whether "programmed instruction" helps you to understand this poem more fully than does simply reading it on your own. Read the poem one or more times. Then work through the programmed instructions for it, which were prepared by Paul Diederich and are reprinted with his permission.

Spring and Fall
by Gerard Manley Hopkins

Margaret, are you grieving
Over Goldengrove unleaving?
Leaves, like the things of man, you
With your fresh thoughts care for, can you?
Ah! as the heart grows older   5
It will come to such sights colder
By and by, nor spare a sigh
Though worlds of wanwood leafmeal lie;
And yet you *will* weep *and* know why.

Now no matter, child, the name: 10
Sorrow's springs are the same.
Nor mouth had, no nor mind, expressed
What heart heard of, ghost guessed:
It is the blight man was born for,
It is Margaret you mourn for.   15

DIRECTIONS: Cover everything below the item on which you are working with a sheet of paper. Read the item, look back at the poem, and write the number of the best answer in the ( ) at the end of the item. Then move the sheet of paper below the next item. The number in parentheses is the intended answer for the preceding item. If your answer was not the same, put a circle around this parenthesis. If you disagree and want to discuss the item, add a question mark or exclamation point.

1. About how old is the person addressed? 1—five 2—eighteen 3—thirty 4—fifty ( )

(1) 2. What is Goldengrove? 1—some English flower, like goldenrod 2—a particular plant to which she had given this name 3—a patch of woods in autumn 4—a person named Goldengrove ( )

(3) 3. In line 2 "unleaving" means 1—not leaving (i.e., staying) 2—failing to produce leaves 3—unfolding leaves from buds 4—shedding leaves ( )

(4) 4. The *opposite* of "the things of man" in line 3 is 1—the things of woman 2—the things of children 3—the things of nature 4—the ideas of man ( )

(3) 5. In line 3 "leaves" are 1—addressed by the question, "Can you?" 2—the subject of "care for" 3—the subject of "can you" 4—the object of "care for" ( )

Continued

BOX 15-6 (continued)

PROGRAMMED INSTRUCTION FOR A POEM

(4) 6. In line 7 "nor spare a sigh" means 1—not be sparing of sighs (i.e., give many of them) 2—not give so much as a sigh 3—not express sorrow openly 4—not permit anyone to sigh (   )

(2) 7. In line 8 "worlds" means 1—large quantities 2—imaginary worlds 3—planets like our world 4—little worlds (round balls) formed by wanwood (   )

(1) 8. Which of the following is most like "leafmeal" in line 8? 1—oatmeal 2—bone meal 3—piecemeal 4—last meal (   )

(3) 9. Which do you think is the best reading of line 9? 1—Although others may not weep, you will, for you are more sensitive. 2—Yet you will weep in the future, because life will be harder for you then, and you will know what real grief is. 3—Yet you will weep in the future, but about the reality rather than the shadow, and then you will know why you are weeping. 4—But you go right on weeping, in spite of what I have just said, and you want to know why. (   )

(4) (3) 10. Which is the best reading of line 10? 1—Now you are not weeping about anything serious but about a name. 2—Now this knowledge means nothing to you. 3—Never mind now what name we give to the cause of your sorrow. 4—I forget your name, but it does not matter. (   )

(3) 11. Which is the best reading of line 11? 1—Sorrow attacks you now as it will later. 2—The ultimate source of all sorrow is the same. 3—The springtime of sorrow is the same as the later stages. 4—The emotional springs that ease the shocks of life are always the same. (   )

(2) 12. Which is the best reading of line 12? 1—You could not put into words or even conceive as an idea. 2—You do not now have words or concepts to understand why you will weep in the future. 3—And I never told you in words or even in thought why you will weep. 4—Neither literature nor science can tell you why you are weeping. (   )

(1) 13. What is the "ghost" in line 13? 1—the ghost of an idea 2—a departed soul 3—Margaret's soul 4—the writer's soul (   )

(3) 14. What is "the blight man was born for" in line 14? 1—evil in general 2—unhappiness 3—sin 4—death (   )

(4) 15. Why? 1—Because sin is the ultimate source of all unhappiness. 2—Because her soul unconsciously took the death of the leaves as a sign that she, too, would die. 3—Because the overwhelming force of evil in the world is what finally makes us weep. 4—Because man is born for sorrow, and that sorrow springs from unhappiness. (   )

(2) 16. In line 15 why is she mourning for Margaret? 1—Because all sorrow is self-centered. 2—Because the departing leaves make her feel lonely. 3—Because she must die. 4—Because she is dying. (   )

(3) 17. In the title "Spring" stands for 1—sorrow's springs 2—the spring of the year 3—the happiness of youth 4—Margaret's age (   )

(4) 18. In the title "Fall" stands for 1—old age 2—death 3—the last years of Margaret's life 4—the writer's age (   )

(2) Now restudy the items you answered incorrectly.

ready to observe and comment on each other's interpretation of character, but in the beginning the purpose is for all the students to experience for themselves how Sammy feels.

A variation which may be less demanding is to have one student "be" a character—perhaps the mother in *My Brother Sam Is Dead*—and other students, playing no particular role, question her about what she has done or felt or will do.

Role-playing can be done in writing. One example is to have students assume a character from a novel and, in that person, write a Dear Abby letter seeking advice. Many other ideas of this sort are available to you in sources like those listed in Boxes 15-3 and 15-4. Use them and evaluate their effectiveness in stimulating your students to identify with characters in fiction.

Imaginative Writing as a Response to Literature

Responding to a literary work through imitating the style and/or structure of the author develops students as readers and writers, and teachers use this technique as effectively in the primary grades as in senior high school. In grade 3 Ms. Pawlachuk used the traditional tale of the Gingerbread Boy in its many versions (including Ruth Sawyer's *Journey Cake, Ho*), and the children followed the story pattern, which gave support to their plotting, to create a modern-day version featuring a Big Mac. In twelfth grade, Mr. McGuiness had his students examine the structure of famous detective stories, then concocted a mystery for them to solve in the manner and style of their favorite detective. Sixth graders followed the story line of *The 500 Hats of Bartholomew Cubbins* to produce their own stories in the style of Dr. Seuss.

Imitation (*mimesis* is the scholarly term) is an honorable means of learning appreciation for a craft, and teachers have no need to fear it will smother creative instincts. Students should understand why they are following professional patterns as closely as hanging a new story on an old plot frame or rewriting a bit of Dickens in Hemingway style. With most students the aim is not so much to explore their creativity as it is to improve their understanding of literary craftsmanship while at the same time giving them pleasurable reasons for writing.

Some English teachers have students follow professional patterns by replacing words and phrases deleted from a literary selection. Instead of random deletion based on every fifth or seventh word as in a *cloze* exercise, they use deletions to call students' attention to particular characteristics of diction and style. Like *cloze*, this type of exercise invites discussion of the author's choice of words as comparisons are made with the students' restorations. This close inspection of style is a high-level exercise intended only for interested and capable students.

Responding by Asking Questions

All that we have said in Chapter 13 about comprehension resulting from the reader's own questioning and finding answers, predicting and confirming or revising hypotheses applies also to the reading of literature. While readers' questions during fluent reading are almost always subconscious, and seldom if ever articulated, teachers can force questions to the surface so that they can be examined by the reader, the teacher, and fellow students. One way to do this is to divide the reading of a short story into segments and have students jot down questions and sometimes stop to discuss each others' questions and the reasons for them. This idea works well when teachers read the story aloud, interrupting at predetermined points to ask: What questions do you have? What guesses are you making? Students should understand why the teacher is treating the story in this artificial manner—that is, to make them consciously aware of hypothesizing as they read.

Somewhat less artificially students can be asked to write questions for each other, perhaps to prepare study guides, and to defend the centrality of their questions for understanding the story. At first students naturally pattern their questions after the ones they have been asked by teachers and editors. So an appropriate strategy preceding and accompanying the phrasing of one's own questions is to critique those found in anthologies and study guides. The aim of much discussion of literature is to raise questions, judge them, but not necessarily answer them.

I have seen teachers work with poetry in this way. Two or three students are given a cluster of poems to read and raise questions about. The teacher does not insist that all reactions be questions or that all questions go unanswered. But through many previous experiences in listening to poetry the students have come to understand that an appropriate response to a poem may be a question. Discussions of this kind using poetry cards that the teacher has prepared or purchased should be set only for students who are ready to talk to each other about poetry. In any case, make the sessions brief, say, ten minutes at first.

An interesting objective technique originally designed for wide-scale testing of responses to literature can be adapted to teaching. In an investigation of literature study in ten countries, the researchers presented twenty questions to students and asked them to identify five which they would consider appropriate to a particular selection. These questions are reproduced in Box 15-7. Having students regularly consider similar questions in relation to particular readings can be a springboard to thoughtful discussion.

Making Comparisons

Perhaps the most dependable way of eliciting students' responses to literature is one that has been used for many years: asking students to compare two works on a clearly identifiable point of similarity. That's one of the reasons for clustering poems according to theme or subject in the poetry cards just mentioned. Comparisons can be made on other bases than theme—for example, forms, characters, settings, feelings aroused, mood, tone, timeliness. And comparative lessons can be set at any stage of maturity from first grade to twelfth. Many teachers use a comparable selection to arouse interest in a story to be read, saying, for example: "Listen to this poem (or parable or fable). When you finish reading this short story, we'll talk about why I chose this poem to read to you first." Or: "Here's a news item from last week's *Globe* that describes an incident

BOX 15-7

TWENTY QUESTIONS*

Here are Twenty Questions that might be asked about a literary work. Select *five* of these questions which you think would be the most important questions to ask about _____. (Teacher inserts title of the selection being studied.) Be prepared to say why you consider some questions of little or no importance and why the five you selected appear to you to be the most important.

1. Is there a lesson to be learned from _____ ?
2. Is this story well written?
3. How does the story build up? How is it organized?
4. What type of story is it? Is it like any other story I know?
5. How can we explain the way the people behave in this story?
6. Are any of the characters in this story like people I know?
7. Has the writer used words or sentences differently from the way people usually write?
8. What happens in _____ ?
9. Is this story about important things? Is it a trivial or a serious work?
10. Does the story tell me anything about people or ideas in general?
11. How is the way of telling the story related to what _____ is about?
12. Is this a proper subject for a story?
13. Is there anything in this story that has a hidden meaning?
14. When was the story written? What is the historical background of the story and its writer?
15. What kinds of metaphors (or comparisons), images (or references to things outside the story) or other writers' devices are used in this story?
16. Does the story succeed in getting me involved in the situation?
17. What does _____ tell me about the people I know?
18. What emotions does _____ arouse in me?
19. Is there any one part of _____ that explains the whole story?
20. What is the writer's opinion of, or attitude toward, the people in this story?

*These questions were part of the Literature Test in a study undertaken by the International Association for the Evaluation of Educational Achievement (IEA) and reported in Alan C. Purves, *International Studies in Evaluation II: Literature Education in Ten Countries, an Empirical Study* (Stockholm: Almquvist and Wiksell, 1973). A more recent report on both the reading and literature components of this international study can be found in Purves et al., *Reading and Literature: American Achievement in International Perspective*, published by the National Council of Teachers of English, 1111 Kenyon Road, Urbana, Illinois 61801, 1981.

quite similar to the one in _____. When you finish reading, we'll compare them."

Teachers who overlook opportunities to compare selections miss an obvious opportunity to teach students how to read literature.

Journal Entries as Responses to Literature

As students become more articulate in expressing reactions to literature through all of the ways suggested above, they will find journals a natural vehicle for reactions that are personal, tentative, and not yet ready for sharing with others. They may be willing to share these with a trusted teacher, however, who will react to the responses but not grade them. These journal entries may become the basis for more formal writing about literature.

Here is the journal entry one girl wrote as she read and reread Emily Dickinson's poem "I'm Nobody."

> I don't think the poet really believes she is a "nobody," but she's speaking to another person who may not be famous, and she probably doesn't want a lot of publicity. Some people have to be in the public eye—like TV stars and movie stars—and they'll do almost anything to get on TV talk shows or to get their pictures in People magazine or in the newspapers where their public eats up information about them.
>
> I don't know why Emily Dickinson used an expression like "an admiring bog." Did she just want to make a rhyme with "How public like a frog"? It's a funny expression but I guess I know what she means. A bog is something that sucks you in. That's a pretty good image. Today that admiring bog is full of celebrity junkies.

Essays About Literature

Able students in grades 11 and 12 can be taught to write critical reviews in the manner of professional literary critics. They need to study model reviews (preferably of books they have read) under the guidance of a teacher who brings out how the reviewer develops a point of view, supports this by references to the work being reviewed, and avoids unnecessary summarizing. Students are not ready for this formal response to literature until they have had much experience in reacting critically but personally and informally rather than passing judgments. The danger in forcing critical responses too soon is that students will resort to stock responses, expressing not so much what they feel as what they think you want to hear.

Evaluating Imaginative Literature

There comes a time when students must go beyond saying whether they like or dislike a particular piece of work and tell why it affects them as it does. They must react to the quality of the work. A first step in helping students to exercise critical judgments of this kind is to propose statements with which they can agree or disagree and then support by references to the text. This is a safer kind of item for the "third level" of the study guide than application questions, and we have illustrated this type of item in the study guide in Box 15-5. As students move to framing their own critical reactions, they are guided by the classic questions: What did the author set out to do? How well did he or she succeed? Was the goal worth achieving?

Comparing two short stories of similar intent and unequal merit is a good base for developing critical insights. As students discuss why one story is of better quality than the other, they deal with questions such as these: Which incidents in Story A strained your willingness to believe? How did the author of Story B convince you that this might have happened? What details in Story B made the characters seem real? What made the characters in Story A seem flat or lifeless? In what ways did the language (or style) of Story B contribute to your enjoyment? Give examples from Story A of language that interfered with your understanding or detracted from your appreciation.

One problem with setting up this kind of lesson in evaluating literature is that stories of high literary quality are more accessible to teachers than poor examples. When students are just beginning to discriminate between good and poor literary quality, the differences must be dramatic. Really bad short stories are not likely to be anthologized. Some teachers establish departmental files of bad examples, collecting from pulp magazines and Sunday supplements stories that are most likely to be forgotten. (Bad verse seems to be easier to collect—from newspapers, greeting cards, and anonymous sources.)

When the supply of bad examples is low, lessons in evaluation may be based on plot-completion exercises. For a published story, teachers may devise two or three alternate endings. Then students select and defend the one which best fits the situation presented up to this point in the story. They compare the alternate endings with the author's, noting the merits of this one and the defects of the others.

A variation of the alternate endings idea is the comparison of prose styles as in the following exercise:

WHICH DESCRIPTION DO YOU LIKE BEST?

A

The skipper of the Sephora had a straggling red beard that surrounded his face, and the sort of fair complexion that I have noticed that red-haired people always have. His eyes were foggy blue. He was a singularly unprepossessing person, he had high shoulders and was of average height—one leg was a trifle bandy. He shook hands, looking closely at everything. I thought to myself that he was a very tenacious man.

B

The skipper of the Sephora had a red beard and a fair complexion. His eyes were an odd shade of blue. He was not very good looking, of middle height and slightly bandy in one leg. He shook hands and stared absently about. A kind of dumb stubbornness seemed to be his main characteristic.

C

The skipper of the Sephora had a thin red whisker all round his face, and the sort of complexion that goes with hair of that color; also the particular, rather smeary shade of blue in the eyes. He was not exactly a showy figure; his shoulders were high, his stature but middling—one leg slightly more bandy than the other. He shook hands, looking vaguely around. A spiritless tenacity was his main characteristic, I judged.

This exercise was taken from a test of literary judgment by Brian Ash which required not only comparison of prose styles but also response to poetry.[8] An example of the poetry exercises appears below. One of the poems is by a well-known poet. The other two versions were written by Ash as "mutilations" of the original. For Ash's test, students were asked only to identify the original version. For lessons in critical evaluation, teachers encourage students to say why one version appeals to them more than another. The "right" answer is not so important as the students' attempts to articulate their reactions. These discussions help teachers to understand how their students' tastes in literature are developing.

WHICH POEM DO YOU PREFER?

A
Old Mary

I have no fear
Because I'm here.

At last it gives me little pain
To know I cannot go again

Watching birds on mounting wings
Nor listening to the vibrant strings.

B
Old Mary

My last defense
Is the present tense.

It little hurts me now to know
I shall not go

Cathedral-hunting in Spain
Nor cherrying in Michigan
     or Maine.

C
Old Mary

No point in strife
At the end of life.

No regrets for me to know
I cannot go

Wandering in the Grecian Isles
Nor striding out the country miles.

Evaluating Students' Responses to Literature

Teachers have many ways of judging how students are progressing in developing taste and in reacting responsibly to literature. If students are reacting frequently in talk and writing, if teachers know what they are choosing to read, there should be little real need for more formal testing, but since tests are often given without real need, we must say a word about them here. No tests should

---

[8]Brian Ash, "Construction of an Instrument to Measure Some Aspects of Literary Judgment and Its Use as a Tool to Investigate Student Responses to Literature." Ph.D. diss., Syracuse University, 1969. (Of the three descriptions, C is the version that appears in "The Secret Sharer" by Joseph Conrad. Of the three poems, B is poet Gwendolyn Brooks' version.)

be given on a particular literary work unless students are permitted to "look back." When open-book tests are not permitted, the test questions should be open-ended and students should be allowed to draw examples from a range of selections. The best test of ability to read literature presents fresh examples of the kind most recently studied and raises the same type of questions which have been addressed on the similar selections studied. Many tests for junior and senior high school offer this kind of end-of-the-unit testing.

Responses: A Summary

The chief argument we have made in this chapter is that imaginative literature elicits different kinds of responses from those called forth by informational prose and therefore requires different strategies in the classroom. We noted that the level of reading often referred to as "beyond the lines" or "uses of reading" involves two quite distinct kinds of reaction. One is the application of concepts learned. We believe applications of learning from literature are not easily or appropriately measured by objective test items because what may be "learned" is so personal and subjective. On the other hand, it is quite appropriate to test the comprehension of expository prose by having students apply the concepts they were supposed to learn.

The second type of postreading response is evaluative. With imaginative literature, the reader applies standards of taste and personal values. With informational prose, as we said in Chapter 13, readers can make objective judgments, applying criteria of accuracy, completeness, timeliness, logic and documentation.

We believe that the best way to become a critical reader in a number of fields is to read widely, just as we believe that the way to acquire good taste in literature is to read widely. So whatever limits enjoyment in reading is to be avoided; whatever contributes to the likelihood that adolescents will choose to read for whatever reasons is to be preferred over the exercise which focuses on a process that will be applied to no product.

The best teacher is the one who reads selectively and analytically, not just as an adult reads, however, but also as adolescents might read.

RECAPPING MAIN POINTS

Because imaginative literature and informational prose are different genres, having been written to serve different purposes and having quite different effects on readers, they cannot be approached in the same way either by teachers or students. The teacher of literature aims at heightening readers' pleasure in a story by training them in such skills as noticing details of setting and characterization through exercises that do not interrupt the flow of reading a complete work.

Interpretations of literature may vary, but students should be prepared to judge and defend interpretations according to how well they take into account details of the poem or story.

The literature teacher's first problem is selecting both the works to be studied in common and the ones to recommend for individual reading. Because teachers must read widely, they should save time for this by using study materials they have selected carefully and perhaps adapted but have not prepared themselves. Study guides are particularly valuable in training students to notice details and for permitting different levels of response to in-common reading. Objective-type guides prepare students for discussion. Students should be encouraged to respond freely to selections and should not be limited to agreeing or disagreeing with items prepared by an editor or teacher.

One type of study guide initiates teacher-led discussions. Another type is based on programming that gives immediate feedback. This type models the reading of a poem or story by an expert.

Role-playing, a very different approach from study guides, should be given equal emphasis. Another way of developing students' responses to literature is to have them imitate an author's style or follow a plot line.

Asking questions invokes a more realistic, more genuine response to literature than answering someone else's questions. Teachers promote this type of behavior by the cut-up story technique in which students hazard guesses or raise questions about what will happen next. Preparing study guides for each other is another way to elicit students' questions. Teachers also devise multiple-choice exercises aimed at "which questions would you ask?".

Comparing two or more selections sharpens students' perceptions and provides a framework for responses. Less formal and directed is encouraging journal entries centered on reading. Critical analyses of literature should be expected of able students in grades 11 and 12, but they must be taught how to write them. One way is through model reviews. Critical judgment can be developed by having students compare good and not-so-good treatments of the same theme or plot line. Responding to true and mutilated versions of literary works is another device.

Evaluating ability to read literature can be done through observation and discussion, open-book tests, free responses to ideas that can be illustrated from a number of literary sources, and reactions to selections freshly chosen for testing purposes.

FOR DISCUSSION

1. In a small group demonstrate and later discuss the effectiveness of several ways to introduce particular selections of literature.
2. Prepare a study guide for a short story and share it with a group of colleagues who will read the story and critique your guide.
3. What do readers learn through reading literature? To enrich the discussion of this question, refer to one or more of the books or articles by Louise Rosenblatt listed under Further Reading.
4. Discuss the role of the English teacher in a school where all content teachers teach how to read and how to write, and there is also a reading staff to support them. In such a situation, what remains for the English teacher to do?

5. How can content teachers contribute to the goals of the literature program?
6. In what ways are study guides useful in teaching students how to *read* literature? In what ways are they limited in teaching how to *respond* to literature?

FURTHER READING

Burton, Dwight. *Literature Study in the High Schools*. New York: Holt, Rinehart and Winston, 1965.

Chambers, Aidan. *Introducing Books to Children*. Boston: Horn Book, Inc., 1983.
   Part Four, "Response," fills secondary teachers in on how teachers in earlier grades stimulate readers' responses and takes the discussion to adults' approaches to pleasure in books. Altogether, this collection of essays is not to be missed.

Cline, Ruth, and William McBride. *A Guide to Literature for Young Adults: Background, Selection and Use*. Glenview, IL: Scott, Foresman and Co., 1983.
   Pithy treatment in two hundred pages of literature teachers' questions. See Chapter 10 on comics, 12 on television, and especially 13, "Literature in Other Disciplines."

Rosenblatt, Louise M. *Literature as Exploration*. 3d ed. New York: Noble and Noble, Inc., 1976.
   First published in 1938, now in paperback, this is the foundational text in the teaching and study of literature; it is fundamental, too, to current reading research which today emphasizes the role of prior knowledge and the influence of the reader's cultural milieu in studies of comprehension.

Rosenblatt, Louise M. *The Reader, the Text, the Poem*. Carbondale, IL: Southern Illinois University Press, 1978.
   Seven important essays on response to literature. See especially "Efferent and Aesthetic Reading," essential to all teachers of reading.

continued from page iv

Copyrights and Acknowledgments

Illustration Credits:

Index

A

Accountability, competency tests and, 138–40

Accurate reading, 395–96

Achievement motivation, learning to read and, 38–39

Adler, Mortimer, 432–33, 437

Administrative leadership, in reading programs, 125–26

Administrators
  evaluation of use of test results by, 160–62
  See also Principals

Adolescents
  expectations of, 96–97
  extracurriculum and, 93–94
  family patterns and, 94–95
  informational resources for, 315–19
  language of, 21–22
  magazines liked by, 318
  part-time jobs of, 93–95
  statistics on reading habits of, 245–46
  teacher's concerns about, 92–99
  See also High schools

Advance organizers, 379

Almanacs, 323

American Broadcasting Company (ABC), 250

Analysis, *see* Assessment of needs

Anderson, Richard, 330n, 333

Anticipating issues, 377

Armstrong, W. H., 410

Ash, Brian, 461

Asimov, Isaac, 357

Assessment of needs (diagnosis), 141–59
  class profile and, 145–47
  classroom analysis of language performance and, 147–51
  cloze tests and, 149–51
  estimating levels of reading ability and, 151–52
  informal tests for, 152–53
  listening comprehension and, 152
  observation and, 153–55
  oral reading and, 151
  standardized tests and, 142–45
  using the results of, 155–56
  written recall tests and, 147–49
  See also Diagnosis of reading disabilities

Attention, learning to read and, 38

Auckerman, Robert, 44

Average readers
  in high schools, 89–90
  in middle schools, 81–85
  study skills of, 84–85

B

Babbling, 14

Bantam Publishers, 448

Bard College, 92

Barron, Richard, 377n

Basal reading programs, 44–45, 114
  diagnosis of reading disabilities and progress in, 194

Basic Sight Vocabulary, 223

Beginning reading (reading acquisition)
  growing success of, 51–52
  skills that support, 41
  theories of, 41–42
Beginning reading instruction, 40–52
  basal reading series and, 44–45
  computer-assisted, 49–50
  goals in, 40–43
  Language Experience Approach to, 45–48
  materials and strategies for, 43–49
  skills management systems for, 48–49
  weaknesses in, 50–51
  whole language approach to, 48
Bernstein, Basil, 334
Bickel, Linda, 123n
Bilingualism, learning to read and write in English and, 19–21
Biographies, learning about others' learning in, 178
Bohannan, Laura, 64
Bragstad, M. Bernice, 168n
Brain, reading and the, 36
Brokaw, Tom, 245
Brown, Roger, 63
Brown, Rollo, 407
Burn out of teachers, 107–108
Burton, Dwight L., 447

C

California Achievement Tests, 143
Capital Cities Television Reading Program, 249, 250
Carlsen, G. Robert, 447
Carroll, John B., 331
Cassette tapes, for remedial instruction, 233
CBS, Television Reading Program of, 249, 250
Center, Stella, 64
Chambers, Aidan, 447
Children's literature, 118
Chomsky, Noam, 11
Ciardi, John, 453
Class profile, assessment of needs and, 145–47
Cloze tests, 149–51, 294
Codes, books about, 228
Code-switching, 19

Cognitive processes, in reading, 35–36
Cognitive structure, comprehension and, 61, 63, 65
Cole, Sheila, 95
College aspirations, present learning and, 264–65
Comic books, 326
Comparisons, as response to literature, 457–58
Competency movement, reading programs and, 119–20
Competency tests, 138–40
Comprehension, 56–75
  of average readers, 82, 83
  cognitive structure and, 61, 63, 65
  inference and, 65–70
  IQ and, 70–71, 75
  language codes and, 62–63
  levels of, 65–70
  listening, 152
  motivation and, 71–72
  prior knowledge and, 57–59
  rate of, 172, 174
  remedial instruction and, 228–31
  retention and, 59–62
  structural codes and, 63–65
  teachers and, 73–75
  texts and, 72–73
Computer-assisted instruction, 49–50
  for imaginative literature, 453–55
  for remedial reading, 233–34
Concepts, words as, 331–32
Concrete operational period, 26
Consultants, reading, 120–22, 130–31
Content application programs, 112–17
Content fields
  motivation in, 265–67
  patterns of organization in, 387–88
  reading outside, *see* Out-of-school reading
  vocabulary development in, 354–59
Content teachers
  introducing reading to, 130
  textbooks and, 297–98
Content textbooks, reading teacher's use of, 296–97
Context
  decoding skills and, 223–24
  strategy of, 350
  testing students' use of, 347, 348
  vocabulary development and, 338–41

Cooper, Charles R., 417–18
Coordinators, reading, 120–22
Core texts, enriching, 157–58
Corrective reading, 189, 215–16
Counseling, 124
Cramer, Ward, 152n
Critical reading, 373, 394–400
    author's role in communication and,
        396–97
    materials for teaching, 398–400
    self-awareness as a requisite for,
        395–96
    writing as means of learning, 397–98
Curriculum, current and local issues in,
    262–64

D

Dale, Edgar, 65, 351n
Dale–Chall Formula, 285, 287
Decoding, 359
    context and, 223
    definition of, 37
    as goal of beginning reading, 41
    problems with, 360–63
    reading and, 36–37
    treating severe difficulties in, 222–28
    word parts (phonograms) and, 224
Degrees of Reading Power Tests, 143
DeLone, Richard H., 243
Demonstrations, for teaching word
    meanings, 356–57
Denckla, Martha Bridge, 220n
Departmental organization of secondary
    schools, 108–109
Developmental classes, 110–12, 114, 117
Developmental reading instruction, 189
Diagnosis of reading disabilities, 187–211
    clinical, 207–209
    in-school, 194–203
    interpreting diagnostic information
        and, 203–206
    interviewing the student and, 202–203
    permanent record file and, 194–95
    practicality, 209–10
    principles of, 192–94
    student referrals, 190–92
    testing for, 195–201
    trial teaching and, 201–202
Dialects, 19, 21–22

Dictionaries, 354
Diederich, Paul, 452n
Dillard, J. L., 358
Directed Reading Lesson (DRL) (or
    Directed Reading Actvity (DRA)), 44,
        377, 378, 422
Direct reading instruction, 112–17
Disabled readers
    classroom adjustments for, 234–38
    placing, 212–13
    See also Diagnosis of reading disabilities
Discussion, 374
    before reading, 375–76
Dolch, Edward, 223
Dolch List, 223
Donelson, Kenneth L., 447
Dorsey, Suzanne, 152n
Doublespeak, 118
Dramatizations, for teaching word
    meanings, 357
Drill, in remedial instruction, 218–19
Dunning, Stephen, 443n
Durrell, Donald D., 412
Dyslexia, 213, 215, 218
    definition of, 90

E

Earle, Richard, 377n
Early, Margaret, 115
Ease of Reading Formula, 287–89
Educational Development Laboratory,
    233
Elbow, Peter, 405
English department, 122–24
English Journal, 447
English teachers, 122–24
Environment
    learning to read and, 39–40
    vocabulary and, 334
Equilibration, 25
Escape reading, 326–27
Essay answers, writing, 416–19
Essays about literature, 459
Evaluation, 159–63
    adjusting procedures for, 159–60
    of administrators' use of test results
        160–62
    students', of themselves as learners, *see*
        Learning About Ourselves as Learners

Evaluation (*continued*)
  of students' responses to imaginative
    literature, 461–62
  of students' use of scores and grades,
    162–63
  of teachers, 162
Examinations
  reviewing for, 411–12
  See also Tests
Experiences, vocabulary development
    and, 348–50
Eye movements, measuring, 174
Eyes, reading and, 36

F

Faculty study groups, 131
Fader, Daniel, 407
Fadiman, Clifton, 242
Family, *see* Home environment
Farrell, Edmund, 107
Fernald, Grace, 223
Fiction
  responding to, 445–46
  See also Imaginative literature
Films, 234
Filmstrip/tape combinations, for remedial
    instruction, 232–33
FitzGerald, Frances, 300, 301
Flesch, Rudolph F., 287
Forbes, Esther, 67
Formal operational period, 26–27
Foxfire Book, The, 323
Freebody, Richard, 330n, 333

G

Games, for remedial instruction, 231–32
Gates–MacGinitie Reading Tests, 143
Gerjuoy, Herbert, 306
Giermak, Elaine A., 253n
Glass Analysis for Perceptual
    Conditioning, 224, 226
Glass, Gerald, 224
Glossaries, 358
Glosses, marginal, 358, 360
Goodman, Kenneth, 151n
Graham, Patricia, 138, 139

Grant, Gerry, 125
Graphemes, definition of, 37
Gray, William S., 110
Guidance counselors, 124
Guinness Book of World Records, 323

H

Halliday, M. A. K., 16
Hanf, M. Buckley, 420–21
Harris, Theodore L., 37n
Hatch, Diana D., 262n
Henry, Nelson B., 32
Herber, Harold, 377n
Herold, Curtis P., 333n
Herrnstein, R. F., 67, 70–71
High schools
  average readers in, 89–90
  differences among, 78–81
  problem readers in, 90–91
  reading instruction in, 117–19
  superior readers in, 91–92
  See also Adolescents; Secondary schools
Hilkert, Ann, 251
Hillje, Barbara Brown, 343n
Hobbies, 313–14
Hodges, Richard E., 37n
Hoffman Reader, 233
Holistic evaluation of writing, 417–18
Holmes, Oliver Wendell, 331, 332
Home environment
  of average readers, 82–84
  high school students' learning and, 94–95
Horn Book Magazine, The, 447
Huey, Edmund B., 32
Humor, 350, 351

I

Idea Line, 412, 413
Illiteracy, 304–306
Imaginative literature, 436–62
  asking questions as response to, 456–57
  comparisons as response to, 457–58
  computer-aided instruction on, 453–55
  developing responses to, 445–62
  dialogue with the author of, 438
  essays as responses to, 459

evaluating, 459–61
evaluating students' responses to,
    461–62
imitation as a response to, 456
informative text differentiated from,
    437–45
journal entries as response to, 459
role-playing technique for, 453, 456
suspension of disbelief in reading, 438
teacher-led objective questioning on,
    452-53
Infants, language development in, 12–18
Inference, comprehension and, 65–70
Informal notes, 391
Informal reading inventories (IRI's), 198
    readability of textbooks and, 294
Informal tests of reading, 152–53
Informational resources, for young
    adolescents, 315–19
Informative text, imaginative literature
    differentiated from, 437–45
Instructional materials, for beginning
    reading, 43
Intelligence, *see* IQ
Intelligence tests, diagnosis of reading
    disabilities and, 194–95
Interest, vocabulary and, 334–35
International Reading Association, 139
Interview, diagnosis of reading
    disabilities and, 202–203
Iowa Test of Basic Skills, 143
Iowa Tests of Educational Development,
    143–44
I.Q.
    comprehension and, 70–71, 75
    vocabulary and, 333
Iverson, William J., 447

J

Jencks, Christopher, 243
Jobs of adolescents, 93–99
Johns, Jerry L., 32
Johnson, Laura, 250–51
Johnson, Samuel, 312
Joos, Martin, 332n
Journal writing, 407–409
    as response to literature, 459
Journal of Reading, 190, 447

K

Keller, Helen, 9–12
Kitzhaber, Albert, 404
Klare, George R., 285
Know Your World Extra, 235
Kolevzon, Edward R., 290n
Kosoff, T., 202

L

Language
    biological view of, 11
    definition of, 9
    functions of, 16–18
    learning and, 24–27
    mental activity associated with, 10–11
    public versus private, 19, 20
    reference function of, 12–14
    school, 19
    second, 14, 19–21
Language codes, comprehension and,
    62–63
Language development, 31
    early, 12–18
    functions of language and, 16–18
    lexicon acquisition and, 14–15
    phonological system and, 14
    reference function of language and,
        12–14
    syntax development and, 15–16
    textbooks in, 276
    in the upper grades, 18–24
Language Experience Approach, 45–48
Language Master, The, 233
Language skills, relationship among,
    22–24
LaPray, Margaret, 151n
Learning
    language and, 24–27
    Piaget's theory of, 24–27
Learning About Ourselves as Learners,
    118, 166–86
    development of, 170–81
    evaluating writing, 175–76
    goals of, 167
    launching of, 167–70
    learning about others' learning, 176–80

Learning About Ourselves (*continued*)
  learning experiments, 180–81
  listening in, 176
  overview of, 167
  reading/study habits activities, 170–74
  scheduling, 166–67
  self-evaluation reports, 181–83
  suggested readings for students,
    183–86
  writing assignments, 174–76
Learning disability programs, 213–15
Learning skills, *see* Learning About
  Ourselves as Learners
Learning through reading, 55–77
  See also Comprehension
Learning to read, 31–53
  achievement motivation and, 38–39
  attention and, 38
  bilingualism and, 19–21
  perception and, 38
  preschool environment and, 39–40
  socioeconomic background and, 39–40
  See also Beginning reading
Learning to write, bilingualism and,
  19–21
Lecturing before reading, 375
LeGrand–Brodsky, Kathryn, 249*n*
Lesson planning, remedial instruction
  and, 219
Lexical density, 64
Lexicon, acquisition of a, 14–15
Librarians, *see* Media specialists
LiBretto, Ellen V., 234, 236
Linguistic readers, 226
Listen and Do series, 233
Listening, reading and, 23
Listening comprehension, 152
  remedial instruction and, 230–31
Literacy, 304–306
  goal of, 138, 139
  tests of, 138–40
Literature, *see* Imaginative literature
Local issues, in curriculum, 262–64

M

MacAndrew, Michael, 249
McCall–Crabbs *Standard Test Lessons in
  Reading*, 285, 430

McCullough, Constance M., 152–53
McNeil, Elton, 407*n*
Magazines, 319–20, 322, 324
  for adolescents, 318
  for teenaged disabled readers, 234, 235
Mainstreaming, 257–58
Malapropism exercise, 349
Management systems, skills, 48–49
Manzo, Anthony, 230
Mapping, 420–22
Mapping the territory, 376–77
Marginal glosses, 358, 359
Mathematics textbooks, 277
Meanings
  in paragraphs, 385–87
  reading as composing, 373
  words as, 331–32
Media and Methods, 398, 447
Media specialists, 124
Memory
  tests of, 199
  See also Recall; Retention
Mental activity, in reading, 35–36
Mental development, Piaget's stages of,
  26–27
Metropolitan Achievement Test, 144
Middle schools
  average readers in, 81–85
  problem readers in, 86–87
  superior readers in, 87–89
  See also Secondary schools
Mikulecky, 122*n*
Miller, George, 421
Mills Learning Methods Test, 200, 202
Minorities, IQ tests and, 70
Morphemes, 350
  definition of, 37
Motivation
  college aspirations as, 264–65
  comprehension and, 71–72
  in the content fields, 265–67
  of teachers, 267–68
Multisensory approach, for teaching
  whole words, 223

N

National Assessment of Educational
  Progress (NAEP), 140

National Broadcasting Company (NBC), 250
National Council of Teachers of English, 398, 448
New Reader's Press, 235
New York State, competency test in, 139
News for You, 235
Newspapers, 118
  reading, 319–22
  for teenaged disabled readers, 234, 235
Niles, Olive, 362*n*
Nilsen, Alleen Pace, 447
Nonfiction, 118
Nonreaders, 241–69
  college aspirations and present learning, 264–65
  local issues and, 262–64
  parents of, 243–44
  peer tutoring and teaching, 258, 260, 261
  reading aloud to, 251–54, 256–58
  SSR (Sustained Silent Reading) periods for, 248–49, 260, 262
  television and, 244–45, 249–51
  See also Disabled readers; Remedial instruction
Note-taking
  to aid recall, 410–11
  from individual paragraphs, 391
  informal, 391
  for reports, 412–15
  to review for examinations, 411–12

O

O'Connor, Johnson, 333
Objectives, ordering of, 156
Observation, as diagnosis, 153–55
Oral interpretation, 118
Oral language, 9
  book language and, 39
  reading ability and, 22–23
  See also Language development
Oral reading, *see* Reading aloud
Organization, patterns of, *see* Patterns of organization
Outlining, 419–20
Out-of-school reading, 304–29
  informational resources for, 315–19
  functional, 307–12

  on hobbies, 313–14
  magazines, 318–20, 322
  newspapers, 319–22
  for personal satisfaction, 312–14
  reference books, 319, 323
  survival skills and, 307–10
Overgeneralization, language development and, 15

P

Pacers, 234
Paragraphs
  identifying meaning in, 385–87
  identifying patterns in, 390
  note-taking from individual, 391
Parents, will to read and, 243–44
Part-time jobs, of adolescents, 93–95
Patterns of organization, 380–92
  arranging sentences in, 390
  arranging topics and subtopics, 389–90
  arranging topics in, 390
  in content fields, 387–88
  meaning in paragraphs, 385–87
  in paragraphs, 390
  in pictures, 388–89
  recall and, 408, 410–15
  in selections and chapters to be read, 390–91
  sentences, 382–85, 390
  teaching, 388–92
Peer tutoring and teaching, 258, 260, 261
Perception, learning to read and, 38
Permanent record file, diagnosis of reading disabilities and, 194–95
Perrine, Laurence, 444, 453*n*
Personal reading, 118
Personnel of reading programs, 120–25
Persons, Gladys, 64
Peterson, Marilyn L., 86
Petty, Walter, 333*n*
Phonemes, definition of, 37
Phonetic, definition of, 37
Phonics, 50
  definition of, 37
Phonograms (word parts), 42
  decoding using, 224
  Glass analysis for developing recognition of, 224, 226

Phonological system, acquisition of a, 14
Piaget, Jean, 13, 24–27, 58
Pictures
    patterns in, 388–89
    for teaching word meanings, 357
Plays, learning about others' learning
        with, 179
Polysyllabic words, decoding, 361–63
Postman, Neil, 245
Precommunication period, 14
Predicting, 394
Preparation for reading, 375–80
    advance organizers as, 379
    anticipating issues as, 377
    discussion as, 375–76
    lecturing as, 375
    mapping the territory as, 376–77
    preposed questions as, 379–80
    related reading as, 376
    skimming as, 380
    structured overviews as, 377–78
    testing prior knowledge as, 377
Price, David, 91
Principals
    reading programs and, 125–26
    See also Administrators
Prior knowledge
    comprehension and, 57–59
    discussion before reading as, 375–76
    language codes and, 62
    recall of, 61
    testing, 377
Problem readers
    in high schools, 90–91
    in middle schools, 86–87
Proficiency classes, 215
Proficiency tests, 215
    See also Competency tests
Programmed instruction, *see*
        Computer-assisted instruction
Puns, 350, 351
Purposes for reading, setting, 373–80

Q

Quality of instruction, comprehension
        and, 73–74
Questions
    on imaginative literature, 452–53, 456–57

preposed, 379–80
    by students, 393–94

R

Rank, Hugh, 398
Rapid reading, 429–31
Rate of reading, 429–31
Read-along tapes, 254–56
Readability formulas, 285–94
Readability of textbooks, 285–96
Readers
    average, 81–85, 89–90
    problem, 86–87, 90–91
    of students' writing, 405
    superiors, 87–89, 91–92
Reading
    brain–eye relationship in, 36
    as a cognitive activity, 35–36
    decoding and, 36–37
    definition of, 32–38
    learning through, 55–77, *See also*
        Comprehension
    listening and, 23
    oral, *see* Reading aloud
    oral language and, 22–23
    out-of-school, *see* Out-of-school
        reading
    as a receptive language activity, 35
    setting purposes for, 373–80
    writing and, 23–24
    See also Learning to read; *and specific*
        topics
Reading ability, estimating levels of,
        151–52
Reading acquisition, *see* Beginning
        reading; Beginning reading
        instruction
Reading aloud
    books for, 258
    decoding skills and, 360–61
    by students, 256–58
    by teachers, 251–54
    from textbooks, 298–99
Reading committee, 124–25
Reading comprehension, *see*
        Comprehension
Reading consultant/coordinator, 120–22,
        130–31

Reading coordinators' workshops, 131–32
Reading diagnosis, *see* Diagnosis of reading disabilities
Reading disabilities, diagnosis of, *see* Diagnosis of reading disabilities
Reading for Understanding kit, 398
Reading habits, Learning About Ourselves as Learners and, 170–74
Reading instruction, 40, 106
    adapting a single textbook for, 157
    direct, 112–17
    grouping for, 158–59
    selecting resources for, 157–58
    in senior high schools, 117–19
    See also Beginning reading instruction
Reading programs
    administrative leadership in, 125–26
    competency movement and, 119–20
    criteria for, 115
    direct versus content application, 112–17
    early secondary grades, 114–17
    improving, at secondary levels, 110–20
    staff development and, *see* Staff development, reading programs and
    staffing of, 120–25
    typical (limited), 140–41
Reading teachers, 122, 133
    content textbooks and, 296–97
    in regular classrooms, 129
    vocabulary development and, 342–54
Reading textbooks, *see* Textbooks
Readmore the Cat, 257, 259
Reasoning, reading as, 372–73
    critical reading, *see* Critical reading
    patterns of organization and, *see* Patterns of organization
    preparing students for, *see* Preparation for reading
    questioning and predicting and, 392–94
    setting purposes for reading and, 373–80
Recall
    patterns of organization and, 408, 410–15
    taking notes to aid, 410–11
    written, assessment of, 147–49
    See also Memory
Recordings, read-along, 254–56

Redundancy, principle of, 337–38
Reeves, Richard, 75
Reference books, 319, 323
Register, 18
Reid, James M., 453*n*
Related reading, as preparation, 376
Remedial instruction, 117–18, 212–40
    attitudes toward remedial readers and remediation, 221–22
    chances for success of, 217–18
    classroom adjustments for, 234–38
    comprehension strategies in, 228–31
    computer-assisted, 233
    decoding difficulties and, 222–28
    direct attention to reading comprehension and, 231
    drill, pacing, and lesson planning in, 218–20
    filmstrip/tape combinations for, 232–33
    games for, 231–32
    goals, methods, and materials of, 222–34
    hardware and software for, 231–34
    learning disability programs, 213–14
    listening comprehension and, 230–31
    meaning of, 187–89
    placing disabled readers and, 212–13
    principles of, 216–22
    proficiency classes, 215
    skills sheets, kits, and workbooks, for, 232
    special reading classes or corrective reading, 215–16
    supporting remedial students and, 220–21
    tape/print materials for, 233
    vocabulary development and, 229–30
Remedial teachers, 124
Repeated encounters, vocabulary development and, 336–38
Reports, taking notes for, 412–15
ReQuest procedure, 230–31
Research, teacher-centered, 132–33
Research papers, writing, 424–28
Retention, comprehension and, 59–62
Reviewing for examinations, 411–12
Robinson, F. P., 410, 422
Robinson, Helen, 39–40
Rodriguez, Richard, 19, 21
Role-playing, 453, 456
Ross, Ramon, 151*n*

S

Safire, William, 351
Salisbury, Rachel, 410
Sanders, Peter, 448
San Diego Quick Assessment, 151–52
Sawyer, D. J., 202
Schafer, Margaret, 257
Scheduling
   direct instruction in study skills, 431–33
   study time, 431
Schemata, 25
Scholastic Action, 235
Scholastic Books, 235, 448
Scholastic Scope, 235
Scholastic Sprint, 235
Schools
   differences among, 78–81
   finding time to read in, 246–49
   high schools, *see* High schools
   secondary, *see* Secondary schools
Science textbooks, 276
Sebesta, Sam Leaton, 447
Secondary schools, 105–35
   competency movements and, 119–20
   definition and categories of, 105
   departmental organization of, 108–109
   reading programs in, *see* Reading
     program
   See also High schools
Self-awareness, critical reading and,
   395–96
Self-evaluation, students', 181–83. *See
   also* Learning About Ourselves as
   Learners
Sensorimotor period, 13–14
Sentences, patterns in, 382–85, 390
*Sequential Tests of Educational Progress
   Series II*, 144
Sevareid, Eric, 244
Shayer, Michael, 58–59
Short stories, learning about others'
   learning with, 177–78
Simpson, Eileen, 218n
Singer, Harry, 295
Skills management systems, 48–49
Skills sheets, kits, and workbooks, 232
Skimming before reading, 380
Slosson, Richard L., 152n
Slosson Oral Reading Test (SORT), 152
Social science textbooks, 276

Socioeconomic background, learning to
   read and, 39–40
Special reading classes, 215–16, 238
Speech, *see* Oral language
Speed reading, 118, 429–31
Spelling, 364–68
   analysis of errors in, 177, 199
   students' self-evaluation of their, 175
Spelling patterns, 42
Spelling test, 199
SQ3R (Survey–Question–Read–Recite–
   Review), 377, 378, 422–25
SSL (Sustained Silent Looking), 248–49
SSR (Sustained Silent Reading), 248–49,
   260, 262
Staff development, reading programs
   and, 126–33
   consultants and, 130–31
   content teachers and, 130
   faculty study groups and, 131
   general principles of, 126–28
   goals for, 128
   teacher-centered research and, 132–33
   teacher centers and, 132
   teachers as students of process and, 131
   team planning and, 128–29
Staffing of reading programs, 120–25
Standardized reading tests, 142–45
Stanford Achievement Test, 144, 145
Stanford Diagnostic Reading Test, 144
Staroscik, Judy, 247n
Stoll, Earline, 333n
Story, need for, 324–26
Strang, Ruth, 152–53
Structural analysis, as word identification
   technique, 37
Structural codes, comprehension and, 63–65
Structured overviews, 377–78
Structures of words, 350–54, 357
Strunk, William, Jr., 365
Study guides for imaginative literature,
   446–52
Study habits, Learning About Ourselves
   as Learners and, 170–74
Study skills
   of average students in middle school,
     84–85
   inventory of, 168, 169
   scheduling direct instruction in, 431–33
   See also Learning About Ourselves as
     Learners

Studying
  increasing independence in, 415–23
  scheduling time for, 431
  SQ3R method of, 377, 378, 422–25
  textbooks, strategies for, 419–23
Subtopics, arranging, 389–90
Sullivan, Anne, 12
Sundance Publishers and Distributors of
    Educational Materials, 448
Superior readers
  in high schools, 91–92
  in middle schools, 87–89
Survival skills, 307–10
Syllabication, 363–64
Syntax, development of, 15–16
Systems 80, 233

T

Tables of contents, patterns in, 390
Tachistoscopes, 234
Taking notes, *see* Note-taking
Tapes
  read-along, 254–56
  for remedial instruction, 233
Taylor, W. L., 294*n*
Teacher-centered research, 132–33
Teacher centers, 132
Teachers
  burn out of, 107–108
  comprehension and, 73–75
  content, introducing reading to, 130
  evaluation of, 162
  individual differences in students and,
      98–99
  motivating, 267–68
  reading, *see* Reading teachers
  remedial, 124
  as students of process, 131
  See also Staff development, reading
      programs and
Team planning
  staff development in reading and, 128–29
Team teaching, 129
Television, 242
  effects on reading, 244–46
  as a stimulant for reading, 249–51
Television Reading Program (CBS), 249, 250
Tests
  cloze, 149–51

competency, 138–40
  diagnostic, 195–201
  informal, 152–53
  proficiency, 215
  standardized reading, 142–45
  of student's use of context, 348
  written recall, 147–49
Textbooks, 275–303
  adapting, 157
  average readers in grades 5 to 8 and, 85
  common characteristics, 276–77
  and comprehension, 72–73
  content, 296–97
  content teacher's use of, 297–98
  core, enriching, 157–58
  cost, 281–82
  for delayed readers, 234
  dialogues attempted by, 282–83
  editorial apparatus, 283–84
  impersonal prose, 282
  language, 298–99
  as mass media, 277–80
  proper use, 299–300
  readability, 285–96
  size of, 280–81
  SQ3R method of studying, 422–25
  state approval, 278–79
  strategies for studying, 419–23
  teachers' manuals, 284–85
  for vocabulary development, 344–47
Thomas, Lewis, 11
Thoreau, Henry David, 56
Thorndike, E. L., 372–73
Thurstone, Thelma Gwinn, 398*n*
Toffler, Alvin, 306*n*
Topics, arranging, 389–90
Tough, Joan, 17–18
Traxler, Arthur E., 152–53
Trial teaching, 200–201

U

Updike, John, 337

V

VAKT method, 223
Van Doren, Charles, 432–33, 437
Viewers' Guides, 250

Vocabulary, 330–59
  conditions for acquisition, 332
  in content fields, 354–59
  context and development, 338–41
  direct approach to development,
    342–54
  and environment, 334
  estimating student's, 347–48
  experiences used to develop, 348–50
  hard words in, 341–42
  interest and, 334–35
  I.Q. and, 333
  language of subject area as framework
    for, 358–59
  reinforcing learning of, 358
  remedial instruction and development
    of, 229–30
  repeated encounters (redundancy) and
    development of, 336–38
  school's influence on, 342
  strategies for developing, 350–54
  structures of words and, 350–54, 357
  textbooks for developing, 344–47
  tools for teachers, 336
  See also Lexicon; Words

W

Walker, Nora, 293*n*
White, E. B., 365*n*
Whole words, 223
Whole-school program, 137–65
  evaluation procedures in, 159–63
  See also Assessment of needs
Will to read, parents and, 243–44
Wilson, Colin, 373
Winn, Marie, 244
Wit, 350
Wittrock, Merlin C., 35*n*
Word factor, 330–31
Word histories, 357–58

Word knowledge, levels of, 335–36
Word play, 350, 351
Word recognition
  analysis of errors in, 199–201
  definition of, 37
Words
  as concepts, 331–32
  as meanings, 331–32
  as physical entities, 360–68
  selecting, for study, 355–56
  spelling, 364–68
  syllabication, 363–64
  See also Vocabulary
Working mothers, 94–95
Writing
  assignments, in Learning About
    Ourselves as Learners, 174–76
  books on, 406
  essay answers, 416–19
  by faculty, 405–406
  frequency, 405
  of holistic evaluation, 417–18
  a journal, 407–409
  learning critical reading through,
    397–98
  practicality of emphasis on, 406
  readers of students', 405
  reading and, 23–24
  research papers, 424–28
  as a way of learning, 403–406

X

Xerox Educational Publications, 235

Z

Zinsser, William, 406
Zip Scale, 152